WHAT THE MOUNTAINS GAVE THEM

A NOVEL OF ELKMONT IN THE GREAT SMOKY MOUNTAINS

CATHERINE ASTL

Published by Smoky Mountain Heritage Press

ISBN 979-8-9947442-0-8 (paperback)

ISBN 979-8-9947442-1-5 (ebook)

DEDICATIONS

To the Elkmont Families.

To "Uncle Levi and Uncle Lem"

*To my most beloved son, Dean, and to my most beloved and
supportive parents, Nick and Cathryn Abernathy.*

To Randy: for everything.

*To my sister, Caroline Fielding Feldman, and my entire family who
have always been there for me.*

Thank you.

ALSO BY CATHERINE ASTL

<u>Non-Fiction:</u>

Behind the Bar - Inside the Paralegal Profession

Behind the Bar - From Intake to Trial

<u>Fiction:</u>

Three Gates

The Colonists

<u>Historical Fiction:</u>

Oliver's Crossing - A Novel of Cades Cove

Gatlin's Gateway - A Novel of Gatlinburg

Mountain Mulekick - A Novel of Moonshine in Cades Cove and Chestnut Flats

Home of the Soul - A Novel of the Walker Sisters of Little Greenbrier Cove

Black Bill - A Novel of Walker Valley and Tremont in the Great Smoky Mountains National Park

Christmas Serenades-A Novel of Traditions with the Families of Cades Cove

CONTENTS

INTRODUCTION

AUTHOR'S NOTE

I often imagine slipping back to the early 1900s to visit Elkmont, Tennessee - a place I've been to many times on my trips to the Great Smoky Mountains National Park. Nowadays, it's a beautiful campground and destination where you can explore vintage cabins and walk down the old street to imagine days gone by. Whenever I'm there, I always ask myself, *what would a typical vacation there have been like*? Luckily, there are some memories and memoirs that remain.

Through meticulous research and a hefty dose of imagination, we know that Elkmont days were filled with hiking, fishing, canoeing, playing in the creeks, dinners, dances, teas on the front porch, meeting new people, and not only fellow vacationers – but locals such as Levi Trentham and Lem Ownby. These two men formed the full flavor of Elkmont, and of the Smoky Mountains themselves. They were so interesting to bring to life! I would've loved to have met them! But then, I *did* get a chance, didn't I? In fact, we *all* get that chance - by reading this book, hearing their stories, honoring their very own place in the history of the Smokies.

So many visitors have come and gone to Elkmont; even today, thousands come to the "ghost town" to walk back through time if only for an hour or so. I have done the same with my own family. Striding down the narrow lane between the rows of cabins and cottages, I close my eyes and imagine: a grizzled old mountain man – wisdom steaming out from years of experience and the ability to feel the air - cussing up a storm over his own government's actions, yet coming back, again and again, to guide, to tell others, to share his spirit of the Smokies. It must've been so hard, this tug of war. Which side would win or lose?

Every single day the fight went on inside Levi Trentham... for years. Sometimes it was one side inching ahead, other days, the other. It's tough to live like that, but he did. I admire these men and women of the Smokies. Not only were they self-sufficient, but very, very wise too. They don't make them like that anymore.

And what about Lem Ownby? Near-blind his entire life, desiring love just like everyone else, fighting to keep his own land. He was also a huge inspiration to me, and many others.

I love writing about days gone by, a slice of American history that is important, but nearly gone. I try to capture the who, what, where, when – the basics. The facts. But the *why* and the *how* are, to me, the two best categories because they reveal a special wisdom that could only be had living through tough times and persevering. Think about it: how would you carve out another life for yourself when you've only known one way to live? Another life you didn't anticipate and didn't want. What resilience! Although most mountain folk would just say, "you just got to get on with what you gotta do."

Many ask why I write about Smoky Mountain history. Beyond the fact that my dad's side of the family hails from the area - Western North Carolina since the 1700s, coming from Abernethy, Scotland (my maiden name is Abernathy- some spell it with an E and some with an A) - the reason is simple: it's because when I'm surrounded by endless wrinkles of blue and misty mountains, I feel the gravity of human history that played out right along their ridges. It's an overwhelming urge to preserve that way of life, to honor it. And I greatly enjoy getting to "know" the many people and communities who once called this place home, before the national park. Before it was all of ours.

Like millions of others, my family drives through the park, stopping for photos, for a hike or two, to enjoy a picnic, and then we simply must go to Elkmont, to marvel at remnants of chimneys, to walk inside and admire the old cottages with their old kitchens, the flooring, the fireplaces, and we make sure to sit on the front porch of The Appalachian Club to imagine how life was during its golden years.

But I also know that only those who actually lived it can truly understand. I try my best to keep true to all details, dates, facts; however, like any historical fiction author, some decisions and creative liberties must be taken. Yet I always keep in mind my mission: to honor and preserve their way of life.

We must cherish and honor our ancestors, our fellow Americans who made such sacrifices so we could all enjoy what is now all of ours - the stunningly beautiful Great Smoky Mountains National Park. I am humbled to contribute to preserving even a bit of its history, for it holds an important place in our human story.

Simple folk and simple living left riches for us all.

I hope you enjoy your stay at Elkmont!

Thank you – *Catherine*

1

THE CLUB – 1912

TRAIN MEANS TO TEACH. IT ALSO MEANS A GREAT STEELY BEAST PLOWIN' THROUGH MY LAND.

~

The Appalachian Club steamed with warm bodies and mountain mist on a mild July night. An iron horse dropped visitors off just this morning; their clothes, hair, and spirit adopting that smoky city smell that clung to faces, hands, and fabric. Most hadn't bothered yet to change from their travel wear, but come tomorrow, the owl would find them in their shorter skirts, linen trousers, even bathing costumes, soaking in the soul of the mountains.

Wading in creeks - shrugging their shoulders up to their chins and ears - they'd exclaim "it's so cold!" Yet twelve minutes later, these same city folk became acclimated to the chill and walked even further, until their waists were submerged.

"Look at this!" Boys clipped rocks between their thumbs and forefingers, flinging them across the water. "I skipped a rock!" Two hits - sometimes four or more - the rock would make as it leapt across the creek's surface. They'd never seen such a thing!

Girls picnicked and hiked, exploring side trails, examining

flowers, choosing just the right walking stick, and marveling at the deer - or two - making an appearance at the edges of groves and forests.

Parents required just about three days in the mountains - the ones dozing in the misty blue clouds - to actually relax. To breathe. So their lungs didn't catch themselves mid-breath with the everyday toils of work and city life. When they did finally fill their bodies and lungs full of that dream-like mountain air, their insides unknotted quickly, souls feeling more at peace than ever before.

A fireplace! Look at the size of this kitchen! Plenty of rooms for all of us... Storage. Look at this corner cabinet. Why, we could live here - and even cook!

Oh, dearest. We are on vacation! I do not wish to cook. The Appalachian Club is supposed to have wonderful food.

A great-horned owl perched on a burly branch. It was dusk, suppertime, and he let out a hoot that bounced off more than three hundred Smoky Mountain peaks, all of them just sitting there, drowsy in the late evening mist. Eyes keen as an eagle, hunting prowess matching that of a wildcat, the owl stalked the myriad kitchen scraps behind The Appalachian Club that always provided a reliable and fine dining experience for the stocky bird seeking a small rat or two.

City folks were settling into their green, blue, red, pink, and white cottages lined in neat rows on each side of the narrow street. The scent of pine mingled with the sharp tang of coal smoke as a train from Knoxville - the *Elkmont Special* - chugged its way into the small mountain station just up the road from the row of cottages.

During this summer of 1912, the iron horse was letting out more than its usual number of vacationers – the entire nation was still reeling from the sinking of the unsinkable Titanic in April, their hearts heavy and ready for a respite. Even President Taft expressed his deep sadness at the loss of life in the icy north Atlantic waters, including his military aide, Major Archibald Butt, who was "like a member of the family," he solemnly memorialized.

But here in the Smokies, life was easy for vacationers. Convenient. No more were passengers forced to ride in the "dog car" or caboose as in years past; daily train service now carried them straight from Knoxville's Southern Station straight into the resort town of Elkmont. Many were taking advantage of the comfortable journey. Why, earlier today, the owl even saw Colonel Townsend himself step off the train, quickly greeting visitors and clients as they settled into a two-week - or even two-month – vacation into the heart of the most beautiful mountains on earth.

IT WASN'T ALWAYS this way.

The owl ate, slept, perched on thick branches, flying a daily surveillance over what was once called the Little River Community, begun back in the mid-1800s. As the cluster of log homes grew, and the logging industry arrived, the area eventually flourished into a town renamed Elkmont.

As with most things, time and progress meandered leisurely, pausing to look this way and that, sometimes turning around and walking backwards towards comfort and familiarity. In the end though, the affairs of humans do change – perhaps adapt is a better word – and even the smallest doses of transformation may eventually fit securely on top of a brand new era.

One particular person saw all of it: the mostly wild and untamed land of his youth. Then, the sprouting up of a small logging community. Now, the beginning of a resort town. Finally - at least in his eyes – he was also seeing the starting seeds being eaten away by the odds and ends of time.

Colonel Wilson Bailey, "W.B." Townsend, stepped off the train and greeted that one particular person, that one very distinct man, the *Prophet of the Smokies*, as Levi Trentham was called. And what an appropriate moniker! Nowadays, Mr. Trentham worked all over these mountains as a hunting and fishing guide, but most importantly, as an informal historian of all things Smoky Mountains. He had either seen, heard, or done it all. Or at least all that mattered. The rest, he prophesized.

"LEVI! Good to see you! Come on over here!" Colonel Townsend motioned to the tall and lanky, grizzled and bearded older man. Smiling, Levi sauntered over to the owner of The Little River Railroad, The Little River Lumber Company, and various other enterprises that had transformed this slice of heaven for the past twelve or so years.

Levi admitted to the Colonel many times: *I like you, Colonel. You're a decent man. But I'll always be angry about some big city man like you comin' in and startin' a business tearin' down all the trees so no bear or deer or man could hide from one another.*

But Levi Trentham also knew enough to know he must adapt, must tamp down the bitterness or it would consume him. Didn't want to be like the south after the War Between the States – a stubborn pupil, rejecting the lessons of the stick-wielding teacher who kept beating his hands until they bled but still clapping back because of near-fatal rage and anger. No. He'd had to be careful of that inner wrath, to not let it get out of control. His thoughts were rigid and well-baked, and he clung to the old ways furiously, yet he also keenly recognized the need to bend and change. *How you deal with life's high summits and deep hollers is what matters*, he'd say, and Levi tried his best to follow his own advice, using his famously favorite word: *goddamn.*

"How's the fishing, Levi?"

"Great, Colonel. Got the folk from Ohio some big ol' rainbow trout, brook trout. A lamprey or two. Them folk are goddamn happy. They're cookin' it up right now up at the club. Havin' it all for their supper I reckon."

"Thank you, Levi. I'll have to try some myself!" Colonel Townsend chuckled to himself at the colorful language this mountain man loved to use. Most would find it offended God and preferred the tamer *doggone, dadgum, daggam*, and *ain't you a son of a biscuit eater?* Trying not to offend God brought out the creativity all over Appalachia. But Levi could get away with saying it outright. It was part of his character – he was the real thing, and somehow, coming from his wise and resigned mouth, his phrasing didn't mean anything religiously offensive. Just another effective word or two to use to emphasize his strong beliefs.

Levi nodded his head at the Colonel, sack of berries over his shoulder. Fishing in the morning turned into collecting berries in the afternoon. He smiled - and puzzled a bit - at the people he guided. Wide citified eyes revealed awe at never-before-seen wild blueberries. Blackberries. A deer or two. A bear. Why, he had been hunting and trapping bear his whole life! Nothin' new about that! But these city folk never grew a radish or carrot, never tilled soil or worried about corn crops, never built a cabin out of only what you saw when first arriving in the wilderness, and certainly never saw a goddamn wild bear!

Later in the evening, he'd join the vacationers on the porch of the club and regale these city folk with that one bear tale he loved to tell. Oh, the looks on their faces!! It happened every other week at least: new visitors from all over the country, stepping off that iron horse with their shiny shoes sinking into leaves, dirt, mud, grass, and water puddling from the creek right over there.

Colonel Townsend especially loved the bear story; his eyes would glint every time this character, Levi Trentham, told the tale, which was often. As the businessman watched the tourists, visitors, vacationers, city folk - whatever you called them - he could see the horror, the fascination, the disbelief as Levi Trentham relayed his famous bear story.

Me and Ben Parton, a friend of mine, struck off up Jake's Creek. We was pursuin' a huge bear. We'd skin it and sell its hide – got about three dollars for a small bear and six dollars or even more for a big one, like the one we was pursuin' that day off Jake's Creek. Now, reckon you may not know this, but we sell our corn for a dollar a bushel and shoes are two to four dollars a pair. So, bear pelts may be risky to get but are worth an awful lot.

Anyhows, we always carry our rifles of course, and our huntin' knives for skinnin' the bear. On that day, we came upon a cave that I said may be that big bear's den. Parton crawled into the cave to flush him out. Now, we had our rifles of course, so though a bear could be crazed, we was well-prepared. Or so we thought...

People who were sipping tea on the front porch stared at this mountain man like *he* was the one crazed. Who goes into a bear's den? Even with a rifle? Pondering such a life, they couldn't imagine! Why, their town's newspaper reported bobcat and bear sightings with regularity, like it was a novelty to see one and it was definitely something to stay away from.

But here, it was just a way of life; in fact, a bear sighting was welcomed! It meant a good amount of money! A soft rug at the very least. This place called Elkmont sure was beautiful, and visitors from cities and towns wondered how it would be to live here. To have grown up within a narrow, but flat valley at the junction of the Little River and Jake's Creek. Such quaint names. But every one of the staff and workers and train porters and maids and cooks knew exactly where Meigs Mountain was and that it was situated to the west; where Sugarland Mountain was - to the east - and Cove Mountain, of course, was right there, that soft peak to the north. Blanket Mountain, Mount Collins, Kuwohi...all were landmarks to these mountain folk, just like street signs and stores and corners were in their hometowns.

Suddenly, 'a thunderous roar came from within the cave'. Levi continued, pausing for effect, looking each of them straight in the eyes. He was quite the storyteller! *Parton found the bear and 'the fight was on'. Never heard such screams...Parton's were like banshees echoing off the walls of the cave and were as loud as those of the bear. It was 'bout half an hour or so when Parton came out. What a sight he was! Bloodied and scratched and bleedin'. But he was draggin' the bear behind him. I done looked at him and you know what I said?*

The people perched at the edge of chairs. Children and men had long ago stood up, shuffling their feet, unable to sit still through such a story.

I paid little heed to Parton's 'ripped flesh and tattered clothing' 'cause I knew he was fine. He was walkin' after all and still had his rifle in one hand and the bear in the other. As Parton would tell it, he said to me 'Levi, you stroked your beard in contemplation and casually asked me, 'you-a-gettin' my bear?' He was miffed that I didn't pay attention to his bloodied condition and screamed back at me: 'Your bear, hell! Go in an' get your own damn bear!'"

"Levi Trentham folks! You gotta love him. What a raconteur!" Colonel Townsend stood from his chair, clapped his hands. He'd heard this story many times – nearly every week in fact, but oh, what a reaction Levi got from every new visitor! Chuckles, laughter, disbelieving glee, eyes dancing to and fro, and dropped jaws from the children.

Word got around quickly. The daily horde of tourists stepping off the iron horse they called the *Elkmont Special* saw this storytelling, cussing mountain man roaming around, picking and choosing who to guide to fish, hunt. Only those who genuinely shared the true spirit of the mountains would he agree to guide. His own keen senses directed him: were these visitors truly interested in his mountains? Or were they here simply for recreation? With no sense of awe or soul...

He took his sweet old time deciding. For he was in no hurry, and no one dared push him.

Levi never worked for The Appalachian Club, nor for Colonel Townsend, nor anyone. No sir. Levi Trentham worked for only one man – himself. Most people loved him. Those who didn't at least respected him. He had grown crops, farmed, tended his land for a good long time, but now his own little slice of heaven was much smaller. Less natural and more crowded. He didn't like it at all yet knew he needed to adapt as progress stomped its feet on his front porch. But he'd be damned if that adaptation wasn't to be on his very own terms.

2

THE PROPHET

MEN MAY MEET, BUT MOUNTAINS NEVER.

It was time for afternoon tea. Such a formal tradition was a bit strange in these mountains where the sky meets the softly scalloped peaks marching their way as far as the eye can see.

People met, gathered, mingled: *This is God's country to be sure. We don't have mountains where we come from.*

Our own drive was a long way...we came from Ohio and drove all the way to Knoxville to catch the train. The train was faster than I expected. Wonderful scenery along the way.

My husband is a banker, needs a vacation. The mountain air is supposed to be good for the lungs. Good for the soul. We're in the blue cabin.

Ah, I saw that one on our walk towards our cabin - we are in the green one, the one up the street from The Appalachian Club. It has a great kitchen.

Ours does too...

But I don't want to cook in it!

I know! Me neither!

I feel bad for not using ours...

Ah now, I don't blame you at all...don't feel bad. I told my husband I don't want to cook on vacation either!

What do you think of that Prophet of the Smokies as they call Mr. Levi Trentham? Such a storyteller! But I love his tales...they say he owned a general store at one time and was a farmer.

Talk spread quickly *like green grass through a goddamn goose* as Mr. Trentham would say. Oh yes, Levi Trentham was well aware he attracted attention with his colorful language, and he'd be damned if he was going to stop now. If these city folk can't take some character-building talk, well, he'd talk even *more* and really give 'em something to run from. *Or at least*, he thought, *I'll ignore 'em and refuse to guide folk to the best fishin' spots they're always askin' me to point out.* Or else he'd take 'em to the dankest and poorest hole in the creek where they'd surely come home empty handed. After he took their money of course.

But if some of them city folk did show some humor and agreement with whatever damn thing he wanted to tell 'em, and if they showed an interest and looked up at the peaks he'd known all his life with wonder and at least some genuine appreciation, *well, I'll still take their money, but at least I'll make it worth their while.*

"Ever wonder why they call him the Prophet of the Smokies?" Mrs. Farr and Mrs. Galyon asked simultaneously to their gathered spouses and children.

There were many families who vacationed in Elkmont every year. The Farrs hailed from Knoxville and constructed a family cabin two years ago, in 1910. Then the Farrs constructed another cabin, and that's when Eugene Galyon purchased their original one for his own family who were always saying he simply had to get away from his desk at the Galyon Lumber Company and Knoxville Lumber and Manufacturing Company!

To which he'd playfully pounce back at his wife, Mayme: "Me? Why, your work with the Red Cross takes up much more time than my two businesses combined! You've got over eight-hundred hours of volunteer work already!" She frowned at that, shaking her head, but they both agreed their busy lives could use a break and never regretted a moment spent in these beautiful Smoky Mountains of Tennessee, full of memories and mysteries and characters like Levi Trentham.

"I hear he sees visions. Things that he's said to others that later came to pass." Mrs. Galyon whispered, looking around to make sure the Prophet was nowhere to be seen.

"Like what?" Children piped up, always curious to hear any new and interesting tale.

"Well, I hear he knows the weather better than the clouds themselves. He once told folk about a disaster about to happen."

"Hmmm. What kind of disaster? It's pretty easy to predict the weather...the Almanac has a whole book about it!" Mr. Galyon scoffed, but pulled up a chair, sat, and poured hot blackberry tea as he listened to his wife and friends.

"Ah true. But apparently, he told his neighbors that heavy rains and flooding were coming and to store food on the highest shelves and stay on higher ground. Some people thought him mad and didn't listen because there was nothing forecasted nor any signs of a storm, but most did, in fact, heed his warning. Sure enough, when the rains came, severe floods swept through the valleys causing landslides. The rivers crested and rose, and they say many homes and farmlands were just... gone. Devastated. Those who listened to Levi thanked the Lord for his advice and avoided the worst of the disaster. Those who didn't, well, some of 'em ain't around anymore to tell him he was right." Mr. Galyon chuckled at his wife's accent, so easily adopted as soon as one stepped off the train straight into the burly and folksy arms of the most beautiful mountains on earth.

"That's an amazing tale, Mayme, to be sure. But still…some of us can tell a bad storm is coming by the clouds and the feel of the air. Why, most of us older folk - our old joints will stiffen and the change in pressure causes headaches and that's when we know rain is coming." Mr. Farr joined in Mr. Galyon's skepticism.

Both men were sipping their third blackberry tea of the day, helped by slipping in a little something from their silver flasks. The businessmen were thus very relaxed, just a few hours into their vacation. The mountains were already performing their magic. Hard-working, routine-oriented souls unknotted; the most industrious and conscientious felt the grind of daily life quieting, gently moving towards peace. Desks, paperwork, meetings and budgets, orders and inventory, the needs of workers and supervisors, all the burdens and responsibilities of running businesses suddenly seemed far, far away.

As for the women, they too had a temporary reprieve from their own "businesses" that nearly always ran out of their homes: cooking, cleaning, laundry, running the household, raising children, grocery shopping, arranging social schedules, shopping, sewing, sweeping; not to mention Mrs. Mayme Galyon's volunteer work with the Red Cross where she comforted and cared for so many by gathering clothes, medicines, and monies. She was just coming off an exhaustive campaign to assist the survivors and grieving families of April's sinking of the Titanic.

"Indeed, we can sometimes tell when the weather's going to be bad or when someone is obviously sick. But can you heal someone who's sick from a mysterious illness?" Mrs. Galyon asked.

"Well, no, but…" Her husband answered warily. Where did his wife hear all these tales? At the Red Cross? She was much,

much more social than he, but still...she had a knack of inserting herself immediately and deeply anywhere she happened to be, including here, right into the local culture of Elkmont, Tennessee. It was one of the things he loved about her. She made her own fun, as they say in the mountains, and always had a good heart attached to her antics. Certainly, life was interesting with her around.

"Well, Mr. Levi Trentham had a neighbor who suffered from something no one could figure out, not even the doctors. They tried and tried, all different treatments, but nothing worked. Everyone said, 'go to the prophet, go to the prophet'... but the neighbor and his family said that was just crazy talk. Until nothing worked and they had nothing else to lose. Then, they finally went to Levi."

The tea cooled as the Farr and Galyon families, along with several other friends, mesmerized their afternoon with tales of this tall and lanky and wary prophet character who hung around The Appalachian Club, picking and choosing carefully who to guide to hike, hunt, and fish; the ones who he thought would appreciate the mountains like he did. Like he wanted them to.

"When the poor sick man arrived at Levi's cabin, apparently, Levi just looked at him, up and down many times, as if studying his body inch by inch. Then, Levi went out into the forest to collect some herbs and plants. Upon returning, everyone present watched in silence as he mixed it all up and gave it to the man with specific instructions on how to use it, along with prayer and meditation. Strange, eh? But according to the story, within about a week or so, the man's condition improved! Dramatically, it is said. And he fully recovered quickly thereafter. No doctor, nobody anywhere, could explain why."

One of the other visitors who was in the corner of the porch sipping tea and listening, suddenly rose, pointing. "Look. There he is! Coming up the road! Levi Trentham. The Prophet of the Smokies."

The intriguing older man was indeed walking along the road between the cabins, stopping to talk to a circle of young boys holding long fishing poles.

"Wonder how long he's seen things in the forest? He grew up here, to be sure, and knows the area very well. I never heard all those other stories ya'll were talking about, but I did hear about the one winter when a local hunter went missing. It may be wise to keep close to Mr. Trentham if we're ever out hunting or hiking or even just fishing." Mr. Galyon murmured, watching the bearded character make his way towards the other side of the street, walking towards the creek, young city boys following him with their fishing poles, barefoot, dirty, and happy.

"Why's that Mr. Galyon?" One of the Farr children piped up, secretly vowing to go fishing with this mysterious man at least once during their stay here in Elkmont.

"Because son, if we're lost, it seems he's the only one who can find us."

The story quickly circulated around the porch. The tea - and whatever else was added - long cold, everyone's attention fiercely set on the legend of the mysterious mountain man who roamed around The Appalachian Club and the streets of Elkmont; the one whom everyone called The Prophet of the Smokies or The Mayor of Elkmont. Some even dared to call him Uncle Levi.

It was Mr. Farr who picked up the story as he chuckled at his friend, Mr. Galyon, who was slumped, half asleep now, having tipped a bit too much into his fragile green and yellow teacup.

"A local hunter went missing one winter not too long ago. He was hunting bear, deer, anything he could find, when a sudden and fierce blizzard arrived. His family and neighbors and friends, and even his dogs, searched for days, but their normal method of tracking was impossible due to snowfall. Desperate, they called on Levi Trentham. As was usual, he listened to the situation and sat quietly, apparently for a long time. For the good part of an hour."

Mr. Galyon rustled just then, grimacing and eyeing Mr. Farr. His eyes closed again, but he was listening to his friend tell the amazing part of the tale.

"Then, he snapped out of it, as they say, and Levi told them he'd had a vision: the lost hunter was trapped beneath a fallen tree near a stream that ran along the eastern side of the mountain. It was so specific! Now, snowfall erases all tracks, everything...so how could he know such things? But they were so desperate that they followed his directions. Well, that's when the miracle happened. Sure enough, after hours of trekking through the heavy snowfall, they found the hunter exactly where Levi had said! Oh, but the hunter was barely alive – pinned beneath a tree. Too weak to call out or even shoot off a shot from his rifle. The men lifted the tree, freed the man, and carried him back to a cabin to recover. And recover he did."

"My Lord. A miracle indeed."

"It must be a true story...everyone knows it."

"Even if it's exaggerated, there's still got to be some truth to it."

"Indeed. But from what folk say, there's no exaggeration at all. They all swear that's exactly what happened. It's quite amazing."

"I wonder...just where did this man come from?"

3

BEGINNINGS – 1840S

GOOD TO BEGIN WELL, BETTER TO END WELL.

~

Colonel Townsend arrived just then. He had been chatting with a group of other businessmen - colleagues and rivals. But he got along with everyone, was always congenial, professional, gentlemanly; his was the type to go from swanky soirees to smoky front porches and feel at home and at ease in both places.

"Colonel! Come on over if you have a moment. We were just discussing Levi Trentham..."

"Oh! Levi. Wouldn't be the same around here without him."

"To be sure!" They laughed.

"Colonel? Can you tell us what you know about Levi?"

"Sure. But...where do I even start?" He greeted the crowd, shook a few hands, sat down, took off his hat, laid it on his knee. Mrs. Galyon and Mrs. Farr both offered him a drink which he happily accepted. Then, he took a breath and told them he had to get back to Townsend soon – the town that bears his name - but that he'd tell them what he knew of Mr. Trentham's history.

"Levi's father was Robert Trentham who arrived in the 1840s. It is said that when he saw this land - so untouched, lush, and fertile; not built up like it is now - that he told his family they simply must settle right here and right now."

Indeed, as one of the first settlers of the area, the inky blue of the Little River greeted Levi's father, along with white oaks, yellow poplars, and the most colorful of nature's decorations: showy pinkish dogwoods, blue and violet wildflowers, green canopies - all decked out in their finest attire.

Colonel Townsend leaned back, balancing a mug on one knee. "Of course, the Cherokee were here long before Robert Trentham ever set eyes on this valley. You can still find the evidence –shards of pottery, remnants of baskets, foodstuffs and such. Very, very old these things."

The crowd nodded and Mrs. Galyon offered, "I think I saw a basket reed sticking up out of the soil after a hard rain. It gave me chills wondering just how long ago it was made."

"Indeed. The Cherokee, as you know, ceded their lands to the thirteen states of the United States of America, in the Treaty of Dumplin Creek. It was on June 10, 1785, if memory serves. And this allowed for the settlement of Tennessee's Sevier, Knox, and Blount counties without resistance from the Cherokee or other American Indians."

They nodded their heads at their knowledge of the famous treaty that opened the path for pioneers like Robert Trentham and another settler, Jacob Houser. Born in 1791, Houser lived the entirety of his life in the depths of this mountain valley. When he died in 1870, despite the isolation of this small slice of the Smoky Mountains, he was quite well-known. The Colonel continued: "that's where Jake's Creek gets its name. Jake's Creek is named for Jacob Houser."

Nodding, fascinated by the history of this place, the vacationers all thought the same way: it seemed as if cabins and cottages and the club were always here. It was hard to picture a wild, untamed, undeveloped, place.

"Soon, a few more settlers came in. They farmed and built cabins and corncribs, barns and mills, and were mostly from two families: Ownby and Trentham, who came to own and cultivate much of the land. We already know Levi Trentham came from one of the original families, but David Ownby was another who came here early on. He was born in...let's see now...1816? Yes, I think that's it. He passed away in 1889, but he came here in the mid-1800s searching for gold and he was the one who called this place "Little River". It was not much of a place though, with only a scattering of homes and farmsteads, until Robert - Levi Trentham's father - arrived in the 1840s and began a community. A small community to be sure, but it thrived: everyone farmed corn and apples, and a few kept bees for honey to consume and sell. Despite its small size, people from mostly the two families came together for the greater good – a few gristmills sprang up, small-scale logging occurred, and a general store or two opened along Jake's Creek. Eventually, the area became known as the Little River Community."

"And that's the environment Levi was born into?"

"Yes sir, Mr. Galyon." Colonel Townsend nodded. "He was born on February 22, 1852, one of ten children of Robert Trentham and Mary R. "Polly" Fancher Trentham. And oh, how he loved his ancestral land! Right from the start. Still does."

It was true. For practically his entire life, he was known as 'a mountain man to the ends of his beard. Through and through, he loved these mountains'. Inheriting his Pa, Robert's, cabin, built in 1845, Levi farmed, trapped bears and sold their hides, owned a store, kept bees and sold honey. But oh, did he scorn outsiders! Years later, as the guests at The Appalachian Club came to know this legendary man, they found him muttering about all the "furriners". He was a man quite content living within his own special and fierce brand of freedom.

Despite his rebuffing anyone who wasn't of these mountains, Levi was clever and astute soon realizing there was money to be made with these *furriners,* who absolutely loved folk like him whom they called the 'native guides and storytellers'. As his own children, along with friends, relatives and neighbors, watched the fiercely independent man adapt to the rapidly changing times of the late 1800s and early 1900s, they'd shake their heads and exclaim, "the fast-talking mountaineer known as Uncle Levi is a natural at tellin' his tales" to all these city folk.

As early as 1885, Levi began to see loggers and their families living on the banks of his little community. In 1901, Colonel Townsend's Little River Lumber Company began purchasing land for lumber and began felling timber for the robust timber market. A bit later, he installed a railroad transfer station so heavy logs could be transferred from the gear-operated trains to rod-operated trains.

By 1908, the Little River Community was known as Elkmont, which was essentially a "temporary logging camp" with "shanty-like housing" for the loggers.

"Seems everyone's callin' it Elkmont nowadays. But there ain't no elk around here!" Levi would lament. He liked his home to be called by its proper name: Little River Community. It seemed only right because, after all, the land was right on the Little River!

But according to Mrs. Maidee Deloach Adams and Earnest Trentham – kinfolk to Levi – the name Elkmont was used more and more because members of the Knoxville Elks Club hunted and fished in the area around 1900, even before Colonel Townsend came in with his Little River Lumber Company. By the time the railroad was established, and logging was underway, the name Elkmont had stuck and was often explained: *it's called Elkmont on account of the "two-legged 'Elks' that now roam this valley and not the four-legged animals".*

Levi saw all this happen, heard the clanging sounds of change, and though he couldn't read or write, he certainly heard enough from his neighbors and kin about *The Maryville Times* and *Pulanski Citizen* newspaper headlines that blared:

Families are moving on Elkmont in Caravans!

All available cabins have been rented this summer and there are demands for many more.

Elkmont is now quite a town and plenty of people and good society is assured every summer, as the houses are owned by different individuals.

Levi knew many of these folk; they were people who had worked in logging, had grown tired of felling logs, but not tired of the area. Thus, they began building their own small cabins for hunting and fishing. Before he knew it, as the seasons meandered through their allotted timeslots in history, word got out about this lush and peaceful place, full of recreation. Soon, Knoxville businessmen and sportsmen, alongside those former logging workers and families, gathered in greater and greater numbers.

Later, it wasn't just the headlines that declared intentions, it was the visitors themselves: *why not build even more cabins and retreats so we can all stay for a while? Make it a real vacation spot? A resort.*

Indeed, Levi saw this mindset grow, saw progress happen, adapted to it - mostly against his will. Yet even he had to admit he'd have to somehow find his new place in this new world. Just how to do that though, remained a half-ripened prophecy still forming in his soul.

4

VACATION LIFE

TEACHING OF OTHERS
TEACHETH THE TEACHER.

∼

The Appalachian Club fell into late afternoon shadows. Well past teatime, guests retreated to their cabins to rest before supper. They soon learned that dinner was lunch and supper was dinner. Such a unique culture here in these mountains! They had words, phrases, habits, all their own. And the people! The tourists had no idea people still lived like this in 1912, without bathrooms or running water, using only the land to sustain them. Why, that curious man, Mr. Trentham - whom everyone called the Prophet of the Smokies or The Mayor of Elkmont or even Uncle Levi- was a strange one indeed! Didn't like foreigners, or as he says it, *"furriners"* – which included all outsiders. Yet he sought out these same outsiders to tell his stories to; sought them out to guide them to the best fishing hole, the best bear caves, or the best waterfall hike.

They'd heard he married Litha Emaline Ownby on January 4, 1872, and had ten children together. Living right here, hugged into these mountains, for most of their lives. What was it like?

To hunt, trap, grow everything? What did they do when they were sick? Injured? What did they do for fun?

Another marvel was that one huge owl who always seemed to be lurking around. Was he merely seeking food? Known to be curious birds of prey, owls prefer to be alone, with time to observe, to be accurate and thorough; yet these independent birds also tend to mate for life, are loyal – at least to their mate and territory – and tend to be wary and vigilant of their surroundings. *Kind of like that Levi Trentham,* they all thought.

Tsgili is the Cherokee name for the great-horned owl, famous for its hooting calls. An owl is known to be prophetic; Cherokee revered the great bird for its wisdom and strength. At the same time, the great creature was feared because it was also said to represent death and defeat. Young men wished to be like an owl – a great hunter - and young girls wished for a husband like an owl – a solid provider with sharp vision for any danger that an owl so clearly sees.

Indeed, the owl and the prophesying mountain man shared many traits, not least that neither owl nor man could read a lick, though both surely knew the weight words could carry.

"CAN'T READ. But I make do."

Levi Trentham was illiterate. In the cities of 1912 America, eighty-eight percent of urban people were literate. But in the mountains of Appalachia, only about half could read or write. Of those, what they did read was limited: the Bible, the Almanac, newspapers, and the Sears Catalog, but not much else.

"No matter. I can't read or write, but I sure can add up some money. See here, I owned a general store at one point. Kept coffee, sugar, cheese, flour, bolts of cloth, farm equipment, grindstones, nails, and some shoes." Levi Trentham was stopped in the middle of the Elkmont street, watching as guests began emerging from their cottages, making their way to the end of the road where The Appalachian Club would welcome them for dinner.

"It's called supper 'round here, actually." He'd gently remind them, catching up to a few families he deemed kindly folk. "S comes after D, or so I'm told. So D for dinner is first. What ya'll city folk call lunch. And S is for supper which comes after D. Reckon that's how you folk can remember what we do 'round here."

They nodded, charmed by the old mountain man.

"How'd you keep track of everything? When you had your store I mean? If you didn't write anything down?"

"Ah, that's easy. A nail."

"A nail?"

"Yessir. And ma'am." He tipped his hat to the ladies in the group. "Simple. See, I hammered a bunch of nails into the walls right behind my counter. One for each of my customers."

"That's a lot of nails."

"Not really. Reckon I only got twenty or so nails. Look around. Not much folk 'round these parts."

They looked. Trees glittered in golden light, swelling with bud, and the air smelled freshly green as the strange owl who loved the daylight argued over its territory with a crow. The vacationers imagined life with only a few neighbors. It was so unlike their cities and towns where people lived on top of one another crammed into grid-like streets. There was so much room here! But it was true that there weren't many full-time residents like Levi – people had been migrating to bigger urban areas in the past few years. More jobs. More opportunities. More comfort.

"See here. Any time a customer didn't have enough eggs or corn or such to buy things in trade, I'd draw a picture of the item and stick it on the customer's nail."

"Seems logical. I bet it worked well."

"Pretty well...except for one time." He laughed, reaching the porch of the club, sitting down on the steps in his dark canvas overalls, beard resting on his knees. Snapping his hat over his forehead, pushing it down a little lower due to the sun coming through the trees, he peered at each one of these guests. *Guess they ain't so bad. Furriners, to be sure, but they seem interested. Oh, and there's that owl, hootin' and hollerin' in the broad daylight. Seems he wants to listen too.*

"So, one day, one of my customers charged into the store like a bear that just done got into a hive of bees. No sooner than he'd come through the door, he was yellin': 'Levi! You cheated me!' Now, I got hot right away 'cause I never cheated no one. And I told him so. 'Sit down here now! Explain this to me.' I said. And he said, 'Levi, you charged me for somethin' I didn't buy'."

The people straightened in their chairs, riveted. One little boy boldly asked, "what happened?", to which Levi just winked in his smirking way, and continued.

"Listen close youngin. So my customer says, 'Well, you charged me for a wheel of cheese and I ain't bought no wheel of cheese.' So I said, 'well what did you buy?' And he said 'I bought a grindstone!' Guess my drawings weren't the best." They laughed, seeing in the mind's eye a crude pencil drawing of a circle that could well resemble a wheel of cheese or a grindstone, but could be a basket or bowl or even a platter.

"Well, I explained to the man, I just forgot to draw the hole in your grindstone and that's why I charged you for cheese." Levi laughed, slapping his knee at his error. "All was well after that. We had a good laugh, and I paid a bit more attention to my drawings."

~

IT WAS SUPPERTIME, around six o'clock. It was early for city folk who sometimes dined at nine or ten o'clock at night bringing their full bellies to bed with them. Here, the sun fell below the peaks much earlier in the mountain world, shrouding forests and boulders and creeks into a dusky darkness, right under what was certainly God's tapestry of heaven.

Early bedtimes were common; early rises essential. Much had to be done by the time the light appeared just behind the mountains with its pinks and yellows, the sun nudging itself up, up as if double checking if it were really time to come out. Satisfied that it was, the shining orb showed itself in its full glory, lighting the stage of already bustling barns and homes, thick smoke rising from chimneys emitting the smells of fresh biscuits and fried eggs and ham.

The Appalachian Club's employees consisted of many locals, accustomed to chores before dawn: collecting eggs, milking cows, pitching hay, sweeping, surveying crops and gardens and fences and roofs, weeding, pruning, cooking, sewing buttons back onto uniforms and such, sweeping yet again. All the while, guest slept peacefully in their cottages lining the one long road leading to the railroad station. When they woke, rested, lungs newly full of fresh mountain air, they were greeted with scrambled eggs, ham, and biscuits so fluffy they were like clouds on a plate. Fruit and cereals rounded out their choices.

After breakfast, the choices were endless! Swimming holes were very popular, girls sat on rocks protruding from the river while little waterfalls spilled themselves down into pools of sunlight. Hikes to nearby Laurel Falls - eighty feet high and stunningly beautiful - were immensely popular.

Afternoons kept company with card games such as poker and whist played on tables in the lobby or on the large porch of The Appalachian Club. Sometimes, players would gather on the smaller front porches or rooms of the individual cottages. Suppers were fine affairs and generally taken at the club. Typical fare would include pickled cucumbers or beets, cornbread with fresh butter and jams, vegetable or potato soup, fried chicken or ham or freshly caught trout from the creeks and river. Perhaps a collard green or green bean side dish or two, roasted potatoes, and biscuits and other breads would round out the hearty down-home meal. Substantial and filling it was, but guests were never ready to return to their cabins just yet. For a peach or blackberry cobbler or sorghum cake were welcome ends to their meal, and they enjoyed every morsel with tea, coffee, and sometimes, home-made cider.

Some of the men disappeared around the side of the club after dessert seeking a bit of cover and privacy, but the women knew exactly what they were doing. They'd heard all about devil's rum, mountain mulekick, white lightning, mountain dew. Oh yes, they'd heard all about the best moonshine in America being produced right here in the Smoky Mountains and they knew their men were tasting a sip or two. It was vacation after all! And as the men sauntered back, sometimes a lot later in the night, they'd exclaim, "This place is heaven. It don't get any better than this."

During a guest's week or two stay, there was bound to be many happenings at The Appalachian Club. From its very beginnings as an exclusive club formed in 1910, it attracted a wealthy crowd, mostly from Knoxville, who wished to escape the city sidewalks for a bit and enjoy the natural beauty of the mountains. Dances, picnics, teas, dinners and suppers, and myriad other gatherings had the wooden building full every single summer night.

A social hub it was and though Levi Trentham wasn't an official member and never truly worked there, every guest knew of him as soon as they stepped off the train and spent their first hour or two settling in. The Prophet. The Mayor.

Uncle. The truest mountain man there ever was. The Legend. And he was present quite often, especially at mealtimes.

IT WAS near the end of suppertime – these city folk still had to get used to not calling it dinner! – as guests of The Appalachian Club finished feasting on fresh trout and biscuits with the greenest green beans imaginable, doused in a bit of bacon scraps and pepper. Some of the visitors, scooping up the remnants of buttery mashed potatoes and feeling mighty well and bold, got the idea of calling on Levi Trentham to tell their fortunes.

"Mr. Trentham! Would you like to join us up here on the porch?" Guests typically moved onto the large deck after supper, to sip coffee, tea, have sorghum cookies or pie for dessert. The view was spectacular, and the evening gave off just the right amount of chill to require a wrap or jacket.

"Mighty kind of you folks. Yessir, I reckon I'll sit a spell with ya'll." Levi Trentham heaved himself up from his chair in the dining room and walked outside to the screened-in porch. At least the mosquitoes wouldn't be able to eat them alive, and the sun had just tucked itself well below the peaks.

"Speaking of spells..." one woman quietly twittered to another. "Let's see if he'll tell our fortunes tonight!"

"Mr. Trentham...?" Called one of the women, a bit of the flirt in her on display.

"Call me Levi."

"Alrighty...Levi..."

Levi narrowed his eyes. *Just what were these folk up to? They always wanted something from him, these furriners. Why can't they just sit and enjoy the sunset? The hoot of that owl that's always lurking around looking for a rat or two behind the kitchen? These folk will never appreciate the mountain life. A few rare ones may feel the soul of the mountains, but most of 'em understand damn nothin' of the heavily forested interior of folk like me. As for me, I don't much understand these city folk. But what I do understand, I don't much like.*

"We hear you're a prophet of sorts."

"Of sorts?" One narrowed eyebrow raised. He nodded, very slightly, curiosity overtaking his instinct to get up and walk away.

"Can you tell us our fortunes?" One of the twittering women boldly asked.

He sighed, squinting his eyes. "You folk really wanna know?"

"Oh yes, yes! We do!" Every last one laid hands in laps, sat up straighter, eager faces pushed towards his own.

"Okay. Alrighty then. I'll tell ya'll what's in store." Pausing, he stood up now, leaned against the wooden railing, making sure no splinters got into the sleeve of his shirt. Pulling on his beard for a moment, he began pacing in front of the crowd.

"You folk may enjoy your time here in the mountains. To be sure, it's the most beautiful place on God's earth. But ya'll will never truly understand this land. All your efforts - some of ya'll are loggers or company men I reckon? Anyways, your efforts to control or what you call 'civilize' this here land will come to nothin'. See those cottages ya'll's families are stayin' at? This grand Appalachian Club building we're standing in right now? The forest will reclaim them all. Eventually. One of them will burn. Not too far from today's date in fact. These cabins you're enjoyin', most will be abandoned, nature overtakin' 'em, reclaiming the wood."

Frowns. Ladies stared into their teacups. Men looked down at their shoes. These weren't the fortunes they were seeking! Expecting more like *good luck will come to you because of that horseshoe hanging over your head,* or *the key to your cottage is the key to your good luck,* or *America will rise with even more industry and your company will be part of it.*

But for someone like Levi Trentham who'd lived here all his life and knew every tree, boulder, creek, peak, bird, and animal, the evidence was clear. For the past few decades, he'd seen the Little River Community turn into what was now called Elkmont, even before The Little River Lumber Company came to town with that keen businessman Colonel William B. Townsend. A good man to be sure, but in the mid 1880s, a logging industry begun roughly fifteen miles away or so if taking the road, was shoved forward by Townsend in 1901. Shortly thereafter, the logging industry landed practically on top of Levi's land, changing Levi's life - and lifestyle -forever.

In short time, Colonel had put in railroad transfer stations so heavy logs could be conveyed from the gear-operated trains to rod-operated trains. Levi watched as logs meandered down the river – making transport much easier - all the way to the sawmill downriver at Tuckaleechee – which was eventually renamed Townsend in the Colonel's honor. He'd brought so many jobs and opportunities to the area after all!

Once at the mill, which was located on a flat and accessible bank of the Little River, all those logs were cut, hewn, smoothed, to be made into lumber for homes, furniture, window frames, countertops, and fenceposts.

If Levi could've read the newspaper, he would've seen the Colonel's own words in *The Maryville Times* newspaper: "even *I* was surprised at the growth of the lumber business! There is very little competition."

Indeed, there was little to stand in his way. There was a Mr. Leander Whaley who had a logging business, harvesting tulip trees, buckeye, and basswood from the upper cove, along Ramsey Prong. But that was during the 1880s and he'd cut down most of his own land's trees by the time Colonel Townsend arrived.

Then there was Andy Huff who began a sawmill in Green-brier Cove in 1898. Huff had claimed the largest and most valuable woods already: cherry, ash, walnut, hickory, and yellow poplar. But that had occurred in surrounding areas; Townsend seemed to have arrived here in the Elkmont vicinity at the right time, for he was the first to log this particular land, thick and full of every kind of tree imaginable.

Levi watched the change to his mountains with an unequal mix of awe and regret: *how did this Colonel Townsend even find out about our place here, hidden so deep inside the Smoky Mountains? How'd a city man get to know about Walker Valley and Tuckaleechee Cove, Tennessee? He came from way up there in damn Pennsylvania after all...*

When Levi learned the truth, he was as surprised as anybody. For, it was the very President of the United States himself who spilled the secret.

President Theodore Roosevelt stated the words, reported in every one of the twenty thousand newspapers, magazines, dailies, and monthlies in America at the turn of the century: *These [Smokies have] the heaviest and most beautiful hard-wood forests of the continent...the finest and largest bodies of spruce in the Southern Appalachians'."*

Levi sighed as he watched Colonel Townsend set up his logging operations and sighed longer and longer thereafter, every night, for years. And now, it was 1912 and The Little River Lumber Company was in its second decade. The logging era had indeed begun and was in high hog heaven right now even if Colonel had logged everything right out of Elkmont itself. Why, he just moved over to another slope is all! And there were plenty of slopes covered with the flush of swelling buds and green canopies. Just waiting.

But no matter how far the Colonel moved his lumber operations, Levi and his few neighbors could still hear the sawing, the machinery, the booming of a large tree thundering down,

down, taking out three others on its way. The clanking of railroad spikes hammered into the fertile soil. Could still hear the iron horse cutting through the noise of the chirping and hooting and water rolling over rocks that had been there for millennia. Could see the smoke coming from that damn train that changed everything for the better. And for the worse. And all these damn *furriners* or city folk wanted to know was *their* very own fortunes.

Well, Levi thought to himself as he eyed the *furriners* all lined up on the porch of The Appalachian Club, full of themselves and cobblers and cookies and their dinner as they call it, forgetting it's actually called supper around here. *I gave 'em what they wanted. I done told them all about the fortune of the land they stand on right now. But I left something out. Their own fortunes will also take a turn. It's gonna be somethin' they don't like. Somethin' they'll try to control, yet they won't be able to. But they'll all have to damn well live with it. Some will take it well and some won't. But I'll keep that particular information to myself for now.*

"TELL US, MR. TRENTHAM – LEVI," one of the men changed the subject, "did you know Colonel Townsend was coming your way with his railroad?"

"Yessir. Saw it all. Felt it too. Saw those three men, who would soon become the Colonel's partners - reckon I recall exactly when they all pitched together their collective fortunes... Speaking of fortunes..." Levi took a turn with his thoughts, "them businessmen, they deal with money, but I deal with the truth. Both are fortunes, but one's worth more. There's a big damn difference between the two. Anyhows, there were three businessmen who done paid $3.00 per acre for 86,000 acres. That's when the Colonel joined up with all three of 'em and then the Colonel became president of The Little River

Lumber Company. As they say, he's the one who pushed it towards what you city folk company men call 'top productivity and capacity'."

Levi remained leaning on the railing of the front porch that evening with the now-silent crowd. He drank some coffee, accepted a bit of shine from one of the men's flasks to splash into his mug, and roamed his memories for when The Little River Lumber Company cut 560 million board feet of lumber out of his very own Smoky Mountains.

By the turn of the century, as Levi was running his successful general store, already very skeptical of the growing number of *all these furriners 'round here*, he remained farming his own land, hunting bear, and selling his honey.

Yet, with each passing season, he felt a bit more exposed; not only because there were less trees in the distance, but also due to more and more folks roaming the slopes, using their machines to snap the quiet surroundings of his beloved green and fertile mountain valley. The only home he'd ever known.

"What made you sell some of your own land as I hear you did? You seem so attached to this place..." One of the twittering women ventured, yet her tone softened with a quiet, almost pitied quality.

"Ah. Well, ma'am, I will always be part of my land, no matter who says they own it. Only God owns this here place. And He put me here forever. Or at least 'til He and I decide when it's time." The group nodded their heads, looking out at the emerging stars covered by a thin veil of mountain mist.

"But as the years went on and the heat to sell got higher, Colonel and his men came 'round more and more, asking about this and that and wavin' money around, and I done told my wife, always with a deep sigh, mind you: 'I'm feelin' more and more pressure to sell our land – these acres and acres inherited from my Pa. What do you think?' And she done told me that one day, the mountains will answer me." He paused, looked out at the darkness, waiting for the crowd's curiosity to peak, as any good storyteller will do. He caught hold of the owl's eyes, gleaming, still.

"Did they? Answer you?"

Works every goddamn time, Levi thought smirking to himself, tearing his gaze away from the creature's sternly fixed stare.

"Yes, they did."

Another pause as that one familiar owl flew away - he didn't need to stick around to listen. He already knew what had happened. Had seen the poor sixty-year old man - the one who loved these mountains as if they were a limb on his own body - cry deep into the nights beside the fireplace his own Pa had built so long ago. Cry so hard, the feathered creature thought he'd put out the roaring fire in the hearth with his tears.

"And what did they say?" Someone dared ask as the crowd stared at this grizzled old, white-bearded fellow wondering just what he heard coming from the voice of the softly scalloped peaks. Perhaps it was only the sounds coming from too much pouring of his flask?

Levi eyed these city folk. Some of 'em were good folk to be sure. But they were so very desperate for answers. To what exact questions, he could only speculate. Questions on what it took to live here in these mountains, their own futures, the very meaning of life? Well - at least this time - he'd give them what the mountains had given him.

"Them mountains told me to live with the questions first. Keep askin'. Don't try to answer yet. One day, you will be sick of asking. And at that exact moment, the answers will come."

It was true. Why, those loggers were pushing him almost every single day to *sell, sell, sell to us!* He refused for a long time, of course, yelling for *you furriners to get offa my land and damn it all, quit pesterin' me!*

But then, in the early 1900s, in his fifties, slowing down just a touch, and seeing how trees were being felled all around him despite his own feelings and desires, he thought of all those questions he was living with: *why not at least have the land surveyed? See how much it's worth. Then, I can decide what to do, if anything.*

He kept asking every day, *what should I do? How much could I get? What more can I do with my land? Maybe I can stay and still get the money?*

And one spring season during those early turn of the century years, as America was rapidly changing, the mountains did, in fact, answer him: *our land and traditions are sacred and cannot be bought. Outside forces cannot reshape our memories; they will remain locked up tight inside our boulders and cliffs, our running waterfalls and soil. It doesn't matter whose name is on some piece of paper in some brick courthouse in a busy town. That piece of paper cannot take away legacies, heritage, your way of life. That's* your responsibility.

Levi Trentham finally relented and sold a portion of his land.

He squeezed his eyes shut and when he did, he returned from his painful memories and told the rest of his story to the surrounding group of strangers from the city – the ones on the front porch of The Appalachian Club - the men in suits and the women in dresses. Finery on full display in the middle of the Tennessee sticks.

"I lived in the questions. Didn't try to answer until I - and everyone else - got sick of me askin'. And then, only then, did the answer come. I had to live with that answer too, no matter if I liked it or not. And I didn't like it, of course. But after I got my land surveyed, much to my own surprise and mixed feelings, I saw an undeniable chance to boost my family. Significantly. You see, I have many grown children, grandchildren and great-grandchildren – I had to think of all of 'em, and I vowed to help my family with their futures. By that time, both my heart and the mountains themselves called me to sell, face the inevitable, 'cause I could see our mountain lifestyle fading away. I could see it when I looked out through the trees that weren't there no more, and I could hear it when I woke in the morning and heard machines. And so, I relented. Sold plots to sport hunters at first, and one big plot in particular to Wilson B. Townsend. Yessir, our very own Colonel Townsend."

"Did you see a vision before it happened?"

He sighed, looked out at the forest cathedral, decorated in its finest blues and greens. "To be sure, I saw men in suits in many visions, comin' to take the land. Ones I didn't recognize. No one I recognized in all my visions. Heck, I still don't recognize 'em." Chuckling, he stood up, gathered his beard into his left hand and stroked it once.

"But one thing I still recognize folks...is myself. If you can hang onto who you are, even when life shoots a goddamn bullet at your head and heart and you duck just in time, there ain't no question in the world that can't be answered."

5

———

CHANGE

CHANGES NEVER ANSWER THE END.

~

Though Levi had sold portions of his land in 1905, he remained living in his cabin with his wife, surrounded by children and grandchildren, growing crops, tending his bees, hunting, fishing; all the rural decorations of a life well lived. Colonel Townsend allowed him to use his now-sold land as long as he wanted, for whatever he wanted, but it wasn't realistic. Loggers felled pretty much every tree they saw. Levi remained owner of his cabin home and the immediate surrounding land, but with each passing day he saw more and more bare peaks surrounding his farmstead. There were very few trunks and leaves standing in the way.

He also saw more and more of those *furriners* stepping off that damn iron horse - or else comin' up the road with their damn automobiles, and even some folk on the backs of real horses - to stay for a week or two, or a month or more, in the place he had called home for over fifty years.

And then, before he knew it, as he approached his sixties, Elkmont was logged out and people began staying in cabins not to work for the logging company, but for recreation. Fishing. Hunting. Breathing in the best air God ever made. Tourists. Visitors. *Furriners*. The Appalachian Club.

During this period - a complete flowing river caught up in quiet pools of memories and isolated rapids of progress - Levi Trentham truly learned to adapt to life's slings and arrows. Perhaps it was his prophecies, or just pure old mountain man wisdom, but he began recognizing the opportunities these Elkmont tourists brought. He wouldn't actually *work* for the railroad, or Colonel Townsend, or The Appalachian Club - indeed, he'd never work for any other man – ever! But he sure could hang around and pick up a visitor or two willing to pay to take them hiking or fishing. May as well make some cash. Which would be easy because he knew everyone – every worker, every cook and landscaper, maid and guide. He'd even grown up with some of these folk! And they could help direct him, along with his own intuition and prophecies, to those visitors who were seeking an authentic mountain experience.

He sighed deeply. Tugged on his beard and drew himself into his prophesizing trance. To be sure, he knew he wasn't losing himself – *that* would never happen. He was too strong, too deeply rooted to where God had planted him.

But his home – the neat pile of stacked logs and sturdy chimney, front porch and gardens and crops, barns, corncrib, springhouse – well, all of that was absolutely losing its battle with progress. He could almost feel the tug and pull of modernity. How did it happen? How was it that nowadays, it felt as natural as a trackless maze to make his way over to the railroad station and roam the road in the middle of Elkmont and hang around to find someone to tell stories to? How to manage this - this fresh and striking contrast between his bearded brashly independent self and these *goddamn furriners* who had heard of The Prophet of the Smokies and The Mayor of Elkmont and called him Uncle when they'd never actually met him before?

Yet they all actively sought him out. Would he go ahead and amuse them? Himself? What was the best way forward, the best way to straddle both worlds? Because he knew he must. There was no hiding; no chance of remaining in the trance, wondering.

Changes. How to answer them.

THE HISTORIAN OF ELKMONT. A new name added to The Prophet, The Mayor. Uncle. So many titles for one man! He'd certainly heard them all. More and more names attached themselves to his faded overalls and white beard, including another relatively recent one: Legend.

Since Elkmont's formal and official establishment in 1907, Levi Trentham glared starkly upon its growth: a post office, a schoolhouse, a hotel, a general goods store. A Baptist church. Houses. The ones cheaply made so they could roll right off the train cars and be moved wherever the loggers needed to move. Wherever there were still trees to fell.

Elkmont was now the second-largest town in Sevier County, Tennessee. Loggers worked six days a week; spent their Sundays at church and then went fishing or watched the local baseball team play; oftentimes, right alongside Colonel Townsend who made his way into their conversations. Most were appreciative – so many logging jobs there were! And it was good pay. With perks such as a free train ride into Townsend on Sundays.

If someone got injured or hurt, the Colonel would pay the logger's family the full wages. If a logger died, he'd pay the family two years of wages. Words, thoughts swirled around many conversations about the Colonel: *generous. Kind. Hardworking. He's right here at the site ain't he? Not in his office up at the mill in Townsend like other businessmen would be, never visitin' the workers and askin' 'em how it really is. No sir. He's right here with us workers.*

As for Levi Trentham, well, he kept his own words and thoughts mostly to himself, but the Colonel certainly made his way into those early morning ponderings and late-night deliberations: a *good man he is, to be sure, but he did change my entire way of life. And now, I, the so-called Mayor of Elkmont, must live with the consequences. Whether I like it or not. Do I like it? No. Well, some of it is okay I guess. Some of the folk I like talkin' to. Most of 'em I don't. They call me 'legend' lately and all that and I guess I do like tellin' my stories. The mountains done told me it's my responsibility to preserve my way of life. And what better way to keep our stories alive than to tell as many folk as possible? And I can make some money as I get older. Farmin' is hard work on an old body. This is much easier money I reckon. But change never answers the end. I think on that and what it means. It means just 'cause you change don't mean a good end. Changin' is just a fact. It's up to us to give it meaning. It sure don't answer on its own just 'cause you change jobs or where you live or decide to talk to folk or not. I must be the one to answer. To give it meaning. And the goddamn jury's still out on my final decision.*

6

LAUREL FALLS

THE WATER THAT COMES FROM THE SAME SPRING CANNOT BE FRESH AND SALT BOTH.

~

ome join us for a picnic this Thursday! Mr. Levi Trentham will be joining us! Hike to Laurel Falls, with a lunch to follow! Right on the banks of the Little River!

The flyer screamed this and that - exclamation marks for every sentence! - and the club urged guests to participate: *All of our visitors from our American cities, immerse yourself in the mountains to walk the trails our pioneers walked! To remember how nature rejuvenates!*

How these people could go into a grocery store to buy tomatoes and greens lined up in rows inside a claustrophobic closed-in white-washed room and walk on paved sidewalks and live in the sky in those buildings that were three, seven, ten stories high, a man like Levi Trentham would never understand. But here they were. And being a man of his word, he had agreed to guide them on a hike in exchange for a fat stack of cash.

Over thirty people gathered for the hike and picnic. He still scorned most of these *furriners*, but hey, they made him money and though his children were all grown and he had many, many self-sufficient grandchildren and even great-grandchildren by this point, he could always use more money. Shoes, a bit of coffee and sugar and salt, bolts of cloth for dresses for the women, trousers for the men, and cotton for tablecloths, napkins, rags, quilts and curtains for every one of the cabins the extended Trentham family required. Yes, indeed. Cash was always welcomed.

"C'mon over here folks. We're a-headin' this way. To Laurel Falls. Used to hike to there all the time, when I was a youngin. Lots of bear 'round these parts. Watch and listen now."

They peered at one another. *Bears?*

"It's ok, folks. I always got my rifle. This here's an Armstrong rifle...not many of 'em made. See here?" He pointed at the foresight and muzzle. "This here barrel has three threads of gold embedded."

"Why is it called an Armstrong rifle?"

"Well, it's a roundabout tale to be sure. This here gun's been altered to a cap and ball type years ago. Ya'll don't know what that is I reckon. But it ain't necessary to know. Alfred Duncan done got one hundred dollars in gold for making the Armstrong gun, though I hear it cost 'im two hundred for the gold he put in it. He made it in 1828 for D.P. Armstrong who then passed it to his son, Marcellus Armstrong. Then, I got it. See here? This here gun is all hit up with ol' McSpadden powder which was made of saltpeter during the War Between the States. Had to be shortened six inches on account of the rotting away of the wood from all that powder. Ain't hunted with it much on account of that. But it does well for trips like these 'cause we're like not to need it. Bear will just run off if they see a crowd like us. But I killed many a bear and deer with this here rifle! D'ya know it worked better than any gun ever made? This here had a range of over five miles."

"Five miles? I never heard of such a range." A man exclaimed.

"Well, you done heard of it now. Lots of things you never heard of before in them cities you folk live in."

They nodded, the women giving each other raised eyebrows wondering just what they were in for today. Just how much embellishment came from the mouth of the prophet?

"We hear, Mr. Trentham, that men around here name their guns. Is that true?

"Yes ma'am. Namin' 'em brings us good luck. And that's about all I got right now is good luck bein' here with you folks." Levi really needed some more money for shoes. Everyone's were so worn out on account of the extra-wet spring that had just passed. Mud cracked leather like nobody's business and his and his wife's shoes were split so bad they had holes right through in three different places. He'd need to get some at the general store or else just order a few pairs of men's black shoes from the Sears Roebuck catalog. Even women wore men's shoes out here in the so-called sticks. They were much sturdier and lasted much longer.

"This here is Bear." He held up his rifle, pride on his face, caressing it like a harmonica stroked the evening with its bright and warbling sound. "I named my rifle Bear 'cause I hunted and trapped a lot of bear in my life."

"What other names do you know of?"

"Don't you city folk have guns?"

A bit sheepish, they replied in tandem. "No sir. No need for 'em. We got the police. Lots of gun manufacturers though. But not enough buyers."

Another man offered his take: "Well, I know pretty much all our past ancestors 'round these parts had rifles. Named 'em Ol' Blue, Persuader, Long Tom, Ol' Death." He sighed, resignedly, as if lamenting his story. "My parents were the first ones of their families to move outta these parts and into town. Once they did, our rifles seemed to be a thing of the past."

Levi shook his head at that.

"What curious names!" A woman exclaimed suddenly, her sturdy black, still-shiny shoes laced tightly for the hike she wasn't sure she wanted to take. "I especially like Persuader."

"Yes ma'am. Me too. Reckon we don't need police 'round here when a well-aimed rifle will *persuade* anyone to give up or go home." Levi answered, eyeing the woman with the tightly laced shoes pacing to and fro. "It's a long hike folks. Make sure ya'll want to go...and *can* go. There's no one to get you out of these here woods 'cept yourself."

The crowd pondered that for a moment, looked around at the seemingly peaceful Smoky Mountains. Wondering about all those rumors of these fiercely independent people doing backbreaking work like chopping wood and bending over to dig up vegetables, not to mention talk of moonshine and revenuers and shootouts. And getting lost. These mountain folk, as it turned out, did so much more than just farm and raise children and go to church! They had an entire culture and lifestyle here. What would it be like to live like this?

There are mountains that ask questions and mountains that answer. But no mountain will ever tell a man how to think. Thus, some of the visitors thought it would be freeing to live here on vast, fertile land with little interference from the outside world - that special kind of freedom certain men craved.

Then again, it would also be unnerving – out here all alone. Having to handle everything – from farms to gardens to neighbors to the law – on your own, with perhaps the help of family or friends and a rifle named Persuader. What *would* they do if they got lost? If they really couldn't make it back from a hike to a waterfall? If they slipped or broke an ankle? Some suddenly realized they'd gone lax in one generation. How provocative softness is! *Or*, the mountains boldly asked, *is it weakness?*

THE GROUP BEGAN its trek to the waterfall, Levi reminding them, "One step at a time, folks. Watch for tree roots. Rocks. Mind this here uprooted tree..."

They trudged on, some huffing and puffing as this was the most amount of exercise they'd had in a long time. It was mostly uphill too, not like their flattened city sidewalks.

"How did this place of Elkmont get its name? Are there any elk here?" The tightly-laced-shoes woman breathlessly asked as she made her way up to the front of the group. She was fearful of bears and wildlife in general and wanted to be close to the mountain man with the rifle that was eaten away by some powder back from the Civil War. The War Between the States is what they called it here in Elkmont.

Levi muttered to himself how someone, in every group he guided, asked how Elkmont got its name because they all assumed elk lived here and so far, there was none to be found. He stopped and reminded them to drink water and rest for a spell. Laurel Falls wasn't too far now, but still, it was humid and even the owl right over there made a daytime appearance to drink from a puddle just far enough away.

"No ma'am. Never seen elk around here. My kin, Earnest Trentham, always said that it was named for the Knoxville Elks Club 'cause their members hunted and fished around here until around 1900. Before the railroad came through."

"And when did that happen?"

Levi continued walking, motioning to everyone to mind the rocks and tree roots sticking up all along the trail. He thought about what he'd seen over the years...the fretting and worried looks that the trees gave as Colonel Townsend's lumber company hacked away their cover. Too fast the landscape changed until one could see a deer a mile away, grazing and skittishly looking for concealment while a lone owl did the same, a bit more successfully due to his long brown feathers disguising its presence in the highest branches possible.

"Just a few years ago, in 1908, there were still plenty of trees for us residents, animals, and the Little River Lumber Company. Colonel's business boomed as ya'll say."

"Now, Colonel used to say there ain't much competition for lumber, but during a few years, before he came in and ran 'em all outta town, these here mountains were bein' run over by loggers lookin' to fell trees for money. These here mountains became very crowded: the W. M. Ritter Lumber Company came to town, operatin' from Hazel Creek, then Montvale Lumber Company began fellin' the forest near the Twenty Mile Creek area, and then Norwood Lumber Company set up operations near Forney Creek. Then, Deep Creek and Greenbrier Cove were overtaken by Champion Coated Paper Company, and that company even went as far as the headwaters of the Oconaluftee River! Finally, the English Lumber Company arrived in these parts, and they were the first ones to strike a deal with a local neighbor - and another legend – William Marion Walker. They call him Black Bill. Ya'll hearda him, right?"

Many nodded their heads, but some frowned, shrugging shoulders and admitting ignorance of another interesting character living deep within these Smoky Mountains. Who knew that within such softly scalloped blue and rocky walls so many local legends were born?

"William Marion Walker– we call him "Black Bill" - is a well-respected man living right over yonder in Walker Valley", Levi explained, pointing to the west. "They call him Black Bill because he was a blacksmith in his younger years and 'cause he has kinda a swarthy complexion." Levi paused to indicate to the crowd to drink from their canteens and water containers. "And he would've been just another mountain man livin' his life farming, keepin' bees, raisin' children, just like everyone else. Except he interpreted the Bible a bit differently, following the stories of David and Solomon and eventually took three wives."

"At the same time?"

"Yes. At the same time. And he sired 'bout twenty-six children." Levi began laughing as he told all about the legendary mountain man. "Truth be told, Black Bill tells folk, 'I stopped countin' at twenty-six youngins!' And he'd good-naturedly chuckle with anyone who asked."

Levi motioned for the group to continue uphill.

"A good man he is – he's still alive, but old now. Reckon he's about seventy-four or so nowadays. Takes care of everyone, and his rifle, Ol' Death, is even more famous than he is! He and I crossed paths every now and then in his younger years. When we was out huntin' or trappin'. Mainly bear. If ya'll think *I'm* a great bear hunter, you shoulda seen Black Bill Walker back in his younger years! He was the greatest bear hunter the Smokies had ever seen." He shook his head in amazement as they walked onwards and upwards towards Laurel Falls, explaining how the waterfall site was named due to the abundance of mountain laurel that blooms near its majestic cascade.

"Mountain laurel can be crushed up and used to treat some skin diseases and infections. And the Cherokee also used its bark to make spoons and trowels. It keeps its leaves year-round too...reckon that's why I always look for bear in mountain laurel - 'cause it provides that thick cover that bear like so much."

"I wonder if Black Bill Walker looked for all his bears in mountain laurel?"

"Reckon he did. He knows everythin' there was to know about huntin' and trappin' and trackin' bear."

Levi didn't quite agree with keeping three wives at the same time – damn, what a hassle that would be! And who had time for three wives? But he did greatly respect Black Bill Walker. After all, that's why these types of men live here in these mountains – for the ability and the freedom to live their own lives as they see fit. No government to contradict what the mountains and God told them to do. Besides, who cares? If they were all fine with it – a man and three women – who was he to judge? That's God's job.

They walked on as the sun nudged itself a bit higher. Soon, they could hear the light din of water roaring past rocks, spilling itself over a cliff. But there was still a good bit of trail ahead and the group of tourists wanted to know more about the history of the land in which they found themselves vacationing.

"Around 1900, that company, England Lumber – part of the England-Walton Company of Philadelphia - came here and built a tannery." Levi continued marching up the slopes, noticing the city folk breathing hard, sweating, huffing and puffing. *Guess I'll slow my pace a bit. They're used to walkin' on flat city sidewalks.* He sighed. *When did all this happen, the trees felling at a rate that left huge scars and balds on every slanted face? What would happen to his beautiful Smoky Mountains when every tree on every peak was gone? And that damn national park they keep screamin' about more and more. What would happen if the goddamn government decided to take this land for the so-called damn greater good?*

But today, he had money to make. And these folk following him weren't the ones who were to blame for the national park or felling trees. So, he put his ire on a wooden shelf above a hearth for now and continued trying to tell these people all about what happened before Elkmont turned into a resort.

"Well, they boiled all those animal skins at the tannery with tree bark and then turned it into some fine leather clothing and saddlebags and such. Accordin' to Colonel Townsend, he had a friend at the England-Walton tannery who said to him, 'Hey

Colonel, there's some huge potential for tree harvesting down by the Little River in Tennessee...come on down from Pennsylvania and explore the area for timber possibilities'. That, along with the dang President who told all about how these here Appalachians have plenty of fine trees."

The tourists hit their stride, walking at a good pace now that they could feel the air turn cooler, could hear the water tumbling over a mountain bluff.

"So, Colonel moved south and, being a big businessman and all, also established another tanning business over in Millers Cove in the Walland community. Not too far from here actually, but far enough that what they call their mountains are actually just foothills. Colonel already owned and ran the Clearfield Lumber Company up in Pennsylvania and some mills, and the Clearfield Southern and Black Lick and Yellow Creek railroad lines. So, he damn well – excuse me – he *very well* knew the business side of things and saw potential - lots of it - in these here Appalachians. And so, Colonel moved down here to our little slice of heaven."

Levi swept his hands across the landscape and watched the tourists frown. For once, mountain man and city folk thought the same thing: slice of heaven? It was beautiful to be sure. And they could see how lush and fertile and blooming it must've been. But right now, at least in the distance, some of it was very bare. Very sparse.

"We folk here in the mountains wondered how we could stop a man like Colonel Townsend. Black Bill Walker over yonder - the one with three wives and twenty-six children - keeps tellin' the Colonel no way in heck he's gonna sell any of his land."

But the owl knew better. He'd flown in to watch the show and to listen. If Levi had what some called 'second sight', then the feathered creature, according to the Cherokee, had ten-fold the power, for he could see a hundred years into the future.

And what he saw, just six short years from now, was Black Bill Walker gaining $1500 from Colonel Townsend in exchange for his heavily treed land on Thunderhead Prong. 96.25 acres. On one condition though: Colonel Townsend could never fell even one tree on said land.

The businessman agreed. And kept his promise. He may have built homes for logging families, owned vast swaths of land for its natural resources – his company was responsible for feeding a lot of people! – but he never once felled one tree of Black Bill Walker's land. He was a man true to his promise.

"Black Bill Walker and I – we both do admire Colonel Townsend...he's a good man and I quite like him. But he was intent on changing my world. Razin' all the trees for his lumber business and demolishing all of it...take a look around. There's trees here and there of course, but really look. Don't you see all the holes? Why, you can see three peaks over...never used to be able to do that. Never used to be able to tell where the forest ended and heaven began." He sighed, still walking uphill, eying the sky for any weather that may be changing course.

"Built thirty-five miles of track so he could take all the lumber to the mill in Townsend. I woke up one day to railroad spikes being pummeled into the rocky grounds of my own little slice of these Smokies. Yes ma'am," he replied to questioning by the now-sweating woman in the sturdy black shoes, "the town of Townsend was named after Colonel Townsend. Used to be called Tuckaleechee Cove until he built the sawmill and moved all the logs there so his workers could saw lumber for houses and furniture and such. Took all the poplar, ash, oak, chestnuts. Maple trees. 86,000 acres he bought when he began The Little River Lumber Company."

The woman nodded her head, "And what did you think?"

A flood washed over his body, the prophecy clear and ready to be shared.

"What did I think?" He stopped, looked her straight in the

eyes. "Takes but a moment in history for ruin and death. I don't want that moment to ever arrive here in the Smokies."

LAUREL FALLS IS a beautiful waterfall thundering eighty feet down its edge before meandering through the steeply sloped slant of Cove Mountain. Aptly named for the abundant mountain laurel - an evergreen shrub - that grows all along its waters, Levi knew it well, spending countless days of his childhood underneath the falls, basking in his mountain world, happy as a tick on a hound that he lived right here, in the most beautiful place on earth.

These city folk – most of them - certainly appreciated the beauty, but could they ever understand how and why families such as his - some in their fourth generation - continue to live in their original cabins deep in the valleys and hollers and cleared unforested areas of the Smokies. How summers were all about picking berries on the sunniest slopes before retreating to the creeks for trout fishing and swimming and bringing home three of the largest trout for Ma's skillet. First, she'd bread them with cornmeal and fry them in the skillet. Then she'd heap them onto steaming platters already full of potatoes and green beans and cornbread because corn was king in Elkmont; every farmer growing acres upon acres every year to feed umpteenth children, animals, neighbors, and themselves.

Could they ever understand watching their way of life disappear and having to adapt quickly? Like his friend, Danny, who lived not too far from Elkmont's main street. One of Black Bill Walker's many children from who knows which one of his three wives, Danny was growing up quickly in Walker Valley and showed an early head for business. He would calculate how many eggs to trade and could barter with the best of grown men at the Maryville markets when he helped his famous father sell honey from his bees.

With a knack for numbers, he devised a way to make money off these *furriners.* Danny asked The Appalachian Club manager if he could deliver milk to their visitors. Confirming that he could, he paid eight cents a quart, plus a small freight charge, and sold the same quart for twelve cents. He also delivered newspapers to the club for twenty-five cents a week.

For a young boy, this was still a lot of money despite the fact that just one candy stick was fifty cents, and a new pair of boots was $2.50-$4.00. A shirt was ninety cents, and a hat for church was $1.95. A new "penny western" or "dime" novel cost a dime, hence the name "dime novels". A Ford Model T, brand new, with enough room for five passengers sold for $690.00. The average wage in America was $750 per year, and the still-young country was being paved and built and developed and connected like never before. It was an exciting time for young people and those with ambition.

Levi and most other mountain folk preferred quite the opposite. He had ambition to be sure, but his came with a healthy dose of trees and animals and towering peaks.

No; indeed, city folk could never understand what it meant to live in the burly arms of these craggy mountains, only to see the very muscles cut to the bone; trees felled, hauled away, leaving only bare skin on the rocks that made up these majestic peaks.

But as much resentment as Danny and Levi and others felt at their changing world, they also knew they must bend, for if they did not, the prophet saw clearly there would be no place left for them.

~

"It's right up here folks. Now, ya'll know the *Elkmont Special* thunders into the station once a day. Reckon that's how most of ya'll got here, though I seen some on horseback or even in those new damn – *dang* - automobiles Ford is makin'. Oh, you think we don't know about such things! We ain't that backwards! We read newspapers. Not me of course, but I do hear about the news. Listenin' is better than readin' in my opinion. Anyhow, I know all about the train - for $1.90, a two-and-a-half-hour scenic tour could be had, stopping in Maryville, Walland, Kinzel Springs, Townsend, Line Springs, Wonderland Park, and here in Elkmont. You should see it in the fall! When the leaves are burnt with orange and rust..." Levi explained as he rounded a corner of the trail and was suddenly upon Laurel Falls. He had timed his talk perfectly; finishing telling the tourists all about the background of how the railroad had quickly morphed from chugging itself right through the heart of Colonel Townsend's logging operations and into its current track towards tourism.

"Here it is!" Levi waved his arms as his group of tourists arrived at Laurel Falls. Rainbows spilled their colors into the mist and the city folk marveled at the coolness of the falls as they found boulders to sit on or lean against.

"Now you can see why we come here. It's a salve for the soul." They looked at the craggy mountain man who certainly had a way with words. One minute he was trying to curtail his cussing and talking about bears and guns and such; the next, he was almost a poet.

"Like I said, before The Appalachian Club was built and the Elkmont resort where ya'll are stayin' in nice cottages and cabins, this whole place was a loggin' camp. You can kinda see it still, but not as much – imagine an entire community sprung up for the loggin' workers and their families. Only when this area was logged out – pretty much no more trees as it is right now – did it turn into a resort. But youngins of loggin' workers would come here all the time to play in the falls, and scootch down the rocks. Be careful, mind. You see how slick these rocks are. They're wet and moss grows on 'em. Makes you slip. Some youngins turn up mighty cut up from these rocks and one or two even hit their heads so hard they were never right afterwards."

A healthy respect murmured through the crowd...their shoes did slip and slide the closer to the falls they got. Some of the women crouched down and used their hands to brace themselves.

"Why not just leave this place entirely after it was logged?"

"Well now," Levi chuckled at the gentleman who asked the question, "Colonel Townsend is a businessman to his bones and once the timber was nearly depleted, he asked himself what he could do with the land. Didn't want to just leave it and let it all grow back. That would take too long. And it ain't profitable."

Levi took the hand of one lady who was struggling to get a footing. "Stay off to the right...it's dry over there." She nodded, thanking him once her sturdy, but smooth shoes gained purchase on the trail.

"Colonel Townsend didn't want to just let the land lie. He'd already done years and years of commercial loggin', with over 560 million board feet of lumber taken from these here hills, mind." Levi told the tourists. "Reckon I don't know any man who'd want to just give that up. He has a vision that one. Even if it's different from mine."

The group frolicked in the mist for another few minutes, then the Prophet looked at the sky and told them they'd better get back if they expected their picnic to be dry because rain would surely arrive in the late afternoon.

7

COLONEL TOWNSEND

...RESERVES THE POSSIBILITY
TO CHANGE COURSE...

What a wonderful morning they'd had at Laurel Falls! Their walk back was much easier because it was downhill, and they made it back within an hour or so. Now it was time for a quick picnic. With clouds rolling in, the hiking group arrived back at the club to enjoy ham and cheese sandwiches, fried chicken, coleslaw, and fried breakfast potatoes. Picnic tables piled high with hearty food greeted the crowd as they sat on wooden slats and in various rocking chairs scattered throughout the resort.

Just as they finished, fat raindrops fell sending everyone dashing under the club's covered porch. Workers scooped up the remaining food to bring inside, while Levi snatched one more ham sandwich with that thick bread that filled his soul. What was left of it anyway.

These tourists come here thinkin' this is their playground for a week or so, pay for it with their hard-earned dollars, but they don't know what that cost folk like me.

"Ah! Here's the famous Colonel now!" One of the "city" men

rose to greet his fellow businessman as he hurried to escape the now-pouring rain.

Townsend loved to visit and speak with the guests of Elkmont. They were so curious about its history! Walking, visiting, dining with them, he relayed the rise of his logging operations in the area, the last tree falling, his moving his operations to the next slope full of trees, and his staring out at the hushed landscape pondering what to do now with this beautiful land that had spectacular wide-open views! Who knew the trees were hiding such beauty? On the other hand, thick foliage has their own appeal, and folk like Levi Trentham, with his *goddamn this* and *goddamn that*, spewed forth his grave unhappiness at his heavily forested mountain landscape ruined by logging operations.

The Colonel could see both sides to be sure, but progress always won, whether you liked it or not, because it is the most serious of causes. That, and if anyone ever wished to make a better, more efficient life, one had to be willing to abandon all baggage to get there – useless friendships, dangerous liaisons, rigidity of opinions, political alliances, and even legitimate and deep-rooted prejudices.

The Colonel was one such rare man.

He was willing to abandon all baggage. Leave it at the last station and get on the next train. But that didn't mean the next train had to go very far.

"Nice to see you folks! How was Laurel Falls? Ah, yes, it is one of our gems. Levi, I am sure, guided you well."

They all answered at once:

Indeed. He's a wealth of information!

A true mountain man.

Loves the mountains as much as anyone I ever saw. Can't wait for the next hike. Perhaps a fishing trip tomorrow?

How long is the rain supposed to last? Levi – the Prophet – says it won't last long. Perhaps another ten minutes he said. Don't know how he knows such things, but he clearly knows these mountains... seems to fit into this landscape like it's his second skin.

Ten minutes later the rain subsided leaving cooler air behind. Glints of light in the thick puddles marched side by side in veins down the street, past still-weeping eaves and the flickering of the river. As the sun emerged once again, the jeweled hills dried with lightning speed.

"Colonel? Would you like to walk with us down the street? I'd love to learn about all these cottages. They're all so different!"

"Of course, Mrs. Turner. My pleasure. I knew your brother when he visited me in Pennsylvania. We were planning to do some business together and indeed, he served me well, selling me some fine gloves for my workers. Please give him my regards when you see him next. I'll likely be calling him for more gloves within a month or so."

"Thank you, Colonel. I surely will tell him." Exchanging pleasantries, the group walked down the street, The Prophet trailing behind. Listening. Watching. Brows furrowing over a fortress-like face.

"As you can see, we have quite the mix of architecture here at Elkmont – traditional folk designs, Craftsman style, and even some marrying of two or more styles." Colonel Townsend pointed to this and that, up and down, towards roofs and porches.

"What about The Appalachian Club here which serves us such fine dinners? How was that built and who came up with the design? It fits in quite nicely, like it came with the mountain straight from a show-window in a furniture store!"

"Ah, Mrs. Turner, that's mighty kind of you to say. Even Levi here would agree!" Slapping him lightly on the back, the mountain man had caught up, eyeing the businessman, but grudgingly smiled. Smirked would be the better term for it, but Colonel paid no mind, continuing to speak to the guests.

"It's what's called balloon-frame construction, which means the builders used a wooden framework of vertical studs that extend from the foundation all the way to the roof of a building. It's simple, but it works. Makes for a building that's better able to withstand wind, which can get mighty strong up here."

"Especially with no goddamn trees to block the wind." Levi murmured, mostly to himself.

Mrs. Turner and a small group of men and women observed the street lined with rustic cottages covered with board-and-batten, weatherboard, drop siding; some with galvanized steel roofs. Bark-peeled porch posts and railings adorned some of the cabins, and chimneys of stone, brick, and concrete soared from the sides of homes. Retaining walls helped create large back porches and patios laid with stone where guests could relax while overlooking the creek and trees and that one owl hanging around the area, wisely seeing everything these humans did while playing upon the spines of some of the oldest mountains on earth.

"How far above the sea level are we up here, Colonel?"

"Ah, I believe we're about 2,000 feet. We're kind of nestled into these mountains and we've got some of the richest soil I've ever seen. We get a lot of rain which is bad for logging because it slows us down with stuck equipment and muddy landings and rutted skid trails and such. But it does clear the air from the fires and chimney smoke." The people nodded their heads. *Makes sense,* they murmured.

"Here in the Smokies, we can get awfully cold, but it's still temperate...it's not too extreme and we can work in our logging industry mostly all year long. Heavy snow bogs us down, but luckily, we don't get too many of those blizzard days where everything gets buried. Ah! There's Mrs. Murphy...Mrs. Murphy! Come on over here and join us!" The Colonel waved his arms, beckoning a well-dressed, elegant woman who had come out of the large cabin to join them.

Smiling, she walked quickly to see her old friend, Colonel Townsend, and a crowd of visitors, most of whom she did not yet know.

"Folks, please meet Mrs. Joseph Murphy. She's one who saw Elkmont from the very beginning, back to 1901."

"Pleased to meet you all! Where are you from? Knoxville? Ohio? Ah, that's a long way. I'm glad to hear you are enjoying Elkmont. Yes, indeed, I recall the beginnings of this place. And I've loved it every time I've come here. It gets into your soul these mountains. And it never lets go!"

"Would you tell us all about it, Mrs. Murphy? Perhaps come on over to my porch for a sip of tea? I made a pitcher this morning, though truth be told, I am really enjoying not cooking dinner or preparing lunch or doing much of anything. The club is so convenient and serves excellent food! It really feels like a vacation." Ladies exclaimed in tandem their invitations to get to know the much talked about Mrs. Murphy while Levi held his tongue over these damn *furriners* calling dinner lunch and supper dinner.

"Ah, so. I understand completely, the curiosity about Elkmont. When my husband, Mr. Joseph Murphy, met Colonel Townsend, he was impressed immediately with his leadership and foresight. My husband, who is also from Pennsylvania and first met the Colonel there, became enamored with joining his lumber enterprise. And so, he did. Became his superintendent and helped him buy over 80,000 acres of land. Colonel Townsend, Mr. J.W. Wrigley of Clearfield, and Mr. F.H. McCormick of Williamsport - all these men came down here to the mountains to stake their claim as we say, in the soils of the Smokies."

She paused, wistfully thinking back to her courtship with Joseph Murphy. Her mother had been right - he was so dashing! Still was. His car also couldn't get a flat, something her mother pointed out. If this handsome young man could think of a way to never worry about a car's tires, why, he was worth something just for that!

Indeed, Joseph Murphy drove a Model T Ford, stripped it of all four tires and installed flanged railroad wheels on the car so it could run on the very tracks of The Little River Railroad.

What of the train? What if it came the same way as the track the Murphy's car was on? She was, yet again, soothed by her mother: "Ah, dear, don't you worry. It goes thirty miles an hour, which is fast, but surely he knows the train schedules. Only once a day it comes through, but once that train has come and gone, the track is empty for the rest of the day and evening."

They only had one issue and that was with the chassis. Relaxing now on the back patio of one of the cottages, the fifth one down from The Appalachian Club on the left, the iced tea was sufficiently sugared, to her delight. What a sweet tooth she had! Just enough to perk up and tell the guests and new neighbors all about the day they heard something fall from their Model T right onto the railroad tracks.

"We were taking a ride, as usual, towards Townsend, when we heard a tremendous crash! The strange thing is, Joseph kept right on going! I looked at him with great concern, but he just laughed it off and told me 'see? It's still running. We'll check it when we stop'."

Eyebrows raised. What was left on the tracks? And what of the train that was bound to come?

"Something fell from the chassis, whatever that was. I know nothing about cars, you see. Still don't. Anyway, when we stopped, he found the crank for the engine was missing! I tried to explain to my mother why it took until 2:00 a.m. to get back from Elkmont, but it did. She never believed it though. She said to me, 'Ivah' – I was named for a Russian princess, you see - 'you'd better get married quickly!' I tried in vain to convince her that nothing could be further from the truth – he was a complete gentleman! – and I, a lady. But, well, I admit it didn't look very good."

Joseph and Ivah eventually married and embarked on their honeymoon in their Model T Ford modified with the flanged railroad wheels. The contraption sparked such interest that *Ford Times* - the newspaper that Henry Ford put out for his employees - carried a story and a picture of this unique set-up just last year, in 1911. *Ford Times* was created to teach Ford employees "better English" and were "filled with articles about Model T offerings, service instructions, parts availability, and advice on marketing and selling what they called the 'Tin Lizzie'." In later years, the newspaper included articles on life-style and travel.

"We came to Elkmont quite often in that contraption. And we never did have any close call with an oncoming train. Joseph did know the train schedules to be sure. He used to triple check them every day just in case. But every time we arrived here, I never truly wanted to leave. Elkmont captured my heart right from the beginning. Our own cottage is just up there," she pointed to the east.

"Millionaire's Row?!"

Mrs. Ivah Murphy laughed. "Well now. Word travels fast around here! I suppose they do call it that. It's on the Little River's East Prong and has spectacular views of the river and the mountains. Moreso these days with all the trees gone." She spoke softly now, fully aware of the desecration all that logging did to the land. Scarred, bare. She recalled a time when it was a lot lusher, canopied, birds twittering in every branch. Now, it was near-barren; one could see three peaks over, even more on a clear day. The current view held its own beauty, but nothing could match being enveloped in the burly arms of mountains when their forests, swelling with bud, could hug anyone as tightly as needed.

Ivah closed her eyes for a moment while the small crowd

rose and walked along the patio's low retaining wall. The creek lay below, silent witness to all the human activity that had occurred in just the past few years. And there was that one owl. She was familiar with it and thought many times that this place wouldn't feel the same without the great feathered creature.

At first, it haunted her a bit; after all, owls are seen as wise and observant, sometimes bringing good luck and fortune, but sometimes, it is said, bringing death and bad omens. What that bird has seen! Living twenty to thirty years, they can inherit memories. At least that's what the Cherokee say, the descendants of those who walked the *Nunna daul Tsuny*, the "trail where they cried". The ones who, in the early 1830s walked west, turned around and walked back east, hiding in the woods, only daring to emerge again when things changed just enough to allow living in the *Shaconage* - "land of the blue smoke" - where they'd roamed from slope to slope for centuries.

Things sure have changed, Ivah thought. *For everyone.* She roamed her mind for those memories back "to around 1907 when Knoxville businessmen went to hunt and fish and soon, wives and husbands hunted and fished together in Elkmont". Those couples, along with businessmen, eventually formed the club.

Nudging a bit forward to 1910, Ivah Murphy stood, recalling to the others: "That was the first big summer when we built our own building. Of course, we called it The Appalachian Club. Colonel Townsend let the club have acreage for its site and for the building of the cottages for the Knoxville families to buy and to rent out to summer travelers. That's when he added an observation car on the logging train, and later, passenger coaches. Suddenly, everyone flocked to Elkmont to vacation. Even Mr. Cochran, who owns the East Tennessee Brewery in Knoxville, was so enamored with the area, he built his own cottage back in 1908 and spends more and more time at this fledgling resort."

Ivah Murphy moved her way over to the nest of ladies in their rocking chairs perched close to the low wall of the back patio with a clear view of the river. All seemed relaxed, savoring their vacation. All was well in their worlds; Ivah hated to break the spell of the mountains. But she was realistic and loved the truth of things – that's one of the reasons why Mr. Joseph Murphy fell in love with her. He often praised his wife: *you do not let yourself drown in the many difficulties of life.*

"Indeed, the trains were wonderful and a fun way - if a bit rocky - to transport us city folk into another world. But it can be dangerous. There's been a few accidents and there was one tragedy that shook us all."

At the mention of that, Colonel Townsend stood, took off his hat, and bowed his head. "It *was* a true tragedy. One I will never forget."

Ivah began relaying the incident while wide eyes of children, joining their parents now, all quieted to hear about the train wreck they'd heard something or other about, but didn't know exactly what had happened. And right in front of them was the woman whose husband had to deliver the news.

"It happened in the summer, June 30, 1909. *Old Three Spot*, as we called the train, raced down the tracks running along Jake's Creek, loaded with logs. It was rainy, and everything - the rails, the soil - everything was very wet. The engineer that day was who we all called Daddy Bryson and Charlie Jenkins was his brakeman. There were others – loggers, workers – riding atop the logs. They were overloaded because everyone wanted to hitch a ride to go to a party that evening."

Guest nodded their heads. They understood going to great lengths for a bit of entertainment. Especially out here in the mountains. What else was there to do besides work, fish, hunt, and go to church on Sundays?

"They were also hauling five cars of logs. Two more than normal. Suddenly, things started jogging back and forth along the tracks a bit too strongly – they were losing control, and a sharp curve was just ahead. They realized they were going to crash. That's when workers and loggers started jumping off the train. In another split second, Daddy Bryson and Jenkins also jumped towards the creek side of the train...but sadly, tragically, both were killed." Ivah sighed; face fallen in sadness.

"The Knoxville newspaper blamed the employees for over-loading the train...and they pointed out very strongly that this was in strict violation of the rules of the company." She sighed again, deeply. It was always a struggle to tell this story without breaking down completely.

"And the newspaper reported 'the engineer Bryson' was fatally injured. He was listed by name, but the only mention of Jenkins was that 'another member of the logging train crew whose name could not be learned was fatally hurt.' What a blow to his family!" She shook her head at such finality. A split second is all it takes for heartbreak and ruin.

"My husband, being an executive for the railroad, was the one tasked with carrying the news to the victim's families. As for Colonel Townsend," she nodded towards the businessman whose head was still bowed and spoke directly to the solemn man, "well, you and I both know logging is a difficult business; very dangerous. A few too many young men were killed by fallen logs, logs that skid down the slopes too fast to get out of the way, and other such things. Colonel - you would always pay the men's families two years' pay. Remember this folks," she turned her attention back towards the ladies and gentlemen standing, riveted in the mood of the calamitous story, "his enterprises come with great danger to be sure, but our Colonel

Townsend is a good man. If catastrophe strikes, he steps up and makes it as right as he can. He cares. A very good man."

And then Ivah walked over to the creek, looked down and decided to turn the mood of the small crowd of visitors.

"The thing is - tourists who came later that same summer of 1909 were fascinated by the wreck! It took weeks to clear, so it was still visible during the busy July holiday month. We had more tourists than ever here at Elkmont and all they wanted was to catch a glimpse of the wreckage, which if you were here to see it like that owl over there, was quite horrific".

8

LEM OWNBY

WHERE THERE IS NO VISION, PEOPLE PERISH.

∾

Lem Ownby was the one who continued telling everyone what happened when his great friend, Daddy Bryson, was killed.

Mr. Ownby and Levi Trentham were friends, and Lem also hung around the Elkmont resort at times. Not too often, for he also despised most *furriners*, and besides, he was too busy with his farm. That and he was near-blind so he liked to stick to his own familiar territory. But like Levi, Lem Ownby also realized the power of adapting, not pushing everything backwards, towards the past. Because it was a losing battle. The past pushed right back. Mostly it shoved. So why not join them, these *furriners* and his friend, Levi Trentham? But only if it suited him. He was, after all, a man born of these mountains, where the fierce independence of will and action ran as deep as the sleep of the coldest winter.

∾

"HEAR YOU FOLK TALKIN' about the train wreck. What a day that was." He had shown up, cane in hand, and sat down near the low retaining wall of the back patio. Near blind as a result of a family condition affecting all of his brothers and a sister, and thought stillborn when emerging from his mother's womb; only a relative noticing a "faint, shuddering breath" saved him. "Somebody better tend to that baby!", were the words uttered to save little Lemuel Ownby "from the horrifying possibility of being buried alive."

From then on, he grew up, attended school - albeit sporadically - and when his father, Tom, sold the family land to Colonel Townsend, Lem helped his father with his new farm above the mouth of Jake's Creek. An indelible part of his childhood was spent helping his parents and siblings "build and maintain a crude weatherboard house where he would live for the rest of his life." Needless to say, life was hard for young Lem, but he held up his share of chores, even working in the lumber industry for a while, managing to navigate his mountain world in the middle of blurry lines and blind spots and wavy vision that dominated his life from boyhood through his later years.

But his disability didn't stop him from living. No sir. He may not be able to see a mud puddle or a tree root, but he could certainly feel when it was about to rain, could sense a horse's lameness, could smell the burnt tinge of train wheels losing their grip, could certainly taste the hunger of the visitors of The Appalachian Club to know exactly what happened to Daddy Bryson and the horror that happened on a lonely stretch of mountain railroad track.

"I CAN STILL SEE Daddy Bryson's weather-beaten face as he throttled the last train down the grade before the day's end. I was about twenty years old and was in that ravine workin' timber the day Daddy Bryson lost his brakes. There was the dreaded whistle and screamin' and mashing of metal when Daddy jumped the track. There was a large hiss of steam. We all knew it was the end for Daddy. Daddy died immediately and his brakeman was severely injured and died within four hours. Three men survived their jump from the runaway train. They wrote a ballad about it. As far as I know, no lyrics were ever written down – ya'll know, we tend to pass down stories and songs just by talkin' or singin' - but there's some mighty fine words in it: 'through the hollers he will ride/with the Smoky mist as his guide', and 'Where the Elkmont rivers flow/he made his mark long ago' - which was strange because he only died on June 30, 1909, three years ago. So it wasn't so long ago."

The crowd sat, rapt. What a tragedy that had occurred right here in Elkmont! A reminder of what was left unfinished.

"I do recall the rest of the ballad – near every word of it. Would ya'll like to hear it?"

> Down the hills on Jake's Creek
> This wicked train did run
> Till the brakeman and conductor
> Saw there must be something done
>
> Poor brakeman Charlie Jenkins
> His last words did relay
> I hope nothing will happen
> On the last trip we make today
>
> The engine speed increasing
> Forrester picked his place and jumped
> There was a mighty crashing
> As he landed on a stump

Old Three Spot she turned over
And the tank by Daddy passed
The logs fell upon him
Poor Daddy breathed his last

"WE MOUNTAIN folk sing songs for long memories to be sure. Let's see here...reckon I recall other lines of the ballad: 'Daddy Bryson, strong and true/on the tracks he always knew/where the trees would bend and fall/he was the mightiest of them all'." Lem stopped singing and opened his eyes.

"Ya'll know this already I reckon - we folk call our lunch dinner - and we all had our dinner buckets holdin' our so-called lunches. Well, when someone dies like Bryson and Jenkins, we make sure to hang their dinner buckets from a tree in Elkmont. They hung there for three years. Just took 'em down earlier this year I reckon."

The crowd paused. Lem Ownby was a unique character; one could see that just by looking at him. Only twenty-three years old in 1912, his skin was smooth, yet he looked aged and already knew these mountains like he was the old, wise owl itself. Known even at this young age as "Uncle Lem", he lived in Elkmont in a tiny cabin that some may call a shack.

The owl liked to perch right outside to peer into his world. By day he farmed and kept 150 bee hives that produced sourwood honey, training his dog, Old Shep, to keep bears away. By night, he sat by a pot-bellied stove filled with wood, and sometimes coal in his later years, retiring early to a bed piled high with faded quilts. A few chairs arranged here and there throughout the one-room wooden structure would eventually see walls blackened from decades of smoke, and an old family clock sat on the mantle, tick-tocking for years and years, slow, methodical, ancient.

"Reckon I recall Daddy Bryson's son used to git very upset every time he heard the ballad – and they sang it a lot to honor his Pa. But his son didn't see it that way. Oh, I reckon he knew they was honorin' his Pa, but he couldn't take it no more and he done quit the Little River Lumber Company – he worked there too – before he finally just moved away."

"Were there any other train incidents? Or tragedies?" One of the crowd tentatively asked.

"Oh sure. Sure there was. Engine Number 1 derailed and wound up in the Little River near Townsend around 1901. Then Number 4 – a Shay named for a fella called Ephraim Shay – fell through a bridge at West Fork in 1904. The workers were badly hurt, but the bridge was repaired, and they got the Number 4 goin' again. Number 9 Shay had a boiler problem causin' the cab to separate. Good men all of 'em. Hard workers. 'Tis a shame. But it's hard and dangerous work workin' on the railroads and workin' in lumber. I done it myself even though I can't see good. Used to cut thirteen trees a day on a good day. I just sawed until they tol' me to stop. A two-man crew on a crosscut saw and a leader to tell us which way the tree was fallin'. The biggest one we sawed was a poplar, nine feet around. Old Granddad we called it."

The owl perched quietly, watching Lem Ownby, whom some also called a prophet. The feathered beast felt something crawl inside and he saw that Lem felt it too. Both man and bird saw two years hence, in 1914, when Number 4 again would have a boiler explode, killing Sam McClanahan and almost killing Walter Hall. Five years hence would see a caboose derailing and the deaths of J.N. Badgett, Pleas Myers, and Earl Dockery. Dangerous work this logging operation, yet Colonel Townsend would take care of all of these families, as he always did.

"How much do ya'll earn logging?" Ever the businessmen, they weren't afraid to ask about money and profits and how much for this and that.

"Got $1.50 a day for eleven hours and we was all grateful for it." He smiled widely as the businessmen contemplated their own salaries versus the loggers' earnings. Why, their salaries were $15,000 a year or more! But they also had to buy just about everything and pay for their mortgages and insurance and equipment and other such things that come with this kind of life. It wasn't easy. Stores charged thirty-four cents a pound for a chuck roast and twenty-five to thirty-five cents for a dozen eggs.

Here, in rural Tennessee however, people grew their own food, raised hens for eggs, pigs and cattle for meat; had their own homes which they built themselves with no mortgage. Different advantages, different worries, different lives.

"Lem Ownby! Whatcha doin' up here? Sellin' some honey?" Ivah Murphy had run back to her own cabin for a bit of freshening up and was just returning when she glimpsed young Mr. Ownby with whom she had a friendly, if strange-bedfellows type of relationship. It was one of those symbiotic affections where the odds and ends making up the sophisticated townswoman and the rooted mountain man recognized each other. And what made it work was that both appreciated each other's place in the world.

She hadn't seen him come to the back patio as she left for her brief respite and she smiled widely at the sight of Lem, knowing he'd filled in the blanks on all the horrific train accidents.

Walking over to him, Ivah got close to his face so he'd be able to see the outline of her appearance and person, warmly taking his hand, and giving him a quick hug. He smelled of earth and field.

"Or are you lookin' for some, Lem? Heh heh." Ivah did have

a wicked sense of humor which she loved to show, especially in front of men like Lem Ownby and Levi Trentham, the Prophet of the Smokies, who had by now also joined the crowd.

It was almost dinnertime. *Oh excuse me - suppertime!* They corrected themselves. Tourists still couldn't get used to the fact that lunch was dinner, and dinner was supper around these parts.

Yet no matter what they called their meals or where these men and women came from – the land right over yonder or hailing from the bigger cities and towns of America - people loved stories. Even the owl noticed, nudging his feathered breast closer, closer, to hear what would come next.

Mrs. Ivah Murphy, Levi Trentham, and Lem Ownby, along with a gathering of guests of The Appalachian Club walked down the street and were now settled on the wide porch, taking tea and a bit of a snack. After all, it was still about an hour before *supper* and all the hiking and walking and running from the rain and general activity made them just as hungry as if they hadn't eaten anything at all since breakfast!

"That's 'cause we're always movin'." Lem Ownby answered the city folk who commented on their constant hunger since they stepped off the train. "Reckon you folk don't hike or fish or swim or tend crops all day long back in your part of the country."

Heads nodded. It was true. They walked to work and grocery stores and such, but just as often, if not more, they stepped into their automobiles and let machines do the work. They murmured to one another, "city living is convenient and comfortable. But it's true – we don't move." And one too many tugged on their snug trousers and suddenly realized how the weight of city life can certainly press on a body.

Colonel Townsend, usually a man of many words, had been unusually silent since talk of the train accident, and now, suddenly, stood and bid a quick goodbye. "I must make my way back to Townsend now folks. Mighty nice to meet you all. Enjoy your stay here in Elkmont."

Laments of *please stay for supper at least!*, and *I hope all is well*, and finally, *we hope to see you again in a few days!* Colonel Townsend smiled and tipped his hat, assuring everyone that he simply caught on to an idea and wished to return to the mill in Townsend, and would see them soon. "All is well." He smiled. "But when a businessman gets an idea, well, it's not to be shaken from his every thought anytime soon. At least until it's put on paper and mulled over while sitting at an office desk."

The crowd shook hands, waved, watched the Colonel make his way up the road to the railroad station. *He is the best businessman I ever met. Wonder what he's up to now?*

Levi Trentham and Lem Ownby sat with the knot of tourists as they turned their attention back to their vacation.

"Supper is at 5:00 p.m., as you know. I hear we're having trout, meatloaf, and potatoes. Perhaps a pie or two. Mr. Ownby? Mr. Trentham? Will you be joining us?" Mrs. Ivah Murphy asked.

The two mountain men looked at one another. Levi seeing confirmation in his friend's eyes, Lem seeing a slight blurry nod of Levi's head, Lem replied, "Yes ma'am. We both will be there. I like the good ole speckled trout I catch myself – it's my favorite. You city folk are like to call it brook trout, but we call it speckled. Either way you say it, there ain't nothin' better!"

"Oh I'm so glad! We wish to hear more of your wonderful stories!" Ivah smiled, while everyone else nodded vigorously.

Soon, Lem, Levi and the gathering of tourists from Knoxville, Ohio, New York, and beyond were inside The Appalachian Club, dining on the freshest speckled trout, caught just two hours ago from the Little River.

And telling stories of how Elkmont was known as the Little River Community at one point before *all the loggers and then all you furriners came in.*

And how Lem and Levi Trentham were actually kin by marriage due to Levi marrying Lem's father's sister – his aunt - Litha Emaline.

And how Lem was the eighth child of his family, and how their land is so steep that "our mules needed to have two legs shorter than the others in order to stand upright on our land. In fact, it is so steep, one neighbor plants his potatoes in vertical rows instead of horizontal so they roll right down the hill to him".

Afterwards, bodies satisfied, minds still reeling from all the stories and amazingly intertwining lives of these mountain folk, the tourists sighed, reflecting for just a moment as the mountains invite you to do. They looked straight ahead. Down at the river. Up to the sky which was in its nightly process of turning itself into shades of carrot and cherry. People from the cities of America took in the heads of all the peaks marching in ragged lines, some with crowns of green, some completely bald. The owl was right up there, on his favored thick branch, like a liquid shadow slipping its way through the night. Watching.

Seen from above, these humans were pale, dressed in the colors of summer – many were promising buds, a few, doomed blossoms. All appealed to the owl's sympathies, and he let out a hoot or two, but which ones were truly listening for the beautiful memories not yet made?

As for Levi and Lem, this evening was just one more day of realization: beautiful memories of life in the mountains *already* made. They had grown up expecting them to continue. Yearned for them to continue. But doesn't history always have such big ideas that get lost in the debris of necessities? It's the wise man who doesn't like it, doesn't invite it or want it, but at least sees it coming. Levi and Lem were two such men and thank goodness for that, the owl thought, because how could they have survived what was coming?

THE *FURRINERS* NEEDED domestic help for cooking, cleaning, maintenance of cabins, guiding to hikes and waterfalls and fishing holes. But the mountain folk like Lem and Levi also needed said *furriners,* for income from guiding, selling honey, and farm products. Both men had the power of prophecy, of knowing it's a fine and useless enterprise to try to fix destiny. May as well join the parade. You have to get down the street one way or another, so may as well straighten the smile and get on with it. Maybe pick up the pace so you're not left behind.

And that's how folk like Levi and Lem adapted.

Seeing this clearly, albeit through eyes clouded with bad luck and dubious change, Lem Ownby decided right then and there, in the supper room of The Appalachian Club, just how to make these new ways work for him.

He was still a renowned bear hunter, despite his sight being impaired. With a good rifle and steady hands, one could mostly rely on smell, shadows and skill, and he always managed to find the bears with the best, thickest fur.

Lem had sold his bearskins during his childhood and young adulthood, traveling to Gatlinburg, Maryville, and Happy Valley to sell and trade. Why not forget all that traveling and sell to these folk right here? The ones itching for things to take home from their mountain vacation. Imagine the look on their friends' faces when they stepped inside a townhome right onto the fur of a black bear!

And so, by the very next week, he began selling his bear skins for seven dollars each, and the bear meat to the kitchens. But he didn't stop there. His favorite trout, rabbits, and vegetables he also sold, sometimes to faraway customers. Packed in sawdust and ice, his efforts were soon hauled by the *Elkmont Special* train from his farm in Elkmont to Knoxville and beyond, sometimes all the way to the northern states.

Past, present, future – all working together. At least for now. The days passed, Lem ate at the club during many of those summer nights, tipped his hat to bid his goodbyes after visiting and dessert on the porch, and walked down the street to the sound of the owl, towards his home deep in the sparse woods of Elkmont, Tennessee.

But one week, he noticed the sound of the owl had changed. It was hooting not with amusement or alarm or longing, but with curiosity over the opening of that other, much larger building to the north. The one that they've been building this summer. The one that looked down the southern slope towards The Appalachian Club with a wide smile, but a soon-to-be emerging look of scorn.

9

WONDERLAND - JUNE 1912

THISTLES MAKE THE GREATEST CRACKLING.

~

By the hot summer of 1912, Elkmont was a full-fledged mountain playground for Knoxville's elite families, The Appalachian Club the hub of everything. Colonel Townsend had even built his own cabin south of the club in 1910 and loved spending as much time as possible amongst the guests.

Though rising in popularity, Elkmont wasn't a large region. The entire area may have been eighty thousand acres or so, but the resort section itself was only about a mile or so wide and perhaps a couple of miles long. Despite its compactness, Colonel Townsend was, as usual, the one who saw the potential of luring even more tourists to the area.

~

JUST LAST YEAR, in 1911, The Little River Lumber Company made a deal with Charles B. Carter, another savvy and productive businessman. Townsend and Carter got along well, and

Townsend trusted him. The Little River Lumber Company sold acreage just north of the Elkmont resort community to Mr. Carter, on the condition that Carter build a hotel within a year.

It was a good price, a good opportunity, and Carter agreed. Along with his equally entrepreneurial brothers, the Carters founded Wonderland Park Company and constructed the Wonderland Park Hotel.

The Wonderland, as they called it, was that other building to the north, the one opening this summer - June 1912 - with fifty rooms that looked down its southern slope with a smile.

At first.

It only took a few years though, until it began glaring down the hill towards The Appalachian Club with a sneering grin and scornful eyes; the sturdy building inciting some unfriendly competition.

THE APPALACHIAN CLUB WAS POPULAR, folksy; The Wonderland Hotel aspired for a bit more panache. Style. Luxury. Less than two miles from Elkmont's main road and its Appalachian Club, it was evident nearly from the start that the two sets of clientele would steer clear of one another. Oftentimes, The Appalachian Club sent its regrets that there were no more tables available for Wonderland guests who wanted to try dinner – *remember, here, it's called supper!* – somewhere different.

Likewise, if The Appalachian Club guests ventured uphill, they too were told The Wonderland Hotel was full, the dining room was full, they had no more chairs, not enough waiters, they ran out of food, or other such regrets.

But the demand for lodging and dining in the heart of the Great Smoky Mountains was so great – growing larger every year – that there was plenty of room for both resorts. And both flourished in their own ways.

The ideal summer resort in the Great Smokies!

The Wonderland was well-advertised in the newspaper and via word of mouth in the city of Knoxville and beyond. They boasted in glossy brochures: *Our very own Wonderland Station platform will drop you off right in front of the hotel. Rooms can be let for $1.50 to $2.50 a night or you can stay for a month for $25. Meals are 75 cents for adults and 50 cents for children. Lots are also for sale for $25 and up.*

As for Elkmont's Appalachian Club, they upped their game to include *teas, dances, and taffy pulls at the club. Prizes are cigars for the men and sewing baskets for the women. Baskets made from the bark of surrounding trees are awarded for the whitest taffy.*

As TIME WORE ONE, the two enterprises tried to outdo the other and soon the clientele began segregating themselves even further. *Are you going to The Appalachian or The Wonderland?* Groups of families traveling together from Knoxville had to ensure they'd stay at the same resort, because if they didn't, they'd never see each other for the entirety of their trip such was the separation.

Levi and Lem couldn't understand the dispute. Wasn't it all the Great Smoky Mountains? Weren't both buildings and cottages and rooms and porches just somewhere to eat and stay? What's the big deal if folk can't try another restaurant up or down the hill? *Heck, for most of our lives, we only had one place to eat and that's right here in Elkmont in our own kitchens! We may visit one another's homes, and nowadays we may eat at The Appalachian Club, but we all eat the same dang things and we're mighty grateful for it.*

The owl heard the mutterings, the slights, the offensive little verbal pushes and shoves that came out in loud whispers. The two groups so sure of their respective sides, but the owl couldn't make out how normally religious and faithful people could feel completely free to talk poorly of others who chose to stay up the narrow road or down the sloped lane. God and his Saints must surely be asleep in these here hills. Because no rebuke by lightning or storm or mudslide came. And so, the comments and undertones continued from both resorts: *Surely, He agrees with us. We are the better because we're nicer. Welcoming. A family place.*

While two mountain men rolled their eyes, day by day, week by week, and laughed and puzzled about it all. "Goddamn *furriners.* 'Bout the only thing the regulars can agree on nowadays is comin' after July 1ˢᵗ when the black gnat season is over. Them bitin' varmints come through the screens of every porch and they make everyone from city folk to us mountain folk dang miserable."

"Yessir, you're mighty right, Levi. But we got the castor oil to put in our lanterns. And that peppermint oil from Wayne County, New York we get at the general store. Repels the mice too."

"Yep. Sure does. Reckon I ain't seen no mice around during black gnat season. Well, what do ya say to goin' to both the club *and* the hotel and sellin' em both our trout and bear meat? We could use the money and they'd be eatin' the same things! How 'bout that?"

"Reckon that's the best idea I heard all week, Levi. Let's go."

"Thank yo, Lom. Let's sell 'em some of our corn too. There's a sayin' about corn: he that hath much may be content with some thistles. These *furriners* – there may be some thistles in the bunch, but hey. We need the money and let's get as much of it as we can from these city folk who don't know a thistle is a fat salad for an ass's mouth."

10

OL' GLORY - JUNE 16, 1918

WAR, HUNTING, AND LOVE ARE AS FULL OF TROUBLES AS PLEASURES.

~

Damn Germans. They're gonna ruin the world. They ain't done neither. Even if this great war is over soon. You watch. They're so mad — like a hungry tick on a fat hound - and they're so dang sure they're right about everythin'. They'll be back you know. They won't just go away. No sir - they ain't done yet.

Such were Levi Trentham's sentiments during the waning days of the Great War, begun in June 1914, when Archduke Ferdinand was assassinated by The Black Hand, a shadowy, Serbian terrorist group.

Elkmont, and the rest of the world, read about it in *The Maryville Times* and all other newspapers they could get their hands on.

Headlines blared: *Austria-Hungary is outraged! They're going to destroy Serbia — The Black Hand is a Serbian terrorist group after all. Kaiser Wilhelm II is giving Austria a "blank check". But Austria-Hungary needs the backing of Germany, their powerful ally. And if*

Austria-Hungary goes to war against Serbia, Russia will come in, and quickly too, to protect their Slavic brothers.

The newspapers tried to make it simple for people to understand the tangled vines of world politics and chess moves.

...and if Russia comes in, as they certainly will, Germany will declare war on Russia. If that happens France is bound by treaty to come to Russia's defense. And when Germany moves against France – marching through neutral Belgium to do so - Great Britain will also have no choice but to enter the war. And if Britain joins the war, so will Canada, Australia, New Zealand, South Africa, and India.

It had been almost four years, but the words uttered by Sir Edward Grey in August 1914, Britain's Foreign Secretary were the ones defining a generation of men and women facing large hopes and short lives: *The lamps are going out all over Europe. We shall not see them lit again in our lifetime.*

The United States had tried to stay out of it. But on April 1, 1917, Americans woke to fresh outrage and horror:

We wanted to stay neutral, the newspapers declared, *but now that Germany has attacked our steamship, the Aztec—after the sinking of the* Lusitania *and the* Zimmermann Telegram *urging Mexico to attack the United States—we will join the war effort and support our troops in Europe.*

On April 2, 1917, President Woodrow Wilson stood before Congress and asked for a declaration of war.

On April 4, 1917, the Senate voted to declare war against Germany by a vote of 82-6.

At 3:12 a.m. on April 6th, the House of Representatives passed the resolution in a vote of 373 to 50.

The United States of America had entered the Great War stating it would "make the world safe for democracy".

~

Damn furriners!

Oh, how Levi Trentham hated this war! He spoke out against it as much as possible. But as is human nature, what was under his own roof of Heaven was more important than something going on halfway around the world that had nothing much to do with him. War was raging in Europe to be sure, but another, more personal war was being waged against the land he was born on. The startled grasses and corn stalks stood, waiting, like the owl over there, trying to anticipate the next move of this government hell bent on taking this land and doing what with it? Building townhouses? Dams? Paving the whole goddamn place so *furriners'* damn automobiles can smoke up this whole place? If that happens, the beautiful blue – *natural* - smoke of the Smoky Mountains will flee to where walls of trees once stood, leaving only the yellow fog of mankind's fumes. Goddamn it.

Levi Trentham's rage bubbled; in time, its inflamed red clouds turned him into the top general of his own army of one.

Plant them all along the way! From Knoxville, into Townsend, and then all along the rail line into Elkmont! Every store and cabin and flagpole and building we will be flyin' Ol' Glory. A thousand American flags! That'll show those Germans who's stronger!

Guests, tourists, residents – pretty much everyone – applauded the patriotic efforts. Showing support with Liberty Bonds to finance the war, Victory Gardens to help food production, and women entering the workforce to help make the weapons of war and to replace the men who were off fighting "over there".

Elkmont proudly did their part, inundating their little mountain world with bigger gardens and a show of pride in the form of American flags flapping in the winds of sweeter harmonies. Everywhere, red, white, and blue bunting hung from eaves, people ran flags up many flagpoles scattered throughout the area, and many trees had the colorful fabric flying proudly at their tops. Elkmont's ten cottages closest to the club had the most flags, The Appalachian Club itself had the second largest, and Colonel Townsend's own cabin had the brightest - all working together to show their patriotism.

Over at The Wonderland Hotel, the biggest flag in the area wafted atop a white pine tree. Even the daily train had flags dangling from its windows and doors and sides; a red, white, and blue-draped iron horse galloping into the station.

Residents and visitors alike helped plant the flags, maintaining these important banners of independence. Both new and seasoned guests soon realized how tightly these mountaineers gripped the still-new American ideals of freedom and fierce individuality – the ability to do what they wanted on their own land. That was how moonshiners especially flourished in this area of the country, taking extraordinary risks for a chance at complete liberty. And liberty for the world was on everyone's mind during these still-raging days of the Great War.

JUNE 16, 1918, dawned bright, the sky blue as a robin's egg. The Appalachian Club decided to hoist an even bigger flag in response to turning tides in the war. Germans were still fiercely fighting, but the Allies were beginning to cut their way through the fog of war, clearing the way. Things were looking better.

Throughout Elkmont, the main road seemed one huge banner of reds, whites and blues. It was as if laundry day had arrived, and everyone had hung out their favorite fineries –flags and bunting festively snapping in the summer breeze.

Levi Trentham emerged from his cabin that morning and saw the usual green and browns of the mountains, the blue gray of the river, the big triangles of open mountain walls – but all that was now masked with the unnatural clashing of manmade and government sanctioned colors of the brightest reds, whites, and blues.

For some reason – perhaps it was that Levi finally decided to exercise his freedom of speech and expression about the hated war, or some say he was fed up with feuding with another storekeeper and neighbor; others say it was because the top of one of his favorite pine trees had been chopped off, and still others say he was just a rickety and salty ol' timer - but whatever it was on this fine mountain morning, the contrast of wild summer flowers and handsewn fabric set him off on a path towards an angry, but useless bone to pick with the world. And oh, no matter how futile, he planned to pick that bone like it was an open sore on the back of a fat and wild hog.

The Prophet of the Smokies, The Mayor of Elkmont, the man who was born and raised in the husky arms of ancient mountains, found himself walking, walking, and before he knew it, he was standing stock-still in the middle of Elkmont's road. Rage could be seen behind his eyes if one dared close enough. But no one did. Because they were all finishing breakfast and going about their business, making plans for the day. Feeling better about the war and grateful to be here, on vacation with their families in the playground of the Smokies.

It was right then, as ladies sipped tea and men made sure their flasks were full for the day that Levi Trentham put his hands on his hips and screamed as loudly as a hundred cackling crows, cursing the government and the war and the storekeeper and neighbors and visitors and the loggers and everyone and anyone who was in the middle of changing everything.

Corporations were taking all the land around him it seemed; lately, the American government had been trying to sweet talk him into selling them even more of his own land. For a national park. They wanted to *buy* his land for *everyone!* Ha! It was more like, *well, we will give you money for it — fair market value, but you must leave. Eminent domain, blah, blah, blah. Here let me explain it to you. You mountain folk never wrote or read any contract before...what it means is...*

Eminent domain my ass, he muttered to himself. Cussing was, as always, a very ingrained habit of his, especially when goaded by the hated government whose only job should be protecting the country as a whole and making roads and stoppin' this goddamn war over in Europe and staying the hell out of his business. *They'll never get my land, those bastards. I already done sold some of it to a corporate goddamn company! Now, they're comin' for more. Companies! My very own Government! And all these damn furriners have the nerve to fly Ol' Glory all up and down the street. Which is mostly paved! It ain't natural to have paved roads in these parts! Gimme the dirt paths and roads I had as a kid. Things are changin' too fast. Clubs and cabins and railroad tracks and a train comin' every day and now this place lookin' like a dang flag factory done set up shop and threw up its insides right in the middle of the Smoky Mountains. Well, goddamn it all...I'm done with it all. Pass the ammunition!*

But for all the huff and puff and railing against progress and the war and the government and change and tiffs with neighbors and colorful patriotic fabric attached to everything he saw, his real anger came from a deeper place, a dark cave of recognition. Because the Prophet of the Smokies knew better, knew what was coming, could see as clear as that owl the future when his entire mountain world would be altered forever, when the government could, and would, gain this land for themselves. For the greater good.

All these cursed visions and realizations came together allowing for a fiery eruption on that June morning in the middle of Elkmont's paved street.

"Goddamn Old Glory!" He yelled at the top of his lungs.

"Goddaaaamn Ol' Glory!"

"Goddamn it all! Goddaaaamn Ooool' Gloooryyyy!!!"

He repeated this so many times, screaming like an old cantankerous man. Because he was. Sixty-six years of living just like he wanted, and now...damn it all! Unwelcomed change had already happened, but it was *still* happening and now it was happening even faster.

A hysterical rage spewed from deep within and he just wasn't about to hide his blanched mood any longer.

"Levi! What's gotten into you? I'm gonna have to arrest you if you don't quiet down and go home!" The Sheriff arrived, marching right on over to the raging mountain man. He knew Levi well, liked him too, but the old man with the white beard and a tendency to cuss at just about everything simply wouldn't shut up about the war! And his land being taken! And he was disturbing the guests of Elkmont, whose revenue and taxes supported his paycheck.

"We can't have this yellin' and cussin' going on in a resort town, Levi. It'll drive everyone away and word will get out about an old grizzled bearded prophet showing up in the middle of the street yelling about a goddamn flag and the goddamn government and goddamn *furriners* and even goddamn damnation itself!"

Levi's eyes stabbed at the Sheriff over that description of himself. But he couldn't deny it was true. "Didn't do nothin', Sheriff! I got my freedom of speech you know."

"That ain't freedom of speech, Levi. You can't just come around here on private property and spew out hatred. There's youngins around!"

"Don't care. Goddamn flags everywhere. Why are they glorifyin' Ol' Glory? What's Ol' Glory doin' for them? Fightin' the Great War, and for what? What're we gettin' for sendin' our youngins over to God-knows-where-Europe and for what? We ain't gettin' any more land out of it! Or money. Or power. Oh, but that same goddamn government is taking this here land next, that's what! They're fightin' over in Europe for *no* land at all while they're fightin' *over here over our very own land!* Reckon they've got their heads up the wrong way of a pig's behind. Gonna take all these little towns and houses and fences so they can make a national park. They'll take all these cottages away. This here Appalachian Club even!" He pointed up the road, jabbed his finger toward the wooden building where a crowd had formed, watching the show.

"I bet these here *furriners* won't fly Ol' Glory so high when the government takes their own places here in the mountains that they say they love so much but most don't care a lick about! Done sold some of my own land already. To Colonel. But that was *my* choice. This daggum government - they're talkin' about how they're gonna force me to sell the rest of it for a goddamn national park. And soon. Goddamn it all!"

"Alright, Levi. Let's calm down now. I'm going to have to arrest you."

"I ain't see no handcuffs." Levi stepped back two paces. Of course he had his rifle with him. But the Sheriff's pistol was faster. Besides, Levi didn't want to shoot anyone. Preferred to let his words do the shooting.

And his words did just that for the next fifteen minutes while people peeked through curtained windows and came out on to porches and gathered at the club to see *what in tarnation was going on.* Amazing how quickly city folk adopted the folksy mountain lingo.

"Levi. I'm gonna have to banish you to your own land. For the duration of the Great War. Don't bother no one 'round here. You can yell all you want on your own land. But don't do it around here."

"Oh no. *No no.* Can't have *that* now can we! Because then the rich little townsfolk - all these goddamn *furriners* - won't be coming to *my* land anymore 'cause there's some hillbilly in the middle of street yellin' about a flag! Well, too goddamn bad! If they can't handle that, then they're weaker than a dyin' pig in a poke.

"Levi." The Sheriff folded his arms across his broad chest. The pistol was still at his side. "This is the last time I'm gonna say it. Come with me. Please. I'll escort you back to your own land instead of takin' you right to jail. Gonna have to fine you $100 though. And permission is only granted for you to visit the store and other such essentials. Nothin' more."

"$100! That's goddamn robbery! Who's the crook now?!"

"Do you want me to bring you into the jail, Levi? The pokey as you like to call it?"

Levi grumbled something about he *would be the one doing the pokin' to someone somewhere with somethin',* but the Sheriff let it pass, staying silent, ushering Levi Trentham towards his mountain home.

Where he stayed for a while, some say for almost the entire remainder of the Great War, managing to make a few appearances here and there at The Appalachian Club by the next summer.

But when he did meander his way to Elkmont's street again, it was evident he still could not keep his mouth shut.

"Not goin' to pay one goddamn cent of that $100. Ever. Did nothin' wrong. It's in the Constitution and I'm just exercisin' my rights as an American even though I'm not at all in agreement with America's government. Oh, and those Red Cross women – the ones helping our soldiers? They're also helpin' the German ones! Well, they're all 'a goddamn set of whores'."

America's women helping the enemy's soldiers?! Even if it was a benevolent, kind, humane thing to do – that kind of thing just could not be tolerated in Levi Trentham's world. Why,

Elkmont's own Mrs. Galyon volunteered with the Red Cross, and she put in over 800 hours! 800 hours gathering clothes and food and bandages for the damn bleedin' Germans! It was treasonous! Traitors, all of them.

He repeated these sentiments one too many times: "all of 'em - a goddamn set of Red Cross whores!"

The Sheriff made another trip to the middle of the road in Elkmont to talk to the man who was supposed to be confined to his own land.

"Levi! Again?! I'm takin' you to jail for this one. You can't be doin' this! And I'm addin' to your fines. The fine for this one'll be $250."

"Well, goddamn it all! Don't care who says what. I ain't paying one goddamn penny!"

The owl had been watching this show since that bearded ol' timer yelled about the flags in the middle of the road. Now he was yelling about the women helping the war effort, the ones showing mercy even to the enemy. The wise feathered creature eyed the suspicion, the desperation, the yellow and foul mood emitting from this man who could always see the future.

What a curse this old man had! Oh, it had served him well over the years to be sure, but once those visions crystallized into a narrow-focused tunnel of lost land and lifestyle, of perceived wrongs and slights, of people daring to counter his personal views, the highest mountain of bitterness and anger released its boulders, overtaking him

No one was going to tell a man like Levi Trentham what to do. Not neighbors, fellow storekeepers. Not *furriners* nor city folk. And especially not condescending and patronizing government men – even ones like the Sheriff whom he knew well and actually liked. Most of the time. And to think the men in Washington in their fancy and soft and dull suits acted like they were handing out charity! *We're fighting this Great War for democracy. To save lives. For liberty.* They don't even know what liberty is! And all the while, the bigger, more immediate problem is the one they're smilin' about and walkin' around about and paradin' their fat bellies all over the country makin' plans with *my* land! *Our* land! *Don't worry,* they say, sneers hinting just underneath their goddamn soft smiles. *You'll be more comfortable in town what with electric and indoor plumbing and running water. Don't you worry! We'll pay you good money for your land!*

Well, goddamn right you will! Mountain folk ain't beggars!

But he didn't want to be paid for his land. He didn't want to leave the soil, his home, crops and creeks, at all. Ever. He wanted to go back in time to our Founding Fathers - they understood small government balanced with individual liberty. Today's government was intrusive, regulating American lives more and more and more. Maybe that worked in the big cities. But it sure didn't work here in the Smoky Mountains of Tennessee. And it sure didn't work for folk like him.

War, love - both as full of troubles as pleasures. Maybe even more. Especially love. Because that one, when enough time has passed, allows the ability to see too many sides at once. And the love for his land had been in him since his birth in the rich, fertile soil of the Smokies and goddamn it if he was going to give any more of it up for anyone, especially not his country which he loved, yet was deeply angry at for entering a war they had no business in. And he was especially angry at those Washington men for muttering this and that about a national park that may take his and Lem's homes, Ivah and Joseph Murphy's vacation home, Mr. and Mrs. Galyon's – *even if she was a goddamn Red Cross whore* - and the Farr's cottages, along with the Colonel's business and railroad and homes and such.

And everything else that's left.

11

SUMMER - 1919

COMING TOGETHER IS A BEGINNING;
KEEPING TOGETHER IS PROGRESS;
WORKING TOGETHER IS SUCCESS.
SOMETIMES ALL THREE CANNOT OCCUR.

~

As the summer of 1919 bloomed, Elkmont – and the world – was at peace. The Great War was officially over by the signing of an armistice on November 11, 1918. America was about to roar; many of its citizens flocking to the beautiful and well-established Smoky Mountain resort in Tennessee.

People had heard all about the town of Elkmont morphing from a logging town into a premier family vacation destination. Daily train service brought more and more visitors, desperate to find themselves once again within the softly scalloped peaks, the ones misty with memories and traditions. The ones filled with people whose ancestors' bodies are forever rooting into the soil, spirits making their way into hearths and homes, sitting down with you at every meal and at every Bible reading and every time you visit. Everything and everyone feeding you so well you never, ever, want to leave.

It took some time but three distinct areas of Elkmont eventually emerged.

"Daisytown" established itself as an accessible row of vacation cottages between the mouths of Jake's Creek and Bearwallow Branch. It got its flowery name due to the vast number of daisies that grow in the summer months – all along the meadows and creek sides. Why, at their peak, some areas looked like one big carpet of white and yellow! A certain Mrs. Daisy, last name unknown, liked to think it was because she visited Elkmont since its inception and, as she was prominent and well-known, it was thus named for her. But the owl knew better. If she was so well known, why didn't anyone remember her? Why doesn't anyone know who she was? History is sacred to these people and if anyone knew who a famous Mrs. Daisy was, it would be Levi Trentham. And he was still mostly holed up at home after his non-arrest-arrests, perfectly happy to yell on his own land about this and that and certainly did not know any Mrs. Daisy who was supposedly so famous an entire section of a popular resort town was named for her.

Besides, look at those daisies! It made sense this area of Elkmont was named solely for nature's pure and honeyed creations! Some were even purplish and could be crushed and used in teas for coughs and bruises and he swore they could be chewed up and before he knew it, his cold would be gone! Mountain folk didn't have the scientific and medical knowledge that confirmed daisies have nearly as much Vitamin C as lemons. But they somehow knew it had an effect. Knew by trial and error and tasting this and that and knowledge passed down from mothers and grandmothers. There were only so many resources in these mountains and most had been tried before by people both observant and desperate.

From the section known as Daisytown, another area named "Society Hill" was just to the south, still along Jake's Creek, boasting larger, airier cottages, with white wicker chairs in the living rooms and blue and green swings on the front porches.

Finally, "Millionaire's Row" displayed the best homes sitting along the banks of the Little River to the east of the club. As in many societies, the affluence of the owners dictated the layout of Elkmont's sections.

Nearby sat the remnants of the Little River Logging Company's Stringtown – so named because the thin wooden structures had been built in rows, creating the look of a "string" of homes. Little more than shanties or shacks, the logging town did have all the amenities families needed: a post office, a hotel, commissary for groceries, movies projected onto a big screen in the logging company's commissary, and various barns and sheds holding logging and railroad equipment.

Then there was the Elkmont Baptist Church, built in 1916, where dancing, alcohol, and card playing was forbidden, of course, but thirty gallons of ice cream were doled out on the hottest summer days. People were happy, men were working for good wages, and families and friends flocked to the area to join them on weekends to enjoy the fishing, hiking, and beauty of the mountains.

LEVI TRENTHAM and Lem Ownby explained all this to a group of tourists settled at a corner table. It was time for supper – *dinner for you townfolk* - at The Appalachian Club and the summer of 1919 was turning out to be a banner one. They'd never seen so many visitors! Indeed, the idea of a national park had broken ground and people flocked to the area to see just where this newest playground would be and what amenities were planned.

Oh, it wasn't inevitable yet. Levi and Lem had heard all the talk of the past two decades or so and were almost convinced it would never happen. The Appalachian National Park Association formed in the early 1900s to advocate for a park in the Appalachian region. Just where it would be though remained undetermined. Logging had come to town in the late 1800s, and to Elkmont in 1901. Soon thereafter, Colonel Townsend sent half of the trees down the river and to his sawmill in Townsend so the bald heads of the mountains could be seen by residents, visitors, and an owl as it roosted higher and higher up on the rocky crowns.

1913 dawned with Horace Kephart's book, "Our Southern Highlanders", which raised awareness of the region. And by 1916, just three years ago, The National Park Service was created by the government to oversee national parks.

Whispers became bold talk and soon, the air was filled with the real possibility of America's newest national park finding itself right here, where natural wonders abound. Creeks, rivers, beauty, hikes, waterfalls. Why, this place already had roads too! Crisscrossing from Walker Valley and Tremont to Cades Cove, Little Greenbrier Cove, Gatlinburg, down to Sugarlands and Mingus Mill, down further to Oconaluftee, and even east towards Cataloochee. And the views! Those endless blue peaks marching like soldiers into the mist dared the soul to take on anything, dream anything, create and reignite all passions, do anything at all. And the faces of those mountains stared back at you, holding both glares and gazes, eventually making all efforts and toil seem like the easiest thing in the world.

Inside these burly arms of one of the oldest mountain ranges on earth is what drove men like Levi Trentham and Lem Ownby to continue living their lifestyle, doing whatever they wanted on their own land, yet taking care of family and farm and community. It was these same rocky waves of peaks that dared the two men to hope the national park would never happen – the stony expressions and ancient bravado of the mountains fueling their freedom-loving determination.

DESPITE HIS HOUSE arrests and the Sheriff sneaking around just a bit too often, Levi managed to slink off his land at certain times of his own choosing. He never did pay the $100 or the $250. Or spent a night in jail. But he also never got over the slights – or the whispers - of the darker side of fate, snickering at his resistance to change. Yet when it served him, he was not above hitching a ride on the train of progress. Such willingness – or was it a resignation that fate could not be stopped? – included him selling some of his land to Colonel Townsend in 1905, and now again, in 1919, selling a few more acres to the businessman.

As for Lem Ownby, though the Colonel asked him on a regular basis and though Lem had also previously sold some of his land, he made it known he was not willing to part with any other acreage. At least not right now.

Lem may have been almost blind at this point, but his mind was not shaded so much that it didn't see the future notching itself into the walls of his home. He knew things must change. Eventually. He often sat on his front porch, Old Shep at his feet, thinking of the children playing in the creeks and meadows, collecting berries in the summertime. Helping with the harvest in autumn. What would happen to these youngins if this national park came into being? They wouldn't be able to log anymore. Couldn't learn in their school – 'cause there'd *be* no school. Couldn't hunt. Trap. Keep bees. Towns would beckon with their hard desks and chairs and paperwork and sidewalks and houses that were five stories high – living right up in the air! It was all so unnatural! He sighed, rubbing Old Shep and listening to the hooting owl who was trying to join in with knots of children running barefoot and laughing in their mountain world.

Lem would rise and make his way inside for the evening. Levi would do the same. Early morning chores waited for the men to sleep, reassured that, for now at least, both mountain men still had plenty of acreage and plenty of room to keep bees, farm, and yell to their heart's content that they were never, ever going to give up the bulk of their land.

The owl sat there, equally amused and saddened, for it knew what was to come. That no amount of yelling or ignoring or confining a cussing man to a house - nor overall-clad and cotton-dress wearing folk turning their backs on one paved street in the middle of nowhere to concentrate instead on their crops and cabins and corncribs - could keep progress from encroaching onto their ancestral slices of Smoky Mountain heaven.

ADAPTING. The effort dominated their lives.

People find new ways of coping even through the most egregious acts. Within about six weeks, humans emerge with a new way to cope that will ultimately be successful. Or they emerge with a new way to cope that's not successful and then they revert to their own poor decisions. Those are the stubborn pupils; ones who refuse to adapt and change when it is absolutely mandatory to do so. Levi and Lem had vision and tried to be the successful type.

Were they, in fact, succeeding?

Oh, those two mountain men – one now sixty-seven years old with a wife and ten children, and the other one, the near-blind thirty-year old bachelor - tried so hard to make it so! To rail against such rapid progress! To pick and choose which advancements to adopt and which ones to shoo away! On lighter days, they'd come together with others. Listen. Maybe even try to merge with others' mindsets for a while, playing the game of heeding the words of city folk and nodding their heads and showing up to talk. But working together? Ah, there was the rub. Sometimes all three – coming together, keeping together, and working together – cannot occur.

Levi's prophecies began to take him over, and he saw so clearly - like a shining lamp that never went out - that within four, seven, ten short years, life would change drastically and both he and Lem Ownby, along with The Wonderland Hotel and The Appalachian Club would have to alter their entire way of life. Or at least modify the view of their lifestyle, all from a smaller and shorter vantage point.

Adapt they did. But from the outside looking in, it didn't seem like it.

The two well-known mountain men still lived like the mountain farmers they were. They "made do or done without" for just about everything; even, at times, shoes. The valley was scattered with homesteads and farms connected by all widths of trails and wagon roads, and their homes, while dear and cozy to themselves, looked like "unpainted tumbledown shacks" with tin roofs and black smoke blowing from the chimneys. Firewood stood precariously on the front porch, on the sides of the home; brooms, tools, herbs, and hats hung on pegs on porches and from nails pounded into rafters inside the house. From the hearth draped skillets, pots, pans, rifles, rags, garlic and herbs. The smell of smoke was ever-present, heavily lingering in the hair and clothes and eyelashes forever.

Their way of adapting came mostly from the inside.

Levi and Lem sat staring into their respective fires encased in their bib overalls; for Lem, perhaps a tin or two of Blood Hound tobacco nearby, spit cup on the floor by the rocking chair. Everything in its place. But inside those flames, the ones licking the hearth walls and filling the cabin air with tangy smoke, the mountains spoke, and the prophecies came: religion, family, government, education, media, arts and entertainment, and business.

Seven categories of life.

Seven summits.

Seven mountains.

Damn it. They knew they'd never be able to capture – preserve really - these seven classifications before the government did.

Or could they?

The two men - one all-seeing and old, the other blind and younger - took them over quietly, in the dead of night. In the heat of the day. In the middle of the road. On a hike or at a fishing hole. At the supper table – *not the dinner table!* - at The Appalachian Club.

They did all this by telling their own stories, sharing experiences, remembering ancestors and showing how to craft a horseshoe in a homemade blacksmith shop. The tips and tricks and art of cooking bear meat, seasoning it and cooking it low and slow so the toughness would ease.

Levi's wife did her part by sewing everything for ten children and countless grandchildren while tending the kitchen garden and sweeping the floors a million times a day.

Lem did it by tending his bees, listening for children's laughter which always made everything better, and dispensing such advice as he did on those who saw Halley's Comet make its pass from May 14 through May 22, back in 1910. To the ones who loudly predicted doom and gloom and the end of the world, he advised: "you better go ahead and salt a little something away, just in case you're wrong."

These two men – Levi and Lem – and their families preserved these seven summits by keeping their culture alive and kicking. By thriving in their learned arts and crafts and specialties. By making a dough bowl carved from buckeye wood to withstand many washings. Weaving together all sizes and sorts of baskets to corral sewing supplies, eggs, berries, nuts, or extra ham or cornbread or green beans to bring to a relative or neighbor.

By making all their own furniture.

By listening.

The mountains and God Himself told the two rooted men and their families that whoever celebrates true value and virtue would mold the minds and reap the harvest of Elkmont. *Even if Elkmont would be soon owned by someone else.*

Levi's trancelike state called to him, comforted his most hopeless of days: *the government can buy all the open land they want, but one cannot rule a heart always laid open to the good ol' days.*

Heart and eyes open, sometimes reluctantly of course. The Prophet of the Smokies nonetheless stared into the fire, those red and orange tongues in constant shifts of highs and lows, flushes and embers. Change does not have to appear to everyone else; is not the same for each set of eyes. It can be silently ticking away, like the clock in Lem Ownby's house – present, but biding its time. Understanding it must be wound continuously or else stop dead, to look old, timeless, never to be useful again.

12

———

IMPROVEMENTS – SUMMER 1919

BETTER A LITTLE FIRE TO WARM US
THAN A GREAT ONE TO BURN US.

~

Extensive improvements have been made!

Our club house and annex are now in position to serve its members better than ever before.

A complete water and sewerage system is in place, and we have electric lighting throughout our resort!

Visitors will marvel at the "fireflies" lighting the browns and reds of our wooden ceiling!

Attention-grabbing headlines dominated new brochures for The Appalachian Club. A select group of people received these glossy and lively advertisements, making membership to the club even more exclusive. Indeed, it was tougher than ever to gain entry. Though all visitors and tourists of the resort town of Elkmont could continue to dine at the rustic club, people were required to be members to use the building for special events, access to certain dances, teas, socials, and such. There was one exception, however. If you were staying at The Wonderland Hotel and wished to dine at The Appalachian Club, you would be told, *I am sorry but there is no more food. No more tables. I apolo-*

gize, but please return to your resort to dine there. We do not have the staff to accommodate your party.

The visitors loved the club's improvements, which featured not only electric lighting, but a water tank near Hommel Orchard. This meant water didn't have to be hauled or piped from a spring near Jake's Creek. And water supplies were finally reliable; never again would staff have to deal with unknown water levels and sometimes too-rapid currents after a hard rain or during spring snowmelt. This did wonders for the resort and their staff. All workers had to do was dip their containers into the calm tank, and they always knew exactly how much they had left and when they were running low.

So many improvements! Elkmont was a very comfortable place to relax, with hearty food, good mountain air, soft beds, kitchens in every cottage – even if they weren't used much – and healthy and fun activities. The road was maintained. Train service was reliable. And now, the resort had electric! Which brought even more *furriners* to this little wedge of American paradise, even if the water-powered generator provided electricity for just two hours a day.

The owl was amazed at lights flickering on and off in the evenings *inside* of buildings. Just by twisting a key-shaped handle or by pulling a chain, a room could light up like a thousand fireflies or like the shiniest silver moonlight! Two hours of electric lighting was a lot – it felt like adding two more hours to every day and made all these city folk feel right at home, not to mention more spirited – enough to buy one more hour of revelry and two more drinks. Or desserts for everyone in the family. Or three hearty scoops of ice cream for the kids, the ones who stayed up later than they did during the school year and slept better than they had in all their lives.

LEVI STUCK a fork into a flaky piece of breaded and fried river trout, enjoying the slightly nutty flavor. It was *suppertime* again at the club. Lights weren't yet turned on; dusk was still an hour or so away. During these waning days of his house arrest, he evaded the sheriff long enough - and well enough - to lead a couple good men to a fishing hole, and all were now eating their rewards.

"Back in 1912, just seven years ago, they done built The Wonderland Hotel. Ya'll have seen it. It's that one up the hill." Levi began, the raconteur in him on full display this evening.

Guests nodded. The fishermen, Mr. Galyan, Mr. Farr, Mrs. Ivah Murphy and her husband – all the regulars - were there for this banner summer season of 1919. The pull of the mountains was just too much, and no summer would feel right if they couldn't enter their beloved mountain cathedral for at least a couple of weeks. These regulars looked around as Levi lazily finished his trout, chewing slowly.

The Appalachian Club was at capacity. It had never seen so many visitors! Indeed, word spread like mountain laurel on summer creekbanks – the Smoky Mountains were a fantastic place to vacation with family! Days of hiking, hunting, fishing, eating their very own catch for dinner, sleeping under the creaky wooden beams of comfortable cottages, only after meeting so many fascinating people with so many stories to tell! It was another world; one they fell in love with.

It was within this lazy and sated atmosphere that some of the guests dared talk about trying out The Wonderland Hotel next season.

The owl flew in to listen as Levi visibly rankled.

"Why would you *godda*...why would you folk do that? Ya'll have your own cottages right here! And you pay for 'em too. Why would you pay double?"

"Yessir, Levi. You're right. But too many people have fallen in love with Elkmont, and, quite frankly, sometimes there's no longer enough room at The Appalachian Club to hold all of us."

"Ain't enough room? Whyn't you make more room? Build another room! You got plenty of it!" He waived his arms around as if sweeping the entirety of the resort into one big embrace.

The businessmen looked at one another. It was true. But it wasn't that easy and Mr. Murphy was the one who dared tell the truth. "Well. What we mean is, we can build a bigger building to be sure. But even another ten rooms can't hold the lot of us. There's some fine folk who only stay at The Wonderland. And we stay here in Elkmont. But there isn't one building that can hold all of us, even if we build it. Not when our minds are so different." Levi watched Mr. Murphy as he stood, stretching his legs.

"But it would be nice to try. I guess that's why, perhaps, some of us may stay at The Wonderland – to try for a meeting of the minds. We're all in business together after all. It's strange to talk in town and in meetings but have such a split when we're all on vacation!"

Wildflowers sprung from a small vase, a water carafe gleamed in the candlelight. Electric lights wouldn't flick on for another few hours and only for two hours when it became fully dark. More and more homes in American cities were being plugged in, but still, only about 6% of all the homes in the United States had electric, and practically none in the Smokies.

"How did The Wonderland Hotel come to be again? I recall it being built, but I don't quite recall how it came so popular." One of the children of Mr. and Mrs. Galyon asked, too young to remember the entire story.

"Ah, youngin. Listen here and I'll tell ya." Levi began and hunched down a bit to meet the child's eyes.

"You know Colonel Townsend, right? Well, he done realized he'd logged just about all there was to log here in Elkmont. All the trees gone. Cut down. But he still had the land. So, in 1911 –

          CATHERINE ASTL

reckon that's before you was even born! - he tells one Charles Carter, who was another businessman 'round these parts, 'hey, I'll give you several acres of land on a hill overlooking Elkmont if you build on it within a year'. Well, Carter agreed right away, and held true to his promise. That buildin' up there to the north - where all the workers are and we can hear their repairin' and smell their cookin' all day long - is The Wonderland Hotel. It opened to guests back in 1912."

"That's a nice name – The Wonderland. But I like these cottages here in Elkmont! What's so special about The Wonderland anyway? It's right up there so it's not like it has different views or it's in a completely different place! And as far as I can see, it's got the same river and trails and fishing holes." The child asked what many had been thinking. Guests turned to look out the window, up towards the north hill where the large structure called The Wonderland stood for the past seven years.

"Not much difference, to be sure." Levi eyed the hotel. He occasionally went there too, to scoop up city folk – *furriners* – who wanted to fish and hike. Money was money whether it was "Wonder money" or "Appalachian money". But truth be told, he preferred "Appalachian money". Something about the *clientele* as these city folk call themselves. People were different here on Elkmont's tidy street. A little more down to earth. Friendlier. More about family, less about business.

"The Wonderland's got balconies overlookin' the valley and you can see Meigs Mountain from the site. Way back in 1802, there was a Colonel Jonathan Meigs who came to the area to survey the Hawkins Line, what they called the 'craggy and ragged border between Tennessee and North Carolina'. Well, they done named the mountain after him. Lots of Colonels 'round here, eh?!" Levi winked at the young Galyon boy and smiled at the crowd of familiar people.

"Anyways, on a clear day, we used to be able to see the

brightly colored blanket Meigs had spread atop the adjacent mountain so he could more easily train his compass reference point."

Levi huffed out his breath and added, "Nowadays, we can see pretty much anythin' atop every nearby mountain top; they're completely bald from all the loggin'. That's the only good thing that may - I say *may* - come from this national park. If it ever happens. A park will stop all the loggin' and try to restore the trees and slopes and natural runoff and all those things that loggin' took away from these here mountains. That'll be a good thing to be sure."

Businessmen and their wives and children looked at him, mouth agape. Was he actually agreeing with the government? But Levi quickly scowled, coming to his own defense.

"Oh now, don't get me wrong folks. Ain't want no national park comin' in to take my land. No sir. But it would be nice to see some more trees 'round here. Like it used to be."

Talk of the national park edged closer with each passing month; crept its way into the nooks of their lives in the way blue morning mist moved up, up, on fitful breezes.

But tonight, Levi set aside his worries and swirling issues and suddenly stood, wiping his mouth, dropping the red checked cloth napkin on the table. Donning his hat again, picking up his cane, he bid his goodbyes. "Now folks, let's all get to bed early. Tomorrow night's the big dance!" Levi lightheartedly scolded the children's parents, causing their youngins to chuckle. What he didn't add was: *tomorrow is a big day for Elkmont. For The Wonderland Hotel up there on the hill is turning into another club. One that none of you will ever be able to get into.*

13

THE DANCE - 1919

AN IRON ANVIL SHOULD HAVE
A HAMMER OF FEATHERS.

~

It was Saturday evening, and the front porch dance and party was in full swing. The best local musicians were brought in and *Yellow Dog Blues* and the slower *Banjoland* were performed. City folk clapped hands and stomped feet to fast-paced rhythmic patterns and plucking for the first time in their lives. They could only take so much though! All that jumping and moving in a line and do-si-do activity was tiring! Ladies fanned themselves, sitting down, finally, with cold iced tea while the men tipped back their heads for another sip from their fooling-nobody flasks.

Everyone was feeling good and talk soon turned to the newest advertising campaigns running in local newspapers and tourist spots: *The Wonderland Hotel has two daily rail lines on which run the Elkmont Special. Are you seeking relaxation and recreation in a mountain landscape? We offer fishing, horseback riding and mountain climbing, as well as social events and formal dances.*

"Seems Wonderland is tryin' to outdo us here in Elkmont. Reckon they're takin' up the whole second page of all the newspapers!" Southern accents took about three days to emerge, and they were out in full force on this Saturday summer evening at The Appalachian Club. Even Levi Trentham – still technically on house arrest – was here, as was Lem Ownby, his near-blind eyes closed so he could simply listen to the rolls and drones of the banjos. Tapping his feet lightly, nodding his head, he was one with the music of the mountains, which he described as "a hive of happy buzzin' bees swarmin' all around your head and no amount of wavin' your arms can get 'em to go away. But then again, you don't want 'em to go away, 'cause them banjos make music that aids the whisperings of the woods. Along with the winds of sweeter harmonies."

"That's lovely, Lem."

"Thank ya. Reckon ya'll don't have music like this. It empties your glass and calls you to your feet, boots and all."

Nods all around. Ladies' faces stared at the mountain man whose carefully spoken thoughts were sometimes so deep, they dared think his well was dug clear through to the other side of the world. Indeed, their *town music* or whatever these mountain men called their musical style, was nothing like this. *This* was awfully fun! So different! But the tunes fit the atmosphere and people like Levi Trentham and Lem Ownby who grew up in these parts. As rooted to the land as all the remaining trees combined.

"Those newspaper ads. They sound a lot like our cottages and our Appalachian Club what with their dances and activities and cottages and rooms to let. I know it's been seven years now since The Wonderland Hotel opened, but I wonder why they opened another hotel right up the road in the first place? I mean, we have so many cottages right here in Elkmont..."

"Well now. Seems too many folk wanted to come here to... *our* mountains." He stopped short of saying 'my mountains', but Levi Trentham thought exactly that as he chimed in. "As ya'll know, word got out pretty fast and there's enough folk who want to come here for there to be two resorts. Heck, there's probably enough for five! But it won't be a hotel for much longer."

"What do you mean, Levi?" Businessmen prided themselves on knowing everything two weeks before everyone else. But this was news to them, and they perked up, flasks in hand, listening intently as the banjos and harmonicas slid their sounds through the screened-in porch and out towards the sparse treetops.

"What I mean is, The Wonderland Hotel opened on a Tuesday. On June 11th it was, in the summer of 1912. By that weekend, the hotel had no vacancy."

"Indeed, and it's been pretty full every summer. But we've been full too. So has our club here. Daisytown, Society Hill, Millionaire's Row – all of us here in the heart of Elkmont bought our places here. And we come here all the time! Every summer."

"And rent them out to others even..."

"Our families stay here for months!"

"Yeah, but The Wonderland is more about luxury. Wealthier folk go there." Levi could see the Knoxville businessmen sitting before him squirming. Wealthier than themselves? Why, they worked very hard for their money, and they were *very rich*....

"Reckon they *think* they're wealthier, mind." Levi was one who could read the room and size up the emotions of any crowd. He decided to appease them...and give them a little taste of the prophecies he was so famous for.

"Actin' like it anyway, spendin' more and more of their money here in the mountains. But who knows if they really have that much, or if they're just spendin' it all? Reckon those who are wealthiest are never in a hurry to lose money. In other words, those who hang on to their coins longer are always gonna be wealthier. That and livin' here and meetin' a lot of folk over the last few years have given my so-called prophecies time to practice seein' things even clearer. And when a person with experience meets a person with money, I've seen that the person with experience will get the money and the person with the money will get the experience."

Wisdom abounded from this mountain man. It was quite amazing for the owl to see the gaping mouths of the Knoxville men and their wives. They'd never thought of things in such a straightforward way.

"Colonel Townsend is such a man – he's got the money *and* the experience. A rare combination to be sure. Oh, and he has some of that special power too you see - he's like me in a lot of ways. Can see into the future." They stopped, gasped a bit. Colonel Townsend a prophet? They'd never quite heard that about the railroad and lumber tycoon. Oh, he was smart and experienced and rich to be sure, but...a prophet? No. That can't be. And more than one lady murmured that even if the Colonel did have the second sight so to speak, it couldn't match Levi Trentham's famous prophecies because everyone knew those were very far-reaching. And real. And nearly always came true. Levi Trentham - that's who they wanted to hear from.

"What do *you* see, Levi?" Mrs. Ivah Murphy boldly asked, seeing relief on the faces of the others who desperately wanted to ask but were afraid to.

"Well, ma'am. Mrs. Ivah." He tipped his hat to her. "Reckon what I see changes with the times. And sometimes - in fact, *many* times - I see what I don't wanna see."

"Most things I don't wanna see neither. That's why it ain't so bad bein' blind." Lem Ownby softly added, a lilt to his voice that defied the firmness of his statement.

The mesmerized crowd stood silent, anticipation kneeling on the smallest breeze. The band and banjos were taking a break, and the stifling humid heat of the summer night broke like a fragile vessel of joy; its slightly cooler essence spilling out right when the Prophet of the Smokies sweetened the guests' pot of knowledge.

Nodding heads bobbed frantically – *they remind me of the rotten ones*, Levi thought for just a moment. When bobbing for apples, the sinkers are fine to eat, but it's the floaters that are rotten. The floaters are the ones that bob up and down, up and down, forever waving their foul red heads.

But there was nothing foul here, he realized, softening his stare. Just curious folk on a vacation in the Smoky Mountains – determined to see the future.

Mrs. Ivah Murphy, who was so kind and pretty and bold, sank into her seat and stayed there, rooted to the cane-back rocking chair, resolved to know what was coming, whatever it showed. Persisting, she asked again, eyes raised in earnest: "So…Levi, Mr. Trentham. What *do* you see?"

Levi squinted at the guests, eyed them up and down, determining at a glance who were the bobbing apples and who were the sinkers, and decided most of them were sinkers. Mostly okay folk, he thought, if a bit naïve and annoying. But much less annoying than those folk stayin' up at The Wonderland.

After a moment or so, he gazed up at the sky, prompting them to look up towards the familiar owl perched just to their right on a thick branch.

"Don't much like to talk about it. The future and what I see, that is. But since you folk seem to want to know…" Sighing, he sunk in a chair, threaded his hands through his beard, and began sharing his prophecy.

"Shortly after The Wonderland opened, I was invited to the hotel, and they even offered me money to perform what they called a 'blessing for good fortune'. They told me that they hoped my deep connection to these here mountains would 'ensure prosperity for the hotel'."

"How much money did they offer?" Mr. Galyon, ever the businessman, asked. To which his wife softly poked him and gave him a look as if to say, *please do not talk of money while on vacation! And don't ask Levi Trentham of all people! He doesn't like us 'furriners' - as he calls us - as it is!*

"Oh, it don't matter 'cause I didn't take any of it. Not a penny."

The guests were quiet. Oh, how they wanted to ask why he didn't take the money! And how much it was! But never push a man like Levi Trentham.

And so, they waited. Watched the owl sit so still they would be forgiven to think it had simply stopped living. But then, its talons would've slipped the branch, letting its owner fall, fall to the ground. Sink into the soil. Ah, a sinker this feathered creature was. A good one. Wise.

Eventually, Levi continued. Only when he was good and ready.

"Told 'em no blessing could ensure success of the hotel if they failed to respect the land and its people."

"And did they? Respect the land and the people? It has been seven years since they opened."

Levi rose, dropped his beard and tipped his hat, indicating he was saying goodbye and goodnight. But he did turn to answer the group as he walked down the wooden steps and as the band began playing one final round. A waltz, in three-fourths time.

"Still remains to be seen. Only history will be able to answer that one. But one thing's for sure...I done told you already...it ain't gonna be a hotel for long."

14

A SECOND CLUB - 1919

WONDER IS THE DAUGHTER OF IGNORANCE, AND IGNORANCE HAS AN OWL'S EYES.

≈

Rockefeller controlled the oil market while Andrew Carnegie conquered the steel industry in Pennsylvania, but Colonel Townsend had his Great Smoky Mountains, his Little River Lumber Company, and his railroad. Easily recognizing the value of adapting his various enterprises - and the benefits of the now fully logged, treeless, flat land, easily accessed by a railroad and with fantastic views and natural amenities - he basked in his two most recent ventures: Elkmont's cottages and The Appalachian Club, and The Wonderland Hotel.

Years passed as he watched delighted guests lounging in rustic but comfortable accommodations, alongside Levi and Lem, the deeply-rooted residents.

Elkmont's families gathered in summer on front porches of their cottages, keeping busy fishing, hiking, picnicking and playing in the creek. Children were everywhere, which especially delighted Lem Ownby who could hear their laughter all the way from his front porch. It made him smile every time. And wonder – would he ever have children of his own?

Oh, how he yearned for his own family! People around him to help, to talk to. To navigate the world as he aged. He was only just now thirty years old. And strong and kind. Smart too. Near-blind though. What woman could put up with that? He sighed. Watched the owl, a blurry blob in the tree, who gave away none of its secrets just yet. And that was just fine with him as he wasn't ready for any secrets of the future. He'd thought about it to be sure, but decided long ago he would never ask his prophet friend to tell him what was in store for him. He just didn't want to know. Not yet anyway. Not while there was still time to find a kind and strong and resourceful lady to make a life with. Not while hope's strings still dangled themselves before his face, just enough so he could see its soft outlines.

OF THE TWENTY-SIX guest rooms at The Wonderland Hotel, two or three bedrooms shared one bathroom down a wide hallway. Most visitors spent their days on the front porch, occasionally taking a path down to the Little River to canoe or swim. The railroad took tourists directly to the site of the resort, almost right up to the wraparound front porch that looked out onto the face of Blanket Mountain. Visitors could also fish, hunt, and feed the raccoons that came begging every evening on the front lawn and porch. For many citified people, this was their very first experience in the Smoky Mountains, and they told everyone back home that they simply must visit for 'grand accommodations and socializing in the most picturesque setting'.

LEVI TRENTHAM MADE it his business to make his mark anywhere and everywhere in his Smoky Mountain world, even if reluctantly. This included The Wonderland Hotel and its staff and their guests – *more goddamn furriners* - who arrived and roamed around every summer.

As for all those *furriners*, if they didn't know who Levi was prior to stepping off the train, they certainly knew him within an hour of arriving. How could he not be noticed? Walking around with a bear or beaver pelt over one shoulder, rifle perched on the other, staring out with wise, beady, and discerning eyes, that large owl seemingly following him - and only him – everywhere he went.

The craggy old mountain man seemed to be everywhere – by the river, guiding groups on hikes, to the fishing holes, and to the front porches and dining tables of Elkmont. He showed up almost every day regaling everyone with his stories. In the early days of his so-called house arrest, he'd stay away. For the most part. But lately, he'd just done whatever he damn well pleased and no one - the Sheriff included – uttered a word.

Besides, Levi was relatively quiet lately, not insulting any Red Cross women or yelling about the flag or the war - over now thank goodness – or those government men in Washington or this dang national park they keep talking about or progress that's paving over these mountains or the train's smoke that's fouling up the air or anything else he was railing against this week.

But he was clearly holding it in. Sometimes he seemed so… angry, his lips pressed together in an all-out effort to hold his tongue. Enraged. Bitter. Agitated. Like a gaunt-shanked, leather-faced side of jerked venison ready to be devoured by a beast. The only thing that calmed him was going out his front door, walking down to Elkmont's street, finding someone to tell a story to. Someone needs to keep this way of life going! And he supposed it was all up to him. And his friend, Lem Ownby.

Walking down the street this afternoon, stroking his beard, he found his balm. Lem was there, talking to folk, and was already telling that one story about that one bear. Levi smiled. *Yessir, this here story's a good one.*

"Now folks. See here." Lem began, sitting back in a cane-back chair. "Bearskins fetch top dollar. I'm talkin' *seven* dollars. Sometimes *thirty* dollars! Sometimes even more for a real good one. That's why we mountain folk always take some risks to git one. Well, one time, me and my nephew, Steve, treed a bear and I got flat on my back to get a good shot. Reckon you recall I can't see too good. But I could see that black blob in the tree. She was a big one. Well, I cocked my gun and...folks...'I thought I had seen and done just about everything there was to do, but this was the first time I've ever been shit on by a bear'!"

Oh, how the *furriners* laughed at that!! Especially all their youngins who weren't used to such talk - they couldn't wait to go back home to share this hilarious bear scat story! Imagine! And it was all they could do to remember to say *scat*, because they'd be kicked out of school - and definitely church - if they so much as compromised to say *scit*.

Despite Levi and Lem's jesting with city folk now and then, they continued actively seeking out *these furriners* to do more than just shock – they admitted a certain enjoyment in talking to many of them. Different folk decorated their mountain world. From Ivah Murphy's humor and classy boldness to Mrs. Galyon's Red Cross work, which was, *well, I guess it's good of her to help, even if those...whor...women...helped our enemy too,* Levi grudgingly conceded in rare moments of conciliation. And the Farrs and Colonel Townsend were good folk, as were a lot of the others. Most of all, both Levi and Lem sure got a kick out of all those city youngins! You'd think they'd never seen a deer or a bear or a river so wide it seemed to bracket all the flowers and animals and human feelings in the world!

Well, the kids were quick to scold the two gruff men teasing them, *we really and truly haven't seen any of these before so how could we know? We live in town after all! It's as if we told you to go read a newspaper and go sit in an office all day. You wouldn't know what those things were either. Or how to live like that.*

Indeed. Guiding, fishing, leading a hike, talking about bear stories and sharing suppertime – *not dinnertime!* - as Levi had to remind city folk every single goddamn evening as darkness fell in the dining room. Fine suits and dresses and even lace gloves and top hats mixed with faded overalls and white beards and sturdy black shoes. Or no shoes at all. It all somehow worked in the little sliver of smoky paradise called Elkmont. Yet the two worlds remained strikingly contrasted: on one hand boundless enthusiasm for progress; on the other, a halting intuition, steady nerves, and the need for legacy.

Why did Levi and Lem interact with these townspeople who they had such a mixed and rocky connection? They could've just stayed home! Not interacting at all with these city folk they scorned and saw as *furriners.* Invaders almost. Yes, they could've sat in their homemade rocking chairs, drinking tea or the clearest water on earth, or even a bit of moonshine, whittling a cedar log, cleaning their rifles, hunting, selling pelts and meat, tending their crops, handling their bees, mending roofs and fences and barns, checking on animals, spending time with their families.

And they certainly did all these things and then some.

Yet, the reality of life in the Smoky Mountains in 1919 urged them to seek these *furriners* out. To offer to guide them to the best fishing holes, known since childhood. To catch a fish, take it to the kitchen, share a meal. Oftentimes, there were two personalities at the table within the same mountain man: one was cordial and welcoming. Friendly even. The other was eyeing them up and down, suspicious. Scornful. Even mocking.

It crossed more than one visitor's mind: why did these mountain men even bother if it made them so upset?

The two men kept that reason to themselves.

Or so they thought.

The owl knew though, could see it all very clearly. And it wasn't too hard to figure out even without its keen vision that could see inside their very souls. For, it wasn't only about the struggle between a rustic cabin, barns, corncribs, and colorful cottages. It wasn't about the battle between an office in the city and a crop full of corn, between a pioneering, farming lifestyle and progress creeping in faster and faster. No. It wasn't about what one prophesizing mountain man and his near-blind bear-hunting friend wanted at all.

It was about the mountains themselves. What did *they* want?

And when they spoke, in their stony, old voices softened by millennia, there were two beings whose lives were as one with this specially crested world - as much a part of the peaks as the peaks themselves. Two beings who always listened to what the mountains had to say, adopting the reasons the mountains gave them.

We don't want to be changed! The mountain voice rang steady. Strong. *We might bend a bit, shake up our boulders and slopes here and there - depending on the whims of progress - but we cannot be fully tamed. Not yet at least. And if we ever choose to invite progress into our valleys, as with humans, we want to have a say in it. We demand the right to decide. When we are ready. Not by force either. Not by pushing, shoving others' ways and habits down our craggy throats. It all must come to pass on our own terms. When it's our idea. Only then will it feel right.*

The owl watched Levi and Lem. *Yes,* he swiveled his head before flying away to find a small rabbit, *the mountains know all about change. More than two hundred million years of it! And that is exactly why these two fiercely independent men bothered to alter their everyday routines to guide and help all these furriners. To talk to them. Because they had no choice. But they wanted the lack of choice to be on their own terms. Just like the mountains when ice and wind and rain continue to shave and scallop their peaks. No choice there. Can't stop the winds or rains or erosion. Or time. But they'd be damned if they couldn't have a say in it.*

And that's why these two men bothered to interact when they could've just stayed home.

That's why the mountains didn't shrug off all their boulders at once, laying waste to anything in its path. Because that would mean the end of everything.

So. Men try to fit in. Mold. Find a way. Mountains do the same. It's their choice, after all, to hide or to install themselves into this life in a different way.

Everyone, everything, wants a say.

Everyone, everything, has a choice.

"Hey, did you see how Levi Trentham clammed up when we were talking about the blessing of The Wonderland Hotel?"

"Yessir, I did, Mrs. Farr. He's stuck between the old ways and the new ways to be sure. I believe I can relate to him on that. Being in these mountains...it's different. Imagine his life – he grew up here. And he saw all this progress from his own front porch. The one he only shared with bears and deer and his crops and that owl. And now..." Mr. Galyon trailed off, looking at the very same bird, its squatted head fixed in place. Listening.

"And now..." Mrs. Ivah Murphy chimed in. The Farr, Galyon, and Murphy families still spent every summer in Elkmont - their souls wouldn't let them stay away for long. "...

now, all he sees are hotels and clubs and our homes and cottages. And of course, The Wonderland Hotel is definitely being turned into a club."

"What?!"

"Well, it's just a rumor right now. Levi Trentham mentioned it – he said it won't be a hotel for long. And all of us acted like we knew nothing about it. Most of us hadn't, to be sure. But I heard some of the staff talking to my husband about their plans for turning it into a club. You know, our Appalachian Club has no more room for any more members. And those prominent men of ours," her head switched to the left and nodded to indicate Mr. Galyon, her own husband, and a knot of other businessmen, "don't like to hear 'no, there's no more room for you'. Especially when they have the means to enter."

"Oh!" One of the other wives suddenly exclaimed. "That's what Levi saw! Or rather, did!"

"Levi? Saw? Did what?"

"Haven't you heard about all the occurrences at The Wonderland?"

The small crowd frowned. None seemed to know what she was talking about.

"Tell us...was it another of his prophecies?"

"Sort of."

Eyebrows raised; surprised they'd heard nothing about the hushed rumor. All eyes were on Mrs. Farr who took up the facts as she knew them to be.

"A few months after Levi Trentham turned down the money for blessing the hotel – this has been a few years ago, remember – the staff and even some guests who we know from town began experiencing...shall we say, strange occurrences."

They shivered. All senses on edge. Their children stopped pretending not to be listening to boring adult talk and made their way over to their parents, making themselves comfortable on the porch steps.

"Guests reported hearing unexplainable noises. One of my friends from town said she felt a sudden cold draft every afternoon at three o'clock, when the sun was hottest. And she said she saw shadowy figures in the woods at night when they were all on their balconies and when looking out the windows of the dining room during dances and such. She said Levi just nodded his head whenever someone relayed such happenings. Like he already knew, and he wasn't surprised at all." Mrs. Farr paused for effect. Lowered her voice.

"Some began saying that the land itself was resisting the intrusion of the hotel and progress onto its formerly pristine head and shoulders. They whispered that Levi Trentham, the Prophet of the Smokies, somehow called forth these disturbances as a reminder that the mountains could never be tamed. No matter how many buildings or logging companies or hotels or clubs or trains tried to lay claim to their rocky bodies."

"Why don't those strange things happen right here at our Appalachian Club? Here in Elkmont?"

"Ah. But they do."

15

____

ELKMONT WILL
SHINE TONIGHT - 1919

EVERY COMPLAINT ALREADY
CONTAINS REVENGE.

~

"It's really a revenge club."

"A what?"

"A revenge club." Levi repeated, sitting down on a stoop to explain things the way he saw them. "See here, ya'll already know that other rich folk are mad that they can't get into The Appalachian Club. It's difficult to obtain membership, as ya'll have arranged."

"Well, it's just too crowded!" Defensiveness ejected from the businessmen. All at once, they answered, firmly trying to justify their acts. "And we already know one another. We all do business together. We simply, truly, do not have room for anyone else!"

"Reckon I can understand that. But they feel snubbed at being rejected. After all, they have money and connections too. So, they figure, why can't they be in?"

"We just don't have the room."

"Reckon that's your choice. But they have a choice too. So

what did they do? They just said, we'll make our own club! And they did."

"What club? They've got to build one."

"No, they don't. They already have the building."

Frowns, looks of confusion. There wasn't any construction going on up the hill.

Levi stood then, nodding to the north. "They done got together and purchased The Wonderland Hotel. So now, it's not a hotel anymore. I told ya'll. They done formed their own club – The Wonderland Club. Usin' the hotel for their club's building."

THE WONDERLAND HOTEL and Elkmont's Daisytown, Society Hill, Millionaire's Row, and The Appalachian Club had danced together fairly well for a few years, albeit far removed from the other in temperament and never crossing the dance floor towards one another. It had always been an eyeing each other across the room type of dynamic, waltzing with arms encircling no one, plenty of room to step and turn.

But now, some of the wealthy Knoxville businessmen - rejected from The Appalachian Club - pooled together and purchased The Wonderland Hotel building. They had indeed formed their own club during this hot summer of 1919 and gazed down the sloped road with even more scorn. Oh, but now they had a bit of a smirk as well because they had quietly built ten more cottages on the hill to accommodate their expanding clientele.

Though separated by less than a couple of miles, both resorts – and their respective clubs - offered similar experiences: comfortable lodging, swimming, horseshoe and card games, horseback riding, lawn tennis, canoeing, dances, parties, hiking, fishing, and delicious dinners and suppers with entertainment.

Still, the tension between the two clubs simmered. Members of The Appalachian Club, clinging to their exclusivity, dismissed their rivals with a sneer, while those who had just formed their own Wonderland Club muttered about "those elitists and snobs who stay in their cottages down the slope." Neither saw a reason to change, although The Wonderland Club eventually allowed the public to dine at their facilities. The two rivals remained at odds with one another, the contention no secret – and most weren't afraid to say it.

"HEAR 'EM SINGIN'" their song? Their parties always end up the same way. With their raucous singin': *Elkmont will shine tonight, Elkmont will shine!* They sing it as loud as they can because they want us up here on the hill at The Wonderland to hear it."

"Well, we'll show them who will shine. We'll make our own club! Oh wait, we just did!" Laughter from The Wonderland members and their guests slipped out into the night. "Bet they feel shut out, just like we did."

The owl heard Levi Trentham's thoughts on the subject during one particularly pleasant evening during that summer of 1919 when suppertime - *folks, it ain't called dinnertime! Dinner was hours ago!* - was finished and the familiar judging and criticizing of "that other club up the hill" was in full swing.

As usual, Levi sat contemplating, stroking his beard and looking at the owl and up at the stars, trancelike, before answering. Everyone else knew to just sit there, patiently, sipping tea and whiskey while the Prophet of the Smokies gathered his feelings on the subject. Never one to be pushed, people quickly learned he'd take his sweet old time. But it was always worth waiting for the great music of mountain wisdom to begin.

"Well now." He finally began, to which everyone sat up, shoulders back, eyes widened, riveted, ready to listen. Because by golly, this mountain man was always right!

"This Wonderland Club they've made has its rightful place here in these mountains. For now. But they're mucked up with deceit. They'll never last."

Heads nodded. Relief appeared. All agreed!

"But neither will this here Appalachian Club."

Surprised looks on faces, frowns. Some men stood abruptly. Looked out into the twilight of the world. Anger appeared in some eyes. Some downturned mouths. What did this old mountain man know anyway? Just because he said something doesn't mean he was always right.

The owl almost laughed; chose to hoot instead of chuckling. Didn't these same people just murmur that The Prophet was never wrong? And now, he may not always be right? Oh, what stubborn pupils humans are! Like stubborn drivers leading a stubborn ass. Neither man nor beast would ever get where they needed to go.

"See here," Levi continued, despite the concerned looks on the guests, on the faces of well-known Mr. Galyon and Mrs. Murphy and Mr. Farr. "Ya'll already know about the Carter brothers. The ones who made a deal with Colonel Townsend to build The Wonderland Hotel within a year. Too aggressive in their land sellin'. And they were deceitful. 'Sign here', they said to some of my neighbors, folk who've lived here near as long as I have. 'No, we're not gonna build', those Carters assured 'em when they asked what they were gonna do with the land. 'Gonna leave your land like it is. See that mountain? You'll always have that view.' Yeah, right. You'll always have the view. From a balcony! Or from a long porch as they're greetin' guests from all over the damn place. Used to be we *all* had that view.

All of us folk who grew up here. Well, we still have that view, but it ain't the same. Ain't the same when you're sittin' on a concrete pad or from twelve feet up in the air. It's all nice and beautiful as you *furriners* say, but it sure ain't what it's supposed to look like. It's supposed to look like it does from when a man sits on the ground. Or when a man like me stands under his favorite tree. Which has been cut down for years and is now the stubby stump where folk like you sit down for a midday meal. Which is *dinner* by the way."

They stopped. All of them. Thinking about this from his point of view for perhaps the very first time. Indeed, Levi had sold some of his land already. When he really didn't want to. He wouldn't have sold unless his second sight told him it was a must, an inevitability. This rugged and rough and wise man had seen the owl go from tree to tree to tree, required to find yet another one that didn't have men underneath its crown with big saws, ready to cut, cut, cut, all the way through.

Imagine living here – for a lifetime like Levi Trentham - and...and all these changes that were so, so unwanted. Why, they themselves didn't want that one extra hotel, now club, right up the road! And when they really thought about it, The Wonderland didn't even affect them or their vacations here in the Smokies one bit! Imagine if there were many clubs, five more hotels, a restaurant, paved roads, another train; all this progress surrounding their lives, pushing against their crops and fields and barns. Obstructing their views of the mountains. Of life.

"They faced legal disputes, didn't they? Those Carter brothers?" Mr. Murphy asked, breaking the brooding silence and snapping Levi back to the present. Who knows what went on behind those eyes of the aging mountain man? Fear? Anger? Hope? The strong hope that his second sight didn't let him down this time? For what good was the gift of prophecy if a big thing like losing your land could slip by undetected?

"Yessir. They sure did." Levi sighed, standing up. Stroking his long, white beard. "Sold all their land to that group of Knoxville businessmen who made the club. Ya'll know most of 'em I reckon. They're the ones who said, 'if we can't get into The Appalachian Club, may as well make our own club'. And they're the very same ones who bought The Wonderland Hotel and made it the Wonderland Club. Mostly for revenge. And look...there it is." He pointed up the hill as if they didn't know it was already there.

"And all those new cabins clustered there together? The ten of 'em? Nearest their new club? That's where they all stay. As close as possible to their site of revenge." He paused, turning his eyes towards the owl, still perched on a sturdy branch. "You know. They're a lot like you. They all want to fish, hunt, hike, picnic, and relax with their families..."

The sky was deep blue above, with only a few moving fluffy clouds to announce that it was a sky rather than an unfinished painting. The morning dew still sparkled, tossing its shimmer right back at the contemplative crowd.

It was Ivah Murphy who tried to extend the white oak branch first.

"Maybe we can all get along? Some day? Make it like one big, long street...two clubs, perhaps, can become one big club in the mountains..." Mrs. Murphy, ever hopeful, stated with a soft tone.

"No, ma'am. Won't happen. Ya'll will only get brought together once. Far in the future. When you both need one another." Levi sniffed the air, suddenly declaring they'd have an overnight rain shower, and he'd better get on home. He bid the group goodbye, leaving the small crowd wondering, as always, if he was right. About the rain. About his prophecies. About two clubs of businessmen forming permanently separate alliances within the mist of less than two miles of the vast Smoky Mountains.

As for the mountain man, he walked away with mixed feelings. To be sure, he liked these folks – most of 'em anyway – but he also hated the scars on his mountain land growing deeper and deeper with each passing season. Disputes, building, felling more logs, more smoke from more chimneys, smaller habitats for animals like the owl and himself. Shaking his head, he thought of his prophesizing ability – his so-called second sight. Yes. It was still there. And strong too.

Appreciating his special gift - used for amusement and gain as well as warning and understanding – he nonetheless recognized the other side: it was also a curse. For on that day, walking home, he knew the owl followed him, knew he had lost none of the blazing whiteness; the clear vision of the future lay before him like a finely carved scene.

Why, oh why, did he have to see what would happen next? Why couldn't he just live his life without knowing the outcome like everyone else? *To mourn in advance, and mourn again when it happens, well goddamn, it's like carryin' a log that you never get to put down.*

And to think, some of these folk think the mountains can be tamed, placated, and they hush and whisper and ask, "Is this mountain land really resisting the intrusion of progress? Or does Levi Trentham, the Prophet of the Smokies, call forth these disturbances as a reminder that the mountains cannot, in fact, be tamed? We don't think so – for either possibility - because we just haven't seen that. No evidence at all. Nothing like that happens – it's just tall tales! Stories! But some people say such corroborating strange things like visions and eerie voices happen over at The Wonderland. Why don't those things happen right here at our Appalachian Club? Here in the heart of Elkmont?"

With the wind bidding him farewell for the evening and the trees bowing in token formality, Levi somehow heard the questions, muttering to himself as he arrived home, climbing the two steps into a wooden house that time almost forgot: *And I get to remind furriners over and over again, 'Ah, but those things do happen right here. The trees talk; mountaintops show their feelings. Yes, even in Elkmont where ya'll build all your fancy cabins and your restrictive clubs. The mountains reveal all answers. Always. When waterfalls halt to a mere skewer of water falling down, down. When trees lay on their sides like barren backs of beasts, shorn of their soft leafy fur. Yes, the bones of the mountains, the spines, always disclose their fractures. Their illness. If you will only watch and listen.*

"WOULD YOU GUIDE US?"

Levi hung around both clubs during the late summer. Had to make sure he knew what was going on in his mountain world, no matter up the street or down. Disdain had gotten so bad between the two clubs that members and their families who took the same *Elkmont Special* to the same train station in Elkmont, made the journey in contemptuous silence. Never once acknowledging one another on the journey, they'd also never interact while staying at their respective resorts. If they walked by each other, or they happened to be on the same trail or crossing paths, there would not be so much as a nod or a smile or any acknowledgment whatsoever. People would look at the trees, the sky, the clouds, the river, the owl, anything to avoid talking to another person who was here for the same reasons, just eating and sleeping in different buildings.

There wasn't even any fundamental difference between the two clubs! They were both comprised of businessmen, families; both wanted to do the same exact things! But even guests of guests were treated with scorn: once, a man visited a friend who was staying in a cottage in Elkmont, while the man planned to stay at The Wonderland. The man caught the *Elkmont Express* from Knoxville and was starving when he arrived. When he stepped off the train to meet his friend, he said thus: *my friend took me to The Appalachian Club, but they said I couldn't dine there because I wasn't a member. Ashamed, my friend, took me to the commissary where the staff took their meals and they foraged around for some sardines, cheese, and crackers. My friend protested my treatment vigorously, but The Appalachian Club never apologized for that slight.*

As for Levi Trentham, he was apt to scorn *furriners* from *either* club – but he seemed to much prefer The Appalachian Club crowd. Where they lay their heads at night though, wasn't the determining factor of his opinions. He equally embraced anyone he felt may actually respect the mountains, honor them, and want to learn about them.

Even with his powers of prophecy, how exactly did he determine such things?

If you asked him - which some dared to - he'd laugh and mutter under his breath, *goddamn furriners*, with perhaps a softened smirk thrown in. But then, as if rewarding their plucky courage, he'd slip into storytelling mode, relishing the chance to share his experiences.

"There was a guest at The Wonderland, just a few weeks ago. You folk are always askin' to see waterfalls and caves and paths that only I know about. And I pick and choose which folk I reckon are worthy of these here mountains. Reckon ya'll known I choose more of ya'll here at The Appalachian than that Wonderland crowd.

They glanced at one another, nodding their heads, secretly happy about that fact.

"Anyhow, one guest up there at 'that other club', well, he tried to hire me to take him on an overnight expedition deep into the mountains."

"Overnight?"

"Yessir, Mr. Murphy. I thought that was funny too and I asked him 'why overnight'? And he just said he wanted to see further into the mountains and see what other men haven't seen, and he could only do that by walking for two days. Well, I looked him up and down and I admit I looked at the pile of cash he waved in my face. Offered me a mighty handsome sum to guide him. Coulda paid for a lot of new shoes for my family. Or coulda given it to Lem to get some youngins new shoes. You know he's always lookin' out for youngins. Has a special soft place in his heart for 'em. Probly 'cause his own childhood was dark on account of his bad eyes...and darkness in childhood is...well, when a thing's done, it may then be no other."

"Where would you take such a man?" Ivah Murphy asked, guiding the Prophet back to his original thoughts.

"Oh, maybe over towards Cades Cove. There's some caves between here and there with rumors of gold. Or maybe I'd take him up towards Little Greenbrier to see those Walker Sisters. Get some of Hettie's apple pie! Reckon I coulda guided the man and visited them Walkers at the same time. Good folk they are. Only one of the seven married and two lost their fiancées in loggin' accidents. Two weeks apart, mind! One of 'em – Polly she's called – was never the same after that. Took to her bed and still does here and there. Sometimes for weeks."

The crowd murmured simultaneously: *That's really a shame...*

...a true tragedy.

Two weeks apart? My word...

What other options do young girls have out here? So isolated...

"Indeed folks. Them two Walker Sisters who lost their fiancées are into their forties now. Too old for children. Too old to marry. And the youngest of all the seven sisters is already thirty. Most men don't want 'em that old."

City people lamented the tales of the sisters, of mountain folk living here inside the walls of towering heaps of earth. If something tragic happened, it had to be tougher than in the city where there were other options. What would life be like with such limited selections? Why there could be only two choices: live in the grayness of heavy stone wrinkles set between two steep hillsides or wait until the springtime when tiny leaves create green auras when the sun finally stabbed through, until a thousand tiny flowers winked in the meadows.

"Did you wind up guiding the man?" Ivah Murphy asked, sitting down once again. She seemed one of the only ones who could ask this gruff, bearded man anything at any time and he never seemed to mind. His own wife never made an appearance on the streets of Elkmont. "Too busy, my wife is," he'd say with affection. "She's a good woman. Like to be up there on the porch right now, sewin' and weavin' on her loom. Likes to watch the youngins – our grandkids - play around the yard. I's always charmed by women. Especially those who love these here mountains. And she sure does. Emaline sure makes it a pleasure to come home to at night."

Ivah nodded. Smiled. "Emaline sounds lovely..." and then, as usual, she gently guided the Prophet back. "Did you ever guide the man from The Wonderland, then?"

"No ma'am."

"Why not?"

Levi paused, turned his body two steps away from everyone else, then turned to answer in his boldest voice. "Cause, as I told him, money don't pay for knowledge the mountains ain't ready to give."

16

THE ARTIST - 1920

NATURE AND ART ARE THE
TWO GREAT PHYSICIANS.

~

The Great War over now since November 1918, it had been a while since the sheriff needed to pay the rare visit to Levi Trentham to check if he was still sticking to his own land as a sort of house arrest. Oh, he had heard the Prophet of the Smokies was seen roaming around Elkmont here and there ever since the flag incident and the name-calling of the Red Cross women, but the lawman simply pretended he hadn't seen. Nor heard anything. The sheriff had looked the other way, and Levi hadn't yelled or screamed since.

The sentence of confinement to his land was mostly a formality, anyway. A message. But Levi did remain close to his farm and homestead during those years, choosing wisely when to venture out. Which was fine by him. Harvesting corn, killing a hog during the first days of frost, talking to his wife and his ten children, and by now, many grandchildren - life was very busy. Too busy to think about any goddamn fines. And he never did pay a cent, just like he promised.

Life on the farm wasn't the only thing busy; gossip and

chatter were also moving faster and faster. Government talk about the national park rose, gaining momentum with each passing season. Visitors and regular guests arrived summer after summer and the owl and mountain man kept their eyes out for those who recognized the true nature of these mountains; those who looked in awe at soft peaks that constantly outdid themselves with their rusty trembling leaves of autumn and the baby sprouts of spring. They were rare, these humans who felt the soul of the mountains.

People asked: *how could you be so sure what another felt?*

Bu it was easy for people like Levi Trentham. His feet knew the soil, the bend of the river, the sway of hemlocks. He listened to the wind, watched the birds, and read *furriners'* hesitations like rows in a well-worn field. Mostly, he simply looked around. Listened. Watched.

For one who clearly made up their own mind; one who showed it on their face and in their eyes. When the overhead stars faded and weary silvery eyes danced recklessly trying to take it all in at once.

For those not looking for the biggest trout, but for the best fishing spot so they could wade to the middle of a creek and simply breathe.

For those hiking not just to top their personal best of distance or height, but to inhale the blue mist of the clearest air on earth.

For those wishing to walk in the evenings and just watch the sun dip its head below the peaks, banners of pink and orange and red so vibrant and stunning it dared the soul to do anything, anything at all. And the people who appreciated this environment would always take the mountains up on their offer.

All Levi had to do was watch with his heart and feel with his sight.

It was in this environment that he found one more of these

rare people. And the owl hooted at night and flew back to its nest to watch yet another curious happening in the resort town of Elkmont.

"WOULD you like to come over to my place after breakfast and make a basket?"

"That would be lovely! Which cottage are you?"

"It's the one that's up the hill - a bit of a walk to be sure. I will meet you at The Appalachian Club and we can walk together. I love the walk. It's right along the creek and halfway through, the water swirls over a few huge boulders. It'll look like a cairn – a big heap of stones where the more you can gather, the more it adds to the general body of work."

Mrs. Galyon closed her eyes for a moment, picturing the scene as only a true artist could describe. It was simply beautiful here in these Smoky Mountains; she, of all people, understood why Mrs. Mayna Avent, the celebrated artist, chose this spot for an artist's studio. After all, Mrs. Galyon and her family had been summering at Elkmont for years now, and it was magical every single time. The only thing better was sharing it with someone who equally appreciated the cool breath of the mountains.

"My husband, Mr. Frank Avent – you'll meet him at supper tonight - bought the cabin for us in 1918 from Mr. Humphrey Ownby, who built it back in 1845."

"Was that the first time you came to Elkmont? In 1918? I don't recall your family here..."

Mayna laughed. "No, no. We had previously built a summer home that was quite near where The Appalachian Club sits, but we hardly ever came. And when we did, it was off-season, when nobody else was around. That's why you and I never met. But when Mr. Ownby's cabin came up for sale, we jumped at the chance to buy it. Mr. Ownby is kin to that blind man, Lem Ownby. Lots of Ownbys around here! Anyway, as you will see, my place a bit of a ways up Jake's Creek and is a bit more secluded."

The two women walked off a bit of their hearty breakfast taken at the club – pancakes, grits, and fruit – and soon arrived at the 'home and studio' as Mrs. Avent called the structure. The path followed the railroad tracks, passing Cucumber Gap, and the steep trail leading to Meigs Mountain. It was a beautiful morning; the sun's rays pierced their way through the green canopy, the river kept time with birds, and that one owl perched close by, the one who loved the daytime as much as the night. Mountain laurel was in full bloom and lined the entire pathway, fragrant in a sweet grape-like and floral way. Before she knew it, Mrs. Galyon was walking up a set of wooden steps into a well-built cabin snuggled tightly into a thicket of trees.

Small, with a stone chimney on one side, the wooden home was rustic yet comfortable; an ample raised porch providing spectacular views of the apple orchards and mostly cleared land. Water was piped into the sink from a nearby spring and large windows provided enough natural light for Mayna. Inside, the interior was warmed with a wood burning stove; a rug or two hanging on the walls and a large spinning wheel completed the coziness. An angled ladder led to the large loft; hardwood floors with baseboards lent a refined air.

"How did you get into art?"

"Ah! It is said that no one gets *into* art. It is the art, instead, that gets into *them*. That, and these mountains. Look." The women gazed out the window at the peaks hiding in the morning mist. A surreal quality to the air was well-mixed with the artful magnificent of the layered history of these glorious mountains.

"Levi Trentham – the one they call the Mayor of Elkmont

and the Prophet of the Smokies - often tells me that only those who see and feel the devoted art of the mountains can truly capture its majesty." Mayna murmured, the artist within constantly inspired by old and gentle peaks draping themselves over the land.

Mrs. Galyon nodded. Her own husband had bought Cabin Number 9, constructed by the Farr family in 1910. Mr. Galyon purchased it in 1911, about a year after its construction, and thank goodness she persuaded him to come back every year since! For he simply *had* to get away from his desk at the Galyon Lumber Company and the Knoxville Lumber and Manufacturing Company.

To which he'd playfully pounce back at his wife, "Me? Why, your work with the Red Cross takes up much more time than my two businesses combined! You've done well over eight-hundred hours of volunteer work already and though the war is over, you're not done yet!"

She laughed at that, nodding her head in agreement. Both agreed their busy lives could use a break and never regretted a moment spent in these beautiful Smoky Mountains of Tennessee, full of memories and mysteries and fascinating people like Mayna Avent.

"Actually, I studied at the Cincinnati Art Academy and the Academie Julien in Paris."

"Paris!" Mrs. Galyon exclaimed. "How fascinating! Our very own Red Cross, in which I am very active, does good work there. I've never been to Paris – yet. But I wish to go, and we - The Red Cross – are still creating repatriation routes in France for prisoners of the Great War. To help them return home. And we're opening libraries and nursing and welfare programs. We're opening them in the Virgin Islands as well!"

"That is wonderful! How did you get into Red Cross work?"

"Ah. For me, even long before the Great War began, I simply wished to be of help. And quite honestly, I always felt an urge to keep busy. The Red Cross was a tiny organization at first, but the war forced us to expand. Out of everything bad comes good, as they say." She almost laughed, but her tone was ironic, dry.

"Actually, most of our recent work has come from tending the sick from the flu pandemic. I think, in the United States, we've lost over 500,000 to the flu since 1918. And it's still going on, although 1918 and 1919 were the worst years. This year and especially during this summer of 1920, it seems to be waning, thank goodness. I've often wondered why this flu and the Great War had to happen at the same time. It seems a cruel fate for the world; seems we must always surrender be it a war or to terrible sickness. Why is that? Who allowed that to happen? I must admit, Mrs. Avent, my faith has wavered." Mrs. Galyon stopped, wondered and worried how she had let such deep thoughts escape to a relative stranger. She was usually so reserved! But she found the artist easy to talk to. Perceptive. Curious. She had the gift of allowing other people in.

"Ah yes. The age-old question: *why*? It's the one that plagues everyone who has ever lived." Mayna quietly smiled, motioning Mrs. Galyon to sit down, inviting her guest to continue asking the deepest questions. But Mayna Avent soon revealed that she had a different perspective on things.

"Mrs. Galyon. I commend you for your service with The Red Cross. Indeed, it's something I admire deeply. And I can only imagine what you've done, seen, heard. But acceptance of something, even accepting that something has happened – like the flu and the war – isn't a surrender. It's not like you must agree with whatever happened to accept that it did, indeed, happen. And it's not like you – or anyone or anything - must answer every time you ask *why*. Acceptance - even without answers - to me, is a liberation."

Mrs. Galyon nodded, struggling to understand this idea of looking at life like a scientist: *It happened. And that's...it?*

Seeing her new friend's internal tussle, Mayna patted her guest's arm, motioning her to rise.

"See this portrait I'm working on?" The women walked over to the window where a canvas was propped on an easel.

"It's a side shot of a woman. I didn't want to paint her straight-on, as if she's looking straight at you."

"That is beautiful...what made you choose a profile angle?"

"You see, it's all about perspective. This lady in the portrait needs to accept something that occurred in her life. And she can't. So, I am painting her so the viewer cannot truly see what's in her eyes."

Mrs. Galyon frowned, not quite getting the intent. Mayna moved towards the center of the room, sat down again, motioning her guest to sit as well. Pouring hot tea into tin cups, the artist sighed in contemplation, holding all the gloomy and gleeful depths of girlhood and experience within her essence.

"Acceptance is liberation. Once you accept – not agree, but *accept* – life's slings and arrows, your injured eyes will correct what they see. In this painting for example, it's all how well I can correct the lady's injured eyes. And if they cannot look at you straight-on, well, they simply must look elsewhere for healing. To the side perhaps, looking out towards the mountains. Or even a little behind her, towards God."

Mrs. Galyon stood again, walked over to the window framing a giant magnolia tree, bursting with white flowers amongst their waxy dark green limbs. Her mind set something brand new into a previously empty place upon hearing Mayna's words.

"Seems we have a lot in common," she murmured, a bit shaken, her mind, hereafter, forever changed, the kind of snapping change that comes from seeing the familiar dark wrinkle of a mountain suddenly bathed in sunshine. The very features of the landscape change.

Her heart, her eyes, grave and heavy from much of her Red

Cross work - however fulfilling it was - suddenly found support in a surprising new way. *My word, I've never thought about perspective in this way. Usually, grief is all about plowing through. Keeping busy. Staying stuck for a long while. But...acceptance can be liberating! What a thought! Acceptance is liberating! And what was it that this artist said? It's how well you correct your injured eyes. My eyes are injured. From war. From sickness. From name-calling — Levi had called us whores! - and the toil of work that you know is good and meaningful but mostly lays itself out on the table of obscurity. But the tools for correction...they are real! And can be found on the vast canvas of life...if, as Mayna says, you look for it. If you work on correcting what your eyes see.*

Mayna watched Mrs. Mayme Galyon's face. Beautiful, high cheekbones, tiny wrinkles right around the eyes, full cheeks flushed with revelation. A softening of the forehead now, a faint smile appearing on the countenance of her new friend, the artist realized her words made an impact. As for herself, even with her fortunate upbringing and great talent, everyone required a bit of correction for their own injured eyes, and this reaction was just the thing she needed.

The artist took a deep breath, smiled. "Would you like to see some other canvases? I work mostly in oil and watercolors, but I also work with wood block prints. It's in the Japanese style."

"Absolutely!" Mrs. Galyon's spell was broken, and she turned to smile at Mayna, a deep and long-lasting connection clearly in the making. After tasting another few sips of tea, the women walked over to the large picture window to view the line of canvases. Landscapes. Portraits. A cabin with a tree in front and a beckoning path leading the way to the front door. A Tennessee wheatfield.

"Have you had any work displayed?"

"The Smithsonian National Portrait Gallery has my portrait of President Polk. And we have homes in Massachusetts and

South Carolina, and my work is displayed there in various local galleries and such."

Mrs. Galyon nodded, took in the numerous details of the cabin and art studio. The bed was magnificent with its intricately carved wood and high pile of colorful quilts. Gardening tools, various baskets and bins, and a large stone fireplace lent warmth and a lived-in look, while a built-in cupboard and a bookcase in a corner held little treasures and leather-bound volumes. All the accoutrements of a serious and talented artist.

Mayna Avent's gift was evident from a young age. It was said she was given an "armful of magnolias and decided to paint them at once. Finding no used canvas about, she removed a wooden door panel and painted on it, exclaiming 'magnolias just won't wait!'."

Mrs. Galyon laughed when Mayna told her that childhood anecdote. "Ah! I envy your passion and talent."

"But Mrs. Galyon, your passion comes through with the Red Cross. It is excellent and important work."

She smiled, indeed, proud of her work. It was exhausting, but it was a true labor of love, and it was comforting to have someone else recognize how important passion was, wherever it was directed.

"Thank you, Mayna. Coming from you, that is a high compliment. It is true that passion comes out in mysterious ways. It can be poured onto a canvas or into tireless work to help others. Or into a person or family. Children. Or even into preserving land and soil and a way of life."

"Everyone should have at least one passion in life."

"I completely agree."

"Or maybe a few!" Mayna laughed. "Whatever it is for someone, it should be personal. Because the passion to work for something packs a lot more joy when it's personal."

Mrs. Galyon nodded. This new artist friend of hers had such a unique way of looking at things, of communicating her ideas. Passions *are* personal, she thought, and she was incredibly lucky to have a few in her life. Red Cross work. Husband and family. And a summer home right here in Elkmont in the middle of the beautiful Smoky Mountains.

"Please, sit right here." Mayna said to her new friend. Pouring more tea, she motioned for the kind woman to sit in a chair over by the cupboard. "Let me show you how to make a basket. That was our original plan was it not?!" She laughed, poking fun at how their conversation spun its web towards this and that, and life and the big questions of why, and back again.

Mayna picked up some smooth reeds. "There's twining, plaiting, ribbing...all kinds of ways to weave a basket. I think we'll do the twining method today. First, you take these reeds, make a few spokes...I feel it best to use cedar – see the color? I like Eastern Red Cedar for the deeper shades and pliability. Then, you just weave another reed through each spoke like this...make sure it's tightly woven..."

"Mayna! Is there anything you can't do?! Painting, basket weaving...my word, you are most impressive. You would make a great teacher!"

She laughed, shaking her head. "It's just what I love to do. And actually, I do teach...I teach painting at some art studios and schools. It's very fulfilling, and I stay active in the art community. Frank is so busy being Railroad Commissioner for the state of Tennessee. And our children, Mary and James, are all grown. James is twenty-five now and moved to China last year for his job at Standard Oil. And Mary married a very nice man, Mr. Adams, and they – including my dear grandchildren! – just bought a cabin in Elkmont and will be here later this summer."

"Ah! So wonderful! It's the perfect place for families to spend year after year. I cannot imagine life without my Elkmont summers!"

Morning turned into afternoon quickly. The baskets were

completed – Mrs. Galyon was surprised it only took about an hour to weave. Talk was easy; topics wove their way between the women - from family to politics to art to the weather. Before long, their conversation turned again towards the Prophet of the Smokies.

"What do you really think of Levi Trentham?" Mayna asked as she wove the last of the cedar strips through the spokes of the newly formed basket. Tying some of the frayed split ends together at the bottom, the artist taught with her actions that a thicker twig here and an errant leaf there is just the art of nature: "art, after all, is all about beginnings – pick up a bit of this or that and you will start to learn a little what there is to love about life."

Levi Trentham was a man who preferred his art straight from the hand of God, but he had certainly noticed the artist. In turn, the artist had made some observations of her own.

"Well, he certainly is a character!" Mrs. Galyon answered. "Did you know, Mr. Trentham called me "a goddamn Red Cross whore?"

"What?!"

"Well, not *me* exactly, but all Red Cross volunteers. *Women* volunteers. For helping wounded soldiers. See, we helped *all* soldiers, even the Germans. Even the enemies. He didn't like that at all. He's a curious creature that one. Most of the time, we even get along surprisingly well – a curious sort of amusement lay between us. But underneath it all, what he's really angry about is his loss of freedom. Of his ability to talk and say what he wants to on his own land. Nowadays, he's angry about all the government talk about taking his land for that national park. That, and the logging industry, and felling all the trees – even if those events happened in the past, he lives as if they occurred just yesterday. He understands progress but wants it on his own terms. Wants a say in it. But I think he feels out of control lately. Like he sees what will happen but cannot quite accept it. And then, he takes his anger out on everything and anyone standing in his way. Can't blame him I suppose..."

"I understand that kind of anger." Mayna answered, thoughtfully sipping tea. "Though I don't quite agree with how his mouth spews out such cursed words! But imagine how he feels? What he's seen from the time his father built the cabin, which has been home to him for, what? Sixty-eight years now? I only imagine what I would feel if the government would take away this cabin and art studio – my sanctuary! Why, I'd fight with everything I had! It might even do me some good because ..." She pondered for a moment, then laughed, "...anger is the fuel of art!"

"Ah so! Another interesting perspective! But what you say is true...I was so angry when Levi called us Red Cross workers *that name,* but afterwards, I worked more and longer hours than ever before. My anger *did* fuel my volunteering, which I suppose is like my art."

She laughed with Mayna, but then Mrs. Galyon turned serious. "Mayna, what *will* you do if it happens? The national park. They say it will..."

Mayna pondered for a moment. "To be honest, I do like the idea of a national park. I mean, look at all the felled trees. It would be nice to have these mountains restored. My husband even supports the idea. I just hope it doesn't involve us giving up our homes. It's like a mixed bag of paint spilling, running all over one another on this huge canvas of change and restoration – it's not orderly and it's messy. And we don't quite know what the picture is supposed to look like."

Mrs. Galyon frowned, cocked her head in thought. This artist's viewpoints were so deep, so reasonable, so communicative! Mayna Avent could put into words what everyone else was thinking. She looked at life differently. Perhaps it was with those corrected eyes that looked at life towards the reflective side while everyone else was looking straight, seeing only what was in front of them.

"Anger *is* the fuel of art." The artist repeated, softer this time, almost to herself. "There is often great anger within great art. Be it writing or painting or something else. But one must be careful to balance that anger with hope. Even baskets can be too tightly bound. If they are, they crack. No one – not even artists or prophets – likes to be outside of major events, to watch while it's all happening without the ability for any say in the matter. No one wants to be the only one left behind the tell the story."

Mrs. Galyon was the one who was suddenly inspired, opening her imagination towards the artist's metaphorical mindset. "But we all must learn to live outside sometimes. To live out in the cold. I think that's what Levi Trentham is trying to do. He is a mountain man through and through. He may not want to, but he is trying so hard to survive the coldness of being trapped outside his own choices."

The women sighed, heavy with future events, wonderings, change.

The artist squeezed the hand of Mrs. Galyon in reassurance. "Thankfully, I feel right at home inside this cabin. By the fire, surrounded by art and good company. Besides, if any changes *do* happen, it won't be for a long while."

The owl heard this and almost chuckled. Did this wonderful artist who captured colors and the soul of the mountains and corrected people's eyes not see that her very own cabin and artist's studio were in the crossfire? Did she not see that her ideal and peaceful sanctuary was right smack in the way of the government takeover for the national park? Ignorance or denial - both blissfully dangerous until one flash of wisdom unravels it all.

17

THE GOLDEN YEARS-1920S
GOLD DUST BLINDS ALL EYES.

~

What began as a logging town in 1901, turned quiet vacation spot in the 1910s, Elkmont was now a bona fide, and immensely popular, resort area complete with hikes, fishing, canoeing, parties, and dances with live music. The river had been dammed to make a safer and deeper swimming hole; horseshoes on the lawn kept the less adventurous entertained. There was always tea on the covered porch, along with plenty of places to read novels, all of which enticed guests to step off the *Elkmont Special* year after year.

Levi Trentham watched as more and more *furriners* – accustomed to living in high-rise apartments surrounded by concrete sidewalks and neighbors practically breathing on each other - arrived in the canopied peace of the Smoky Mountains. It was an abrupt change for citified people: no traffic, no city noise, no telephones, no meetings, no walks to the grocery store in the mornings, no electric lights glaring at you to stay awake, stay at your desk and work. Work more. Harder. Smarter.

Here, the only thing urging visitors is a large great-horned owl: *relax! Sleep. Longer. Better. Listen to the birds, the hooting and tweeting, the rivers and creeks playing their drums to the beat of your soul.* Sunshine all day; by night, the crisp evening air of ancient mountains nudges you inside towards a comfortable chair in front of the double-faced brick fireplace, always boasting a robust fire licking its way through the chilly night. Other visitors made for fast friends, and people were always up for playing cards, or a game, or chatting while writing postcards and letters to send back home.

The Galyon and Farr families, the Avents and Townsends and Murphys continued to gather each summer, staying longer and longer. An extra day or so turned into two more weeks and their souls grew attached to this place where the Cherokee once roamed, where Colonel Townsend made his fortune, where the owl still roams free but with less and less territory to slake his everyday needs.

"Did you see the bulletin board? On the back wall of the lobby of the club? They pinned my photo from last year!" Mrs. Ivah Murphy was excited. For all the years she'd been visiting, this was the first time she submitted a photograph of her and her husband, fishing poles in hand, smiling at the three trout hanging from the braided horsehair lines. Mountain summits stood in the background, and one could see their magnificence through the black and white contrast of the photo.

Mayna Avent glanced at the bulletin board; the artist complimented Ivah's framing of the image, the sharpness of the mountains looking like they were "etched with a fine pencil".

The large board also had a flyer from the staff of The Appalachian Club: *We encourage you to add a photo from your current trip! Please go back home and kindly send us a photo so others can see what fun you had!*

Indeed, numerous pictures showed crowds of people having fun with sing-alongs, square dancing in the first-floor ballroom, eating ice cream, holding up a large fish in triumph. There were pictures of nicely dressed folk seated in the dining room, and the red and white checkerboard tablecloths and ruffled curtains – even shown in black and white – stood out and featured prominently. People loved to take photos of the food, and the left side of the bulletin board was almost entirely taken up with close-ups of plates of venison, rabbit, wild turkey, quail, ruffled grouse, fresh fish, and even rattlesnake sharing space with potatoes and carrots, radishes and corn. Homemade cobbler filling a plate looked especially inviting in such rustic surroundings, and guests were more than satisfied that three meals a day were included with their room fees.

"Ah, look! There's the governor. Mr. Austin Peay," Ivah Murphy exclaimed squinting to look at a slightly blurry black and white print. "He looks mighty satisfied with his meal!"

"But look...he's not here at The Appalachian Club. Look closer...he's at the dining room at The Wonderland!" Mayna exclaimed.

"You're right! How'd that happen?!" Ivah frowned but then smirked. "Guess he's so important they decided to put his photo up here, even if he's dining at the 'revenge club' down the street."

"I bet they think most guests won't notice."

"What they *all* don't notice is Mother Nature herself! She ain't ever been able to be contained. And she won't 'round here neither. So, who cares about some man's picture on the wall over *here* when he eats over *there*? It's the same dang place if you look from the top of a mountain!" Levi Trentham was suddenly behind them, in the evening light of the fire, staring at the bulletin board. When had he come in? No one had noticed his arrival; quiet people have the loudest and most active of minds.

"Ah. Tell us, Levi," Ivah Murphy dared ask, making room for him between the two women, "what do *you* notice?"

He thought a moment, not looking at the women, but straight at the bulletin board. "Well, I'll tell all you *furri*...folks... what I *don't* see. Ain't see hardly any trees. Not like I did growin' up here in these mountains. It's worse than ever if you look around – loggin' is consumin' the next slope over. And the next and the next. I see nothin' stoppin' the rain and snowfall from drainin' into the Little River, which is bringin' higher water levels to most of the Tennessee side of these here Smoky Mountains. And as much as I like and admire Colonel Townsend, I seen his company lay 150 miles of track, hack away 75,000 acres of trees, and from them, cut 560 million board feet of lumber. A hotel, a club – two clubs now - guest cottages, rail-roads, steam, roads, horses, churches, schools, garbage; all these changed the landscape – *my* landscape – in a mighty drastic and extreme way." He paused before taking two steps back and making his way out the door. But then he turned to tip his hat to the two women whom he actually liked and who did indeed have the mountains in their own souls.

"Ladies. Don't care how much money or progress or impor-tant men anyone brings here. The mountains will impose their own control over any man who tries to conquer 'em. And they will *always* win. These here mountains will outlast the grandest human endeavors."

THE OWL KNEW the Prophet of the Smokies was correct, but it hooted throughout the evening its clarification of how things stood. For right now, it wasn't the eternal mountains that stood in the way of the grandest human endeavors - it was their very own government.

Progress on the national park crept closer and closer, and in 1923, the North Carolina General Assembly established the North Carolina Park Commission to begin acquiring land.

Rumors swirled. Worries rose. Rifles readied. Talk spat out like bitter lemon juice, squeezing out, slowly at first, then sharp and quick, each word stinging more than the last. The Smoky Mountain lifestyle that Levi and Lem and so many others embodied and loved was eroding, unraveling its threads of family and land, culture and traditions.

And yet, even as rumors of land acquisition spread, the golden years of Elkmont and The Appalachian Club remained in full bloom. During the summer of 1925, when color erupted from banks and blooms - some as red as deepening wounds, some as white and pink as the lining of shells - it was time to savor a surprising and special kind of tranquil love that only the Smoky Mountains could provide.

18

MIMMIE – SUMMER 1925

AS HE IS SLOW, HE IS SURE.
HE WILL LOVE ME LONG.

~

Seeing mere shadows in front of him didn't stop Lem Ownby from looking for love. He had been near-blind for much of his life and "felt as if he were handicapped when it came to finding a suitable mate". That, and the loggers had snatched up all the young ladies until the so-called slim pickins became the leanest of chances. Still, he hoped.

Years, seasons passed; by the time he was thirty, his "expectations were rather low".

So, when Lem Ownby - the quintessential mountain man - showed up at The Appalachian Club in the summer of 1925 with a wife on his arm, everyone was happy for the thus-far confirmed bachelor, but more than a little stunned.

"Lovely to meet you, Jemima."

"Lovely to meet you as well. Please, call me Mimmie."

"Well...Mimmie, how did you two meet? I'm Mrs. Galyon by the way."

Mimmie looked shyly at her new husband who would be the one to tell their Smoky Mountain love story.

"Well. It's simple really. A feller recommended Mimmie to me and I began writin' to her for a year or so before I ever met her." Lem said, a smirk on his face. "And then we met and courted for a few more years after that first meetin'."

"You was writin' this whole time! Courtin' for years and didn't say a word?" Levi Trentham was there to see for himself this surprise wife of Lem's and was shocked that he hadn't seen any of this in his prophecies. He'd had no feelings, no insights, no *hmmm, I smell somethin' on the wind* or *there's an extra glint in those blind eyes*...no nothing.

"Wait a second now...how'd you write if you can't see too well?" Levi thought he knew everything that went on around Elkmont. He thought he could see everything in the future too! How'd he miss this courtship going on with his good friend? But then, this involved a human heart which kept such things hidden if there was a decent chance of injury; it was only the mountains who bared their souls to the sunny open minds of those who paid attention and smiled back.

"To be sure, I had someone help me write the letters. Ya'll know I can't see and can't write too well neither."

"Who helped you?"

"Well, I woulda asked you, Levi, but you can't write neither. Reckon you recall the time you messed up the whole cheese and millstone in your store with that one customer?"

Levi hung his head in mock shame. "Ah. Reckon you're right."

"Anyhow, we wrote and found we had some things in common. And soon enough, we found we were both the same age and so we began courtin'. She done tol' me she was one of eleven children and when her Ma was cravin' squirrel gravy when she was pregnant with what woulda been her sisters, her Pa went out to shoot a squirrel but accidentally shot himself."

"How the hell did *that* happen?" Levi asked rather pointedly for such an occasion. He was still unnerved by not knowing one bit of this news in advance.

"Reckon, as I heard it from Mimmie here," he nodded to his new, shy wife, "her Pa headed to the woods to find a squirrel and came upon a log lyin' across his path. Well, from what it looked like, he put the butt of his gun on the log to brace himself, like a cane. Well, when he put a foot on the log, it was rotten and his foot done went right through. That wasn't the problem though. Somehow, when he lost his balance, and his finger found the trigger...the gun fired right into his belly. His wife – Mimmie's Ma - and the other children heard the gunshot and those youngins were sent to investigate. Well, they done found their Pa dead." Lem looked at Mimmie who hung her head in sorrow. It had happened a long time ago, but such memories remain fresh as creek waters filtered through miles of stone.

"And your Ma was pregnant at the time? How awful..." Mrs. Mayme Galyon frowned, touching the arm of Lem Ownby's new wife.

"Yes, ma'am." Mimmie nodded, voice soft. A bit more comfortable now, ready to speak. "And after we buried Pa, my Ma went into labor too early and had twin girls – my sisters. But they died too. So, that single gunshot really resulted in us buryin' three people."

"My word! What a story." Mrs. Galyon moved her hand onto Mimmie's shoulder, admiring the inner strength showing in her round cheeks and somber, wise eyes. Thick, straight hair piled onto her neck; she presented a neat, serious, but kind, figure.

"Lem...you got yourself a gem right here!" Levi smiled, patting his friend on the back.

"Thank you, Levi. I think so too!"

"What'd you think when you wrote each other for an entire year and then met?" Levi pushed for more information.

"Well, we can't be choosey about girls as ya'll know. There aren't many of 'em. Especially at this age. It's the same for the ladies. Slim pickins. So we both were like to take whatever was available, I reckon. And we was both available. But if I didn't think we'd get on together, I woulda just let it all go and been alone. As it was, she did pretty well livin' up to my expectations when I first saw her as she was going into church. As much as I could see her anyhows. Well, after we corresponded, we courted for three more years before we got married."

Mimmie nodded, smiling. "I pretty much had given up and was ready to be a spinster. But Lem here was so kind and I thought we could live well together. Could help one another. We're actually third cousins once removed but had never met one another while growing up. I guess we just never had the opportunity. But I am glad we met now. Seems God had his plans all figured out."

The crowd smiled. They'd never seen Lem Ownby so content! Smiling from ear to ear. They were happy for the near-blind man who navigated his mountain world with the ease of a man who had as many eyes as needed. Lem Ownby had the gift of good sense, which was worth more than two eyes that saw everything...yet nothing.

"When did you two get married? And where?"

Mimmie placed her hand into her husband's and answered, "Reverend Otha Ownby married us at his home in Gatlinburg. We didn't want to make a big deal of it. It was just the two of us. We're both thirty-five years old after all. We're just happy we found one another. It's awfully lonely in the mountains by yourself." Her smile fell. "Even if you have family. Brothers and sisters grow up, have families of their own. Grandparents, parents pass."

"But we live together very well so far. We each have our things to do. And my parents," Lem Ownby chimed in, "live with us too. It eases all our workloads, and we get on nicely with one another."

"Indeed, it's nice to have someone to talk to in the evenings while sewing and baking and such. It was a bit lonely at my house on Dudley Creek. Quiet. Now, I am happy with a house full of people."

"And running water!" Lem said proudly.

"Ah yes! Lem here has put in a galvanized pipe from the spring on the side of the mountain, right by our home. It pipes water right into the house! And we can stop the water flow by pluggin' it up with a wooden plug that holds back the water."

"Don't forget I also built you a wringer-type washing machine so you could roll it over to the creek on warshing days!" Lem said proudly, as she smiled at him, acknowledging how her new husband was really trying to make life easier and better for his new wife.

The crowd marveled at these two individuals who, against the odds, had found one another. Mrs. Ivah Murphy was over-joyed. After all, she was the one who helped Lem write his letters. Collaborating back and forth with Lem during summers in Elkmont; writing nine extra letters each summer so he could keep them, mailing one per month until Ivah returned the next summer to help him write more.

And now it was done. The letters had worked, knitting the tenderness and devotion of two people into one as the right words always do.

Ivah Murphy bounded back to her home in town after each summer, beaming with hope as she told her friends all about the letters she was writing to help her near-blind friend court a kind and fine woman. Her friends all thought the resi-dents a bit backwards if they were honest. Whenever Ivah returned from her vacations in the Smokies, all she would talk about is the beauty and magic of her Elkmont summer. But she was greeted with mixed reactions. Sure, it sounded nice, kind of like a-bit-too-long camping trip. But how could people actually live like that? All the time? Especially in the 1920s when there was electricity in almost forty percent of American homes and running water and refrigerators and... and flush toilets...*inside* the house! Of course, these were mostly found in the cities and towns like their own, but still... cooking over a fireplace? Washing clothes in a cold creek? Didn't these people want to move to where life was...less trouble?

Ivah would just smile at her friends and lament that they just haven't visited yet and therefore, couldn't feel the majesty of the Smoky Mountains and the character and resilience of the people who lived there. Besides, she emphasized to her friends, these people could move anywhere they wanted. They *choose* to stay. *And,* she would add in a strong tone, *it is much more than just their homes and land and the fact that they were born there, that their ancestors were born there. It is a lifestyle of farming, community, traditions, seasons, freedom, and peace, that only those who belong could truly understand.*

"You mentioned baking, Mimmie. Do you have a specialty?" Mrs. Galyon asked, as the crowd began walking down the paved street of Elkmont.

"Yes, in fact, I do!" Mimmie smiled, warming up to these kind people who had been in her husband's life, especially Ivah Murphy who had played such a large role in bringing them together.

"It's honey cookies and I swear that's what made Lem finally ask me for my hand in marriage!" They laughed as Lem's eyebrows went up along with his smile.

"My nieces and nephews constantly ask for Aunt Mimmie's honey cookies. And they are yummy if I say so myself! You see," Mimmie lowered her voice, "I believe Lem and I will likely not have any children. We're older – we're both thirty-five after all - and, well, if it happens, that would be wonderful. But the Good

Lord done told me on my wedding night that the blessing of children would be lain on someone else."

Mrs. Mayme Galyon, face falling, reached out her hand to touch Mimmie's once again as the new bride continued. "But that is okay. God's will. I never thought I'd even get married! Yet, here I am! Life does have a way of surprising you. If it happens that I get to be married with no children, that will be okay by me. Besides, with all the youngins around our house and around this place, it seems all my time will be spent makin' my famous cookies for all of 'em!"

Her warm smile consoled any sadness that may have tried to reach the surface. Rosy cheeks, tall stature, a neat figure, and a quiet, warm disposition was just what this fine lady offered to Lem Ownby who thanked his Lord every day for this blessing of a woman. Who did, indeed, make the best cookies on God's earth.

"How do you make them? Your famous cookies?" Ivah Murphy asked. There hadn't been any mention of cookies or any recipe in any of the letters she had seen.

"Ah, the secret is the same secret with any baking: it's the butter. And in this case, the honey."

Ivah nodded her head. She wasn't much of a baker herself, but Mrs. Galyon was listening closely, always thinking about her work with The Red Cross, which packed up hundreds of tins of cookies for soldiers and for people who found themselves amidst a disaster. Cookies were an evergreen comfort.

"I start with about two cups of flour. A teaspoon of ground ginger, and almost a whole cup of sugar. Then, there's half a cup of honey, three tablespoons of butter and almost one tablespoon of vinegar. Crack an egg and pour in some milk until it's nice and creamy. If it's too dry, a bit more milk will do nicely. Now here's the trick. Don't mix all these one by one. Mix the dry ingredients first." She paused, letting the small crowd take it all in. Women were constantly on the lookout for new recipes and instructions were often repeated, albeit with different words.

"Make sure you cream the honey, butter, vinegar, and egg together. Only after it's nice and creamy do you add in the dry ingredients that've been mixed up first. Mix it really, really well. This takes a lot of effort, but it's worth it. Keep adding milk if you need to, but after it's typical cookie dough, you drop a spoonful onto a baking sheet that's nice and greased. Mind, leave space for the cookies to expand, and then bake them in the wood oven until they're brown. If you have an electric oven, bake it at 350, but since we don't have that around here – mostly wood stoves – just watch 'em closely so they don't overbake. Overbaking is usually within a matter of another minute or two."

Lem chimed in just then. "Now, here's Mimmie's special trick. If you don't have enough sugar or if you don't wanna put sugar in, just use more honey. I give her a jar straight from my hives. When they're done and comin' out of the oven, why, they're like little drops of heaven!"

Mr. and Mrs. Lem Ownby lived happily together for forty-two years. During their marriage, Mimmie also helped take care of Lem's parents, Tom and Sarah, until they passed away in 1930 and 1931 respectively. By that time, the happy couple were both in their early forties yet still had lots of energy and spunk, keeping busy with their farm and homestead. Together, they tended 180 fruit trees in the orchard, managed crops of corn and tobacco, and a tub mill on Jake's Creek. Lem also fished for trout and raised animals.

They never did have children of their own but fed every youngin of their extended family and friends batches and batches of Mimmie's honey cookies, along with her scrumptious apple butter, pies, and desserts. Lem maintained his special affection for children throughout his life. He couldn't see them too well; they looked like little blobs of energy bouncing to and fro. But their laughter! Oh, that laughter brought him back to the young boy lurking just inside his sun-drenched and smooth skin, all of it bathed with honey every day making him look younger than his years. The laughter of youngins - it bubbles up in the soul and lightens the load of the world.

And he loved to share with the younger generations the things he excelled at his whole life, even as he approached his forties and fifties: bear hunting and storytelling.

Why, he'd say, *d'ya know youngins...I don't use none of that moonshine myself and neither should you – got no use for it - but I sure like to go bear huntin' by some stills I know of. Why? Well, them bears get into the shine somehow, and they seem to love it! Must be the sweetness. Now, what's strange is, they don't break the glass or jars at all. They just somehow twist off the lids. And start lickin'. So I learned to lay in wait by the still and there they come – one at a time mind – and a mama never brings her cubs...she must know how it makes her stagger and go sleepy for hours. Anyhows, when a bear comes and drinks some shine, he starts dancin' and singin'.*

The children's eyes would widen; they'd look at one another. Was this *true*? It couldn't be! Just another tall tale by an old timer?

"Oh Lem! Enough with those stories!" Mimmie would scold, but when there were youngins around, he'd pay her no heed at all.

"Now, youngins, I seen it with my own eyes, as bad as they are. And I never drank any of it so don't get it in your head that bears singin' happens when old timers like me get into the shine. I never got no use for it, but I know bears like it. And once they get into about half a jar, they start singin': *I got moonshine breath and a honey buzz, drunk on stars and the way it was. If you hear me hummin' through the smoky air, you just done met the moonshine bear!*

The slapping of his knee and the milky twinkling eyes were the only clues that this story was mostly a whim. But the children loved him. What a storyteller! And Mr. Ownby *was* a great bear hunter...maybe, just maybe, he had seen...?

The owl hooted in disbelief and laughter. A singing bear! Indeed! And the looks on the children's faces! Priceless emblems of doubt and adoration all in one joyous package. Folk like Lem Ownby decorated the mountain world, roaming anywhere he pleased on both land and in the mind, a stark contrast to the city folk who walked all over these mountains trying to find their way.

And so what if he told tall tales and untruths and embellishments that knelt on the wind? They all had lessons within, even if the lesson was merely to live with a little joy. Perhaps this was the best lesson of all. For to keep these stories alive meant the Smoky Mountains would remain all fire, wing, and force. Where life clings tightest to the branch that holds a wise owl, chuckling right along with a moonshine-drinking singing bear.

19

CELEBRITIES - 1925

TELL IT TO YOUR CHILDREN, AND LET YOUR CHILDREN TELL IT TO THEIR CHILDREN, AND THEIR CHILDREN - EVERYTHING TO THE NEXT GENERATION.

~

Lem and Levi didn't much care for the social lives of the rich and famous. Or, for that matter, what was happening with a famous trial being conducted in Dayton, Tennessee. The brick courthouse was less than three hours away but may well be as far as the next continent. Lem was busy with his new wife and Levi with his old one; both men tending bees, hunting, fishing, farming, fixing their barns, filling bushels, and visiting the *furriners* who made Elkmont their home for the summer months. But the two men did keep up with news from the outside world and one thing the intricate knots of gossip fixated on during the summer of 1925 was monkeys.

Specifically, teaching that man evolved from them.

~

"THAT MONKEY TRIAL MAN. He's here!"

"Who?" Mrs. Galyon answered Mrs. Farr, both women's voices hushed to a whisper.

"The Scopes Monkey Trial! You've heard of it to be sure…"

"Oh yes! I've read about it almost every day in the newspapers. It's just now over – that biology teacher, Mr. Scopes, was convicted of teaching evolution, which is unlawful."

"The Butler Act. Yes. It's unlawful to teach evolution. Although I dare say," Mrs. Farr's voice tuned down to barely a breath, "it's got very compelling evidence to support this idea of evolution. In fact, I daresay it's probably correct."

"Indeed. I've often thought the same. Science does have the answers. Even if we don't like them."

The two women spoke softly, carefully, about the famous trial, which was held from July 10th through the 21st, 1925. They discussed the fine of $100 and the fact that the judge clarified that the Butler Act itself wasn't on trial, Mr. Scopes was. And he *had* admitted he had taught evolution.

"Therefore, he was guilty. But I wouldn't mind a teacher teaching my children to open up their minds a bit. I mean, if there is evidence for it – strong evidence - why not at least propose it as a possibility? No harm in that, I feel."

"I agree. But let's keep that to ourselves." Mrs. Galyon looked around, seeing a well-dressed man make his way to the cottage of Williston Cox. "Look! There he is! That's the monkey trial attorney. He was the one arguing on the side of the teacher. I can't believe he's really here! Visiting Mr. Cox, I heard."

Indeed, the tangled grapevine of scandal and chitchat spread as if a real fire had erupted, racing down the mountainside.

It was July 26, 1925, and the famous lawyer, Clarence Darrow, had indeed descended upon Elkmont. But he was in a foul mood after losing the trial and all he wanted was a hearty dinner at The Appalachian Club and afterwards, a peaceful setting to fall into the well of a deep sleep.

MIDNIGHT CAME AND WENT. Mr. Ralph Murphy, the manager of the Central Hotel in Sevierville, Tennessee muttered under his breath at the daring plight he'd found himself in. Riding out in the summer darkness to chase down that famous monkey trial lawyer, Mr. Clarence Darrow, in the heart of Elkmont was hardly part of his job responsibilities. Yet here he was, facing that exact situation. Because a reporter from the *Chicago Tribune* had managed to talk him into it.

"Hello?"

"Hello. Is this Mr. Ralph Murphy speaking?"

"Yes. This is Mr. Murphy. Manager of the Central Hotel, Sevierville. Would you like a reservation?"

"No. No, thank you sir. I would like a favor. Please." The man had desperation in his voice, one that sounded the alarm on a critical situation.

"What's that Mister...?"

"Mencken. Mr. H.L. Mencken"

A pause. "Uh. Okay, Mr. Mencken. What can I do for you?"

"Well, I know this is unusual..."

"And it's very late!"

"Yes, I am sorry for that. But I need to track down Mr. Clarence Darrow. The lawyer."

"The monkey trial lawyer?"

"Yes, sir."

"Why?"

"Because the prosecutor – the lawyer that opposed him just died."

Mr. Murphy, the hotel manager nearly dropped the phone. *Died? Right after the biggest trial of his life?*

"Oh my. I am sorry to hear. Do you mean William Jennings Bryan?"

"The very same."

"How did he die?"

"Right now, it is unknown except we know he died in his sleep. Likely stress from the trial that just ended."

The hotelier paused. "Well, Mr. Darrow is a guest of Mr. Cox's and they were just here earlier today – well, I guess it was yesterday since it's after midnight now."

"Where exactly is Mr. Darrow now? I must get a quote from him for the morning newspaper!"

"Ah, I see." The hotelier had but a moment to mine his memory for all details. "Well, I can tell you they stopped by the Central Hotel here before they made their way to Elkmont. They are there now as far as I know. But I must warn you, Elkmont is way up in the mountains and I cannot reach anyone by phone."

"Can you go to Elkmont for me? To interview Darrow?"

"What? That's…"

"Crazy? Yes, I know. It's the middle of the night after all! But I'm a reporter and I need something for the morning papers."

This was indeed crazy. But a bit of a sense of adventure within Mr. Ralph Murphy stirred; if he could somehow be a part of this famous event, this trial that had riveted all of America, well, perhaps… Then again, it was so late…

"Tell you what, Mr. Mencken. I'm unsure I can help you tonight. Why not call my friend in Maryville? There *may* be a way for him to get a phone connection from there to somewhere nearer to Elkmont. Let me give you a name and number…"

Mr. Murphy had exactly seven minutes of peace before the phone rang again.

"I am sorry, Mr. Murphy. But I had no success." The anxious voice of Mr. Mencken flung itself through the phone lines. "Can you *please* go to Elkmont to talk to Mr. Darrow. Please! Or at least get *someone* to go?"

"Mister. It's a hard trip in the daytime. But at night? It will cost a lot to have someone do this..."

"I'll pay! I will pay fifty dollars."

"Fifty dollars! For fifty dollars, I'll do it myself!"

His mind made up to seize the moment - and the money - Mr. Murphy quickly roused a guest who was a regular at the hotel and who had a car, a seven passenger Buick. Promising to split the money, together, they reached Elkmont quicker than he'd ever reached the resort town before.

It was now about two in the morning, and an owl was perching overhead, peering at him with curiosity. It unnerved him, but he was wide awake and intent on his mission. Mr. Murphy walked up the stone steps and lightly rapped on Mr. Cox's door.

Nothing. No response.

Louder now, striking the door with robust force that even startled the owl.

Mr. Cox finally swung open the door – loudly. He was scowling, and none too happy.

"What the *hell* is going on?" His red eyes seared through the two men. "Do you know what time it is? This better be..."

"William Jennings Bryan is dead."

"Oh. Oh boy...oh my goodness..." Mr. Cox's demeanor changed immediately, his face whitened under the moonlight.

Swiftly, he took Mr. Murphy next door to the cottage where Mr. and Mrs. Darrow were staying. "I agree we must wake him. But I must warn you. He's got quite the wrath. An intense temper."

"I know. But I must."

"Yes. I agree."

They managed to knock on the door in the middle of the night until the famous criminal lawyer emerged.

"What's this?" Disheveled, his eyes glared, adjusting to the night's dimmed light. He saw his friend, Mr. Cox and...and some man who had been managing a hotel earlier that day. In Sevierville!

"What's going on?"

"William Jennings Bryan has died. The newspapers...they need a quote from you for the morning papers. What are your thoughts..."

And that's precisely when the owl flew away to escape Clarence Darrow's celebrated temper.

"Waking *me* in the middle of the night for a *quote*?! Asking me what I *think*? About a lawyer who's basically just a politician? Someone who I, myself, interrogated not last week? The so-called expert in the Bible? You can go tell the *Chicago Tribune* to..." And then he caught himself. Ever the lawyer, he knew how to work an audience. And he didn't want this audience in Elkmont, Tennessee to be able to say anything else about his reputation. Or that of his famous client. For he still planned to fight for the rights of Mr. Scopes, to appeal the inane and unfair decision. He was being paid handsomely by the ACLU after all – they were so eager for a test case to overturn that dang Tennessee law prohibiting teaching evolution that they advertised for a volunteer. And John Scopes was the kind high school football coach and science teacher who took them up on their offer.

Darrow took a moment to gather himself, calm himself a bit by taking three deep breaths, unknotting his rage and hiding at least some of his displeasure.

"Tell that reporter from Chicago...that I will call the paper in the morning!"

"Wait! Mr. Darrow...it's just..."

"What!"

"Please, I am so sorry. But if I go back and tell them that you'll call them in the morning...and I have no quote from you, they won't pay me for coming all the way up here."

"Oh? Is that so? How much are they going to pay you?"

"Fifty dollars."

"The cheapskates! You should've asked for five hundred!"

Mr. Murphy's tired eyes hung. He was about to turn around and go home when Mr. Darrow surprised him. "I don't know... tell them this: Bryan was truly a crusader. He believed every damn word he said. Oh hell, tell them I'll call them in the morning!"

MRS. GALYON and Mrs. Ivah Murphy heard the story by breakfast the next morning, repeating it until it mixed in with the folklore and stories of Elkmont. Indeed, Clarence Darrow kept his word, calling the newspaper in the morning. But Mr. Murphy had called Mr. Mencken, the reporter, during the night and the *Chicago Tribune* was the one who ran those first two quoted sentences, edited for decency: *Bryan was truly a crusader. He believed every word he said.*

By dinnertime – *that's lunch, remember?* - Lem and Levi had heard it too, though they didn't much care and left it to Mrs. Ivah Murphy and Mrs. Farr to gossip and spread the word.

Which is exactly what they did.

"And now, that hotel manager Mr. Murphy – no relation to us mind - has something he can brag about for the rest of his life." Mrs. Murphy talked excitedly.

"Did he ever get his money?"

"Yes, he says he did."

"That's good. I mean, he did make a midnight run down here to the mountains to track down a famous lawyer just off one of the most famous trials in American history to see what he had to say about his adversary who had just died! The most creative reporter in the world couldn't have made up such a story! But it's true. Making it even more unbelievable!"

The women chuckled together, marveling at the touch of

celebrity that had entered their summer lives here in Elkmont. The owl hooted along, wondering how certain people and events belonging to the larger world stage wound up right here in the sticks of the Smoky Mountains. As big as the Scopes Monkey Trial was in America, and as profound an event as one of its lawyers visiting Elkmont right after the trial while the other one died, this event wasn't even to be the vacationers' first contact with a star personality.

During the next summer of 1926, when it was dry and hot, the owl watched the same two women marvel at another man. Actually, he was just a boy then, and was known by his given name, Thomas Lanier Williams III. He was visiting his uncle and aunt, Mr. and Mrs. William Brownlow, and staying with them at their cottage.

Later in Thomas's life, he'd write of his time in Elkmont, Tennessee in his memoir: *That summer I learned to swim in a clear mountain stream; it was Aunt Belle who taught me, in the pool of fabulously cool, clear water formed by the dam, which offered a sparkling waterfall over bone-white rocks.*

Many people read that memoir. It was an autobiography entitled, *Tennessee Williams: Memoirs*, and was published after he'd already changed his name and became famous for writing *The Glass Menagerie*, *A Streetcar Named Desire*, and *Cat on a Hot Tin Roof*.

The owl marveled at the brushes with celebrity this little logging town turned summer resort had managed thus far. As the wise feathered beast soared into the warm orange sky, Elkmont wrapped its quiet and famous history in a cloak all its own, guarding cherished memories with the gentle care of a woman in love, moving through the darkness to kiss it goodnight.

20

A NATIONAL PARK

NATURE - SHUT HER OUT OF THE DOOR AND
SHE WILL COME IN THROUGH THE WINDOW.

~

Though there were spacious and fully equipped kitchens in every cottage, these remained rarely used. Dining at The Appalachian Club was so much better! Isn't that one of the most wonderful things about vacation, after all? Meeting other people, talking, gaining new friends? Not having to cook or clean, and being catered to? Indeed, the club thrived on this basic human desire for vacation to be a true and complete respite, setting up wonderful mid-day dinners and suppers every evening, along with planning as many events as possible to keep guests entertained.

Dance on Saturday! The large paper flyer hung on the bulletin board at the back of the hotel, the one boasting photos of vacationers smiling, dining, holding up fish proudly caught from the cold river, mountains, always the mountains, standing guard in the background.

"You must wear shoes to dinner, boys." Mothers admonished, as their younger sons grimaced. Running around the creeks and trails barefoot was one of the best things about this vacation! They could never do that on the dirty sidewalks of their hometown or city.

"Awright, Ma." They obediently replied. "But what could be better than being barefoot in these mountains? I'll never forget the feeling. I want to come back every single summer of my life."

Peaceful mothers smiled and ruffled the hair of their young cubs. Oh, how they loved seeing their sons and daughters embrace such a different lifestyle! At home, they bought groceries in stores with rows and rows of carrots and radishes and lettuce neatly stacked on shelves. Here, the cooks came out every so often and beckoned the children to the nearby gardens to show them how they grew their own food.

Rows and rows of potatoes, onions, garlic, and beans tethered to the earth, the pull of sun and rain their only reason for expanding themselves into sustenance; all for visitors from towns and cities who only knew concrete sidewalks and food grown in other places, shipped to them and spread out conveniently under the yellow lights of a grocery store. Mothers and fathers alike tunneled their thoughts into a similar mindset: *every task has a purpose here. Everyone is so committed to the land. It's a different lifestyle to be sure, but it feels...important.*

Their tunneled thoughts dug even deeper: *could we live like this? Could I? It is mighty tempting for a week or so, or even a couple of months, but long-term?*

As the people sat with those questions, the mountains boldly showed off their finery – wildflowers, green canopies, deer, bear, fish, an owl, an entire tapestry of pure beauty – and continued to burrow their way into the very core of their souls. Once well and settled, the feeling can never leave.

How could a place - a carelessly crumpled section of Earth - arrange such a thing, even a place as ancient and beautiful as this?

"AFTER MY LOGGING company cleared the land, I went ahead and deeded fifty acres to The Appalachian Club but held onto the timber and mineral rights. We built it so the club was south of the railroad workers' town which was the true start of Elkmont. South because the land is flatter here. More conducive to laying the railroad tracks."

The visitors looked towards the north. Indeed, the land was sloped, steeper there.

"Colonel? Do you live here some of the time?" A woman, newly stepped off the *Elkmont Special*, joined the group, eager to talk to someone other than her husband who never spoke more than ten words at dinner on account of being too worn out from his workday. She dragged him here, begging for a vacation together. Thus far, he was still quiet, but more relaxed, taking it all in. She noticed he breathed deeper, as if inhaling the very dewdrops winking from every leaf.

"Yes, ma'am. I built my own cabin south of the clubhouse. This entire area is called Elkmont, but it's actually divided into sections." Colonel Townsend swept his hand all up and down the street. "This section we're standing in right now is called Daisytown. It's kind of the primary piece of the resort. Then, there's Society Hill and Millionaire's Row."

"Thought you would've been on Millionaire's Row, Colonel!"

He laughed. "Ah, well. I like to be around my workers and my visitors. Gives me another perspective. And I dare say, it's much more entertaining!"

The woman, her husband, and the rest of the crowd nodded their heads, laughing at the amiable and easy nature of the famous businessman. A fresh batch of vacationers from Knoxville, Ohio, and even New York City, had just arrived this morning on the *Elkmont Special*. They were all new to the resort - their first time anywhere near the Smoky Mountains - and Levi Trentham was present, listening, eyes squinting in studied foresight. He knew the train schedule and liked to greet the blazingly fresh people stepping off; to see their gazes marvel at the majesty of the mountain world. It was here he looked deep into their eyes as they became glittering caves, staring long enough to feel which ones were worthy. There were some. In every crowd, there were some who suddenly, recklessly, opened themselves up to another world.

The Colonel continued through the crowd, shaking hands, asking who did what and from where they came. He politely and patiently answered their questions.

"Indeed, sir...ma'am...The Appalachian Club is also a hotel. Not many people know about that because they have their own cottages or they rent them from friends and family. Everyone wants their own space and plenty of it. I understand. Heck, I feel the same! You all know - there comes an age where you crave your own space and privacy." He laughed along with the visitors. "But if you have someone staying just for a night or so, or if you're only a couple and not a family, one of our rooms at the club do very nicely. We're adding an annex too, because the hotel seems to fill up all the time. We need more room for all you fine folk who wish to visit us here in the Smokies!"

Ever the businessman, thought Levi. But he remained in admiration of the Colonel. For all the destruction of logging to the trees and land, Levi also knew Colonel Townsend did, in fact, truly love this place.

Besides, Levi reflected, it wasn't much different from his own Pa felling forty trees for the cabin and their barns and corncribs. Or Lem's felling fifty for his smokehouse and spring-house and fences. Townsend's felling of trees was just on a larger scale. So, what was the difference? Was it just the number of trees? The acreage or the size of a now empty patch of land? The purpose was the same after all – to tame the world and make it livable for everyone.

Or was it?

Levi often pondered such questions. Some he answered quickly: perhaps it *was* all about scale, the sheer number of trees felled.

And then he'd sit with other, thicker questions, the ones requiring more thought: beyond sheer facts and figures, was it the *intent,* the *aim* of felling each tree that mattered?

For it was one thing to build a fence and a home for a family unit of ten, twenty or so. A family who used the land, the trees, the lumber, to live. Never taking more than needed.

It was quite another though, to make ships and window frames and furniture and wooden bowls and homes and fences for a hundred and twenty million Americans. Did they really need all those things? But Levi knew that wasn't the true question - because no two people were ever going to have the same answer anyway.

One could say: *yes, it is too much! Who needs three beds? Who needs another bowl? A bigger house?*

And then others would retort: *free will, do what you want on your own land!* All deeply embedded hallmarks of mountain living. Who were they to tell another man how to live? If people wanted a bed for every person in the household, so be it! If they could afford thicker window frames and another story on their home, well, goddamn, go do it!

Levi didn't much bother with those kinds of questions. He knew there were other, more important ones to ask: was the real danger that those same Americans spent most of their time *inside* those perfectly hewn wooden walls? Cut off from the living, breathing world of summer mountain laurel and autumn's cloak of rust and gold? Cut off from nature, a fresh day, every day, but with cautious leaves refusing to unfurl because work needed to be done while sitting behind a desk? Not to mention grocery shopping being done within a lighted boxed building! Meanwhile, while their idea of hiking was merely strolling down flat paved trails with cracks along the seams - all the while sleeping within the confined tight walls of a fourth-floor concrete house.

Did it matter that children grew up with smooth stones under their feet, encased in sturdy shoes, devoid of the ability to roam the woods - firearm in hand - marveling at bear cubs until they had to rush back to milk the cow, collect the chickens' eggs, and clean their rifles?

Goddamn furriners, Levi thought when visitors asked their own questions: "what's for dinner?", forgetting it was called supper. And "how far is the hike to a waterfall because we have a game of pinochle on the porch at three?"

They always asked the wrong questions.

Except the children, Lem Ownby would always say. *Youngins always ask the right questions. 'Cause they only seek the truth of things.*

Levi turned his attention from his internal ponderings towards the knot of children, one boy in particular who was looking up at the tall figure of the Colonel with awe and a bit of fear.

"What do you wanna ask, boy?" Levi smiled a little, urging what he knew was a question the young lad was burning to ask.

"What...what was it like before the club and cottages?" The boy swallowed, took a step back. A bit shy, anxious, but this youngin was genuinely curious, Levi thought, and the old mountain man could see the city boy had never had an opportunity to check traps for furs or pick berries growing high on a steep sunny slope. Levi looked down at the ground...*this boy is one of ours. He wants nature. Craves the cool breath of some of the oldest mountains on earth.*

Colonel Townsend looked out through slightly squinted eyes, saw Levi nodding at him to answer the boy. The sun was setting and the light filtered through the trees onto one particularly mossy spot, lighting up the green stage.

"Come on over here, lad. Let me tell you what it was like."

Colonel Townsend motioned over to a picnic table where Levi and the boy sat down. Listening.

"The Appalachian Club right there," Colonel pointed down the road, "you can see it is rustic, a simple two-story wood frame structure with a wide porch stretching the entire length of the building. It's my favorite part, the porch, because everything happens there! Conversations, meetings, tea, dances, courtships, reckonings with oneself. Fun, joy, loosening of tongues and opening of hearts. You've been inside, right? Well, those two chimneys make me feel all glowing inside, it's a warmth that is especially designed for dining, dancing, having fun together, and finding out about each other. And about ourselves. But before that, it was just these mountains to look at. Trees everywhere and creeks running to the end of time it seemed. Nothing else except cabins of folk like Levi here. You could see chimneys smoking, hear animals. Children. And the wind rustling every leaf. And it's still like that if you look beyond the club and the cottages and the street. It's still like that...if you let the mountains in."

The boy frowned, not quite getting the point.

"In other words, young lad, no matter what this place looks like, or what time period it is, Elkmont is for finding out what the mountains give us. But it's up to you to listen. To learn. To take what the mountains give you, and you alone. Allow them into your soul. They will never let go. And it's the best feeling in the world."

Colonel Townsend sighed, looked out at the trees. All was quiet. No owl. No stirring. Even Levi, the Prophet of the Smokies, was quiet, as if lost in the world of childhood joys.

"If you were to go back just a few years, young man, you'd notice the difference." Colonel Townsend sighed, stood and walked a few paces. Mixed feelings came from the businessman side of his essence: logging, money, opportunity, fame, pride.

And from the other side of him, completely different sentiments: the views of the barns, the smoke of a chimney smoking for fifty years, animals descended from those brought here a hundred years ago. The human history of the Smoky Mountains is what touched him down, down to the very tips of his roots. For this was a place where families farmed, lived, loved. Who knew so much had happened – was still happening - right here in the heart of the Appalachians! Who still thinks it's important? And why?

Look! It is all so peaceful! The mountains – they're just sitting there after all; crumpled up peaks of earth. Moving through millennia, watching. Watching. All under God's blue banner of heaven.

But when you get into its marrow - its very center - you will see that nothing just sits there. Here, in the Smoky Mountains, you will find everything life has to offer: God, peace, war, betrayal, children, animals, fights, schooling, forgiveness, religion, general stores, churches, blacksmith shops, granny women, children living, dying, people bringing food, helping one another, drinking too much, scolding, bringing an extra batch of biscuits. Forgiving. Love. An eagle, a raven. A crow. A deer. An owl.

Somehow, without saying a word of any of this, Levi saw the center of the mountains enter the boy. And something disentangled inside the young vessel. A decision was made.

"And before this resort began, you'd see Stringtown." Colonel Townsend continued, eyeing the boy who was smiling as wide as the front porch of the club.

"Sounds like a fun place! I think…" he closed his eyes. "I think I can even see it…"

The boy suddenly opened his eyes, stood up at the sight of the head waiter coming out to call them inside. "It's time for *supper*, not dinner!", the boy cried, everyone laughing at how each person stepping off the *Elkmont Special* train had to learn what the difference was between dinner – their usual lunch – and supper – their usual dinner.

"D comes first, and lunch comes first and that's how I remember." The boy chimed in, like it was the most natural thing in the world to think such a way.

Levi laughed. "I often said just about the same thing! Now that's a mighty easy way to recall when to eat!"

As they walked towards The Appalachian Club, Colonel Townsend continued doting on the curious boy.

"It *was* fun. It was a real community." Colonel Townsend reached his table inside the dining room. "My workers lived in Stringtown, in homes which were old rail cars converted into dwellings. They called it Stringtown because the houses were portable and when put in place, it looked like a string of homes all along the sides of the railroad tracks. Imagine if we had to build all new houses as we moved all over the slopes for two thousand workers and their families? That is way too expensive and takes too much time. So, we took railroad cars and turned them into what we call "car shacks" or "box car houses". Wooden steps led up to the doorways and steel rings on top of the houses could be hooked up to a crane when the home needed to be moved. I had a whole crew that was dedicated just to move the homes."

"Why build them right by the tracks?" The boy asked.

"Well son, it's because the terrain is so steep, and our crane didn't have a lot of reach and couldn't extend very far from the tracks. So, there they went."

"And when you had to move, when all the trees were gone, you just hooked up the houses? And moved them?"

"Yes, son. That's exactly what we did!"

"I want to live in a Stringtown!" the boy exclaimed.

Colonel Townsend laughed, rustling the boy's thick sandy colored hair. "Well, it would be hard work, but there would be church on Sundays, and you could ride the train free of charge afterwards. Every Sunday my workers and their families and friends could go into Townsend and go to the movie theater and to baseball games."

The little boy imagined only the good fun of such a way of life. Of the stories of children happy to live a life of adventure, something different from how everyone else lived. He closed his eyes and saw the scene as Colonel Townsend relayed what the children of his workers had said about living in Stringtown:

The railroad tracks were in front of our house, and the river was in the back.

The chestnut blight claimed all the chestnut trees. They were full of worm holes, so they were inferior and considered cheap. Was hard for my company, the Little River Lumber Company, to sell those worm-riddled chestnuts, so the construction crews made tables for all the boxcar houses out of it.

Mamas lay out a nice meal and youngins like you would sit around a big and thick table every single night. Some had a lot of worm holes, but they didn't care. Youngins would tell me they hid nuts and even a coin or two inside the deepest ones.

Other Mamas lay out patterns to make clothes and quilts on the big chestnut tables and if you were living there, you would do your homework on the table while your Ma would be cutting cloth. It would likely be the biggest table you'd ever seen. Why, it would take up more than half of the whole boxcar house!

COLONEL TOWNSEND'S Little River Railroad was still laying what would become 150 total miles of train track, and his Little River Lumber Company had already cleared 35,000 of the eventual 75,000 acres of land. Three million board-feet of lumber were now felled, and they would fell another two hundred and sixty million before 1939.

The Colonel expected hard work. But most workers liked it, enjoyed their jobs, and were grateful. Many reported the same sentiments: *The logging operation was a blessing for the mountain people who were given the opportunity to have jobs and earn a living. Colonel Townsend was well-liked and respected for all that he did for the workers in terms of jobs, pay, health care, and the quality of life that came with the community.*

"But young man, make no mistake. We worked hard...and it was dangerous work. Still is." Sighing, the burly businessman looked down at the floor, waiting for his food to arrive. "Don't know if you've heard of those Walker Sisters. There's seven of them and six still live in the home their Pa built. Two were engaged to be married to loggers, but the young men, sadly, lost their lives in logging accidents. First, Martha Ann lost her fiancée, John. And then, two weeks later, Mary Elizabeth, whom they call Polly, lost her fiancée named Cotter. Martha Ann fared well - eventually - accepting her fate, but Polly. Oh, poor Polly...she was never the same. Remained stuck in a hole that her mind made up – I suppose she dug a hole for the two of them – you know, what could've been - and sunk into it often. I paid two years of wages to their families, but still...and then there were some horrific train accidents..." Trailing off, he nodded his head and looked through the window at a tree framed in the waning light.

The owl.

The Colonel closed his eyes, said a silent prayer for all the men and women who risked their lives for a chance at a better one.

As the Colonel and his tablemates, including the curious young boy, pondered the good and the bad about logging – about *everything* – the waiter came with a heaping platter of trout, potatoes and carrots. Smiles, murmurs of the divine smells, the mood shifted and some of the newer visitors took the opportunity to change the subject.

"What's this I hear about this national park that supposed

to come into these parts? And what will that mean to this Elkmont resort?"

"Yes, Colonel. We'd like to hear what you know. After all, two members of The Appalachian Club, Ann and Willie Davis, were the ones who returned from their trip to Yellowstone National Park and immediately began advocating for a park in the Smokies. Even Colonel David Chapman – one of the founders of The Appalachian Club - supported them and has been pushing for it ever since. I'm sure you'd have seen him hosting legislators here at Elkmont to 'sell them on the park'."

Colonel Townsend sighed, his gaze shifting back from the window to his plate and tablemates, a crack of a smile emerging, grateful for the change of subject. "Ah, word gets around."

"It's all we read about in the newspapers these days. *The Maryville Times* seems especially interested in it. They say it's inevitable."

"Well, not if I can help it. I am not in favor of a national park. In fact, I may - *may* - be okay with a national forest, only because they would still allow logging." He watched the faces of the guests and thought of Levi and Lem and all the residents of Elkmont with whom he'd had the same conversation. Too, he'd communicated the same thoughts to committee after legislative committee.

First it had been the North Carolina General Assembly in 1923. They wound up establishing the North Carolina Park Commission to acquire land for a national park.

The Little River Lumber Company relocated in 1923 as well, seeking treed slopes further away in which to continue their highly lucrative logging business.

Then came Congress in 1926, authorizing the establishment of the Great Smoky Mountains National Park.

Now, in 1928, the Rockefeller Foundation pledged five million dollars to purchase land for the park. Another five million was quickly being raised from schoolchildren donating their pennies for the cause.

"And what will you do if the national park does come to fruition, Colonel?" The newcomer asked, curious as to what this man who made a great living off this land would do.

He answered true; ever the businessman, "I look at profits of course, and future sustainability of my enterprise, but also, like any good businessman, I look out at the slopes and see two thousand people - employees and families - that rely on my staying in business. Men with their wives, children; the ones who work hard, have good paying jobs, enough wages to stay and push the logs onto the railroad cars. The ones who built general stores and a post office, a school, a movie house, a church, and are able to host relatives who stay in cottages and rooms at this here Appalachian Club and at The Wonderland Club just up the road to the north."

Guests nodded their heads, thinking it through, breaking down the Colonel's comments that were high with clarity: a national park would change *everything*.

It would surely mean some great things: more trees, less erosion, and the natural world coming back to order. But it would also mean companies like The Little River Lumber Company and The Little River Railroad Company and all their employees being shut down. A lot of men made a good living working on the railroad and felling logs on the slopes of the Smokies. Colonel Townsend had thousands of lumber workers, railroad workers, and workers in his mill in Townsend. Thousands more comprised workers' families who spent money in the general stores, at the movies, in Townsend, in Elkmont, bringing in friends and relatives on the railroad. An entire industry stood tall, tucked into this slice of one of the oldest mountain ranges on earth. Indeed, what would happen to everyone? And everything?

Wasn't there a way to have both park and industry?

Colonel Townsend had tried to think of every convenience and comfort for the guests of what was once his logging land. By now, The Appalachian Club even had a boardwalk connecting the clubhouse to the cottages so guests would be protected from the mud and dirt so prevalent in the mountain world.

Though still a rustic resort to be sure, visiting city folk couldn't help their innermost souls from crawling into the cracks and knotholes of Elkmont's solid wooden beams and planks. Polite social manners and norms were followed, albeit a bit more loosely. Servants accompanied some of the families – the richer ones – and they lived in small buildings behind the main cottages. Nurses looked after children, and meals were served by waiters at the club. Life was so easy here!

Performances and teas and dinners saw formal clothing and there were even formal costume parties and music. But there were no pianos here. Here, it was all about the fiddles and the banjos.

The owl's head bobbed with the lively instruments being played with such passion on the front porch. It was just what those brochures from The Little River Railroad and the Knoxville and Augusta Railroads and The Appalachian Club and even The Wonderland promised: *Natural surroundings, cozy cottages, modern amenities...a taste of a true mountain life.*

"Very enticing indeed...for *furriners* who don't know a fiddle is just a goddamn violin with a southern accent," Levi sniffed the air, squinting at the crowd, murmuring under his breath. He stayed in the shadows, not one for dancing tonight, but watching as the crowd grew and the fireflies boldly flirted with one another, burning bits and pieces of the midsummer night.

Talk turned towards nostalgia, the crowd a mix of older folk and children. That old saying of 'children are meant to be seen and not heard' did not apply here in the mountains. Children's roles were integral within a farming and rural lifestyle, and the youth from America's cities soon learned from the locals that everyone, of every age, was welcomed. Needed. Why, they'd roam a bit off from the resort's main road and see, off in the distance, the people who lived here all the time like those two characters, Levi and Lem. They'd see a few other homesteads with children as young as two holding small milk tins and weeding gardens. Older ones picking berries, pitching hay, and walking into the woods, which the city kids soon learned, meant they were going hunting or trapping with their Pas.

This Smoky Mountain lifestyle melted into its visitors' souls and soon, the youngins - as they now called themselves - would go home and brag to their schoolmates: *My parents took us to Daisytown in Elkmont. That's in the Smoky Mountains. I stayed there for two weeks and never put on a pair of shoes! Well, we did for dinner, but that was about it. All of us would run around the creeks and trails all day barefooted...I even milked a cow! And pulled a carrot straight from the ground! What could be a better place for a kid than in the Smoky Mountains? I sure hope that national park don't come through. Ha! Yes, that's how they talk down there. Doesn't becomes don't. Lunch is dinner and dinner is supper. I like it there. I loved it. It was the most fun I ever had, I reckon. That's another thing they say: I reckon. And I reckon a national park would ruin everything.*

21

RELOCATION – 1928

I WILL PLANT THEM ON THEIR OWN SOIL,
NO MORE TO BE UPROOTED FROM THEIR
LAND, WHICH I GAVE THEM. (AMOS 9:15)

∽

Levi Trentham was out walking with his cane one day and saw Colonel Townsend coming from The Appalachian Club towards Society Hill. The seventy-six-year-old Prophet of the Smokies was just as crusty and blunt as always; he hadn't seen the Colonel much in the past few months, and he thought this a good time to confront him about the rumor he'd been hearing.

"Colonel? Reckon ya'll are shuttin' down I hear?"

Yes sir, Mr. Trentham. Levi." Colonel nodded his head. "I am finally selling. It cannot be helped you see. I don't like the idea of a national park as you know. I told them time and time again that I prefer a national forest which can still be logged. However…well, you know… I lost. I already sold 75,000 acres to the state of Tennessee years ago. And now, I was forced to sell the rest of it. But I get to log on the land for another 15 years."

"Well, goddamn it."

To which the Colonel smiled warmly, almost fatherly. "Ah, Levi. You always have a way with words."

"Well, it's true. Goddamn this and goddamn that and goddamn the government. They already done got me to sell some of my land. But then, that was when it was my choice. Now, it seems they're forcin' us. Both of us. *All* of us."

"It does appear that way, Levi. Five years ago, as you recall, in 1923, they began in earnest. Then, the Rockefellers gave so much money, no inch of Smoky Mountain land could withstand so many offers."

"Offers?! There's no goddamn *offers!* They're more like 'here's what we call an offer, but it's really an *order*. Get offa your land. Here's some goddamn four thousand dollars for it or whatever goddamn amount a judge up in Knoxville or up in Warshington says it's worth.' Now go away and we don't care where, just not on your land that your Pa built an entire legacy on and that you were born on and that all your youngins were born on." He paused to take a break, neck muscles taut, threatening to burst under his faded shirt and overalls.

"I know, Levi. I can only imagine...if it's any consolation, I have a place right here in Elkmont too you know. Not to mention two businesses with thousands of workers who rely on my companies. They're forcing me out too. After all I've done for this place!" Colonel looked around, angry.

"I've created jobs. Opportunities. Made a lot of people a lot of money. Helped families..." He continued looking into the distance, into the changing world. Not many trees left. Steam from engines and machinery and a few stills up high that the moonshiners were fiercely trying to hide and hold onto.

Colonel continued his laments to Levi - the old mountain man standing right in front of him who so fully and completely represented a dying way of life.

"Moved my operations when the trees were all gone. But there were always trees over on the next slope. More money to be made. More families to make a living in logging. I had to take a lot of chances to keep everyone happy. Then, people –

mostly city folk – flocked here to Elkmont. Their experiences wonderful: picnicking, fishing, hiking, dancing on the front porches of The Wonderland and The Appalachian Club on Saturday nights... I made a lot of people happy...don't understand how the government wants to take all this away."

"One good thing," Levi murmured stroking his long white beard and poking at the air with his cane, "is that this here resort – both clubs – done hired a lot of the former loggers. They're caretakers, cooks, gardeners, guides, housekeeping."

Colonel Townsend was surprised that Levi Trentham of all people, was looking on the bright side of this situation.

"Indeed, Levi! The rough-and-tumble lumberjacks have been replaced by a genteel group from high society." Colonel Townsend ruefully smiled at Levi's narrowing eyes before continuing.

"Think of all who visited here in recent years. Their influence is tough to fight. Senator Joseph Robinson, from Arkansas. He's a strong supporter of the park...he's very busy securing more federal support for the park's establishment. Then there's John McGhee. Pretty big businessman from Knoxville – he's a big supporter of our Appalachian Club and the national park. He advocates conservation..."

"Look around Colonel!" Levi interrupted, his tone turning angry. "There ain't any conservation happenin'! Even that dang owl has stopped hootin' and if you noticed, he'd been hootin' for a whole goddamn hour!"

Colonel Townsend looked up. Sure enough, the great bird was silent, staring down at the two of them.

Levi softened just a tad. "He's listenin' that owl. Yessir, he's listenin'. And he's rehashin' everything that's already happened. He feels he has to yell at us: 'wake up! Look what's already happened! It's a change that cannot be stopped. So, you'd better see what place you have in this new world.' Look back into the early 1900s - that dang Appalachian National Park

Association was formed. 'We want a national park in the Appalachians!' they yelled. Then, we move to now, 1928... Colonel, you've been fellin' trees for decades!"

Townsend nodded, silent, watching the familiar bird. He couldn't believe it, but it *did* seem as if the owl *was* listening. But both creature and businessman remained silent, allowing this old, slightly stooped mountain fellow his say.

"Way back, in 1916, the government got that National Park Service started. To oversee national parks. By the start of these here 1920s, they was snappin' up land like a crazed coon. In 1926...our American Congress - our freedom loving country..." Levi snorted, "authorized for the establishment the Great Smoky Mountains National Park provided they got the land. So they said 'okay, we're going to acquire the rest of the land we want. And if we can't persuade folk to sell when we dangle a check in front of 'em, well, we'll just force 'em out. Pay 'em what we think is fair.' Fair!! Did you hear me?! And then they said, you gotta get out 'cause of goddamn eminent domain, and when folk hear that, they think it's all fancy talk and don't know what the hell eminent domain is, but when other folk say, well it's just the government's right to force you outta your land and it's even in the Constitution, well, all the fight goes out of a man and he cashes that check and gets a few more wagons to move his stuff to town."

Levi was out of breath by now, his long-winded and wounded rage kneeling on the breeze, circling the two men, daring either of them to refute even one word.

Levi sat down on the stump of a felled tree, still wrathful, not quite finished. "And that dang Rockefeller feller...he done gave five million dollars to *purchase* – which is just another word for forcin' us to sell – *our own* land!"

"Nowadays, here we are, 1928, and the government is startin' to really go all in. Buyin' land from private owners. Cades Cove. Cataloochee. They were quiet about it at first. Didn't want everyone to get all riled up. But now the news is well known even in the darkest holler. Gonna be more and more folk sellin' out, collectin' that check and fleein' faster than green grass through a goose."

The owl flew away then, taking the past and present with it.

Only the future remained, standing in the middle of the Little River, walking up the slope, tripping, uncertain as to where to go for the best vantage point. But there was none, for every place was blocked by a cottage, a hotel. A building. The government.

Levi Trentham, the Prophet of the Smokies, vowed to walk with the future, side by side, perhaps even rushing ahead a bit if his old body could handle it.

So far, his powers saw everything. And nothing.

Walking away finally, he tipped his hat to the Colonel. Both men from vastly different backgrounds affected by the same events.

"And then what?" Levi said over his shoulder as he walked to his home and stayed there for a year.

22

FIGHT – 1930

AND WHEN THEY CAME, WE YELLED
'COME OUT OF YOUR BUG-HUTCHES
AND FIGHT!' AS WE WAITED BEHIND
ANOTHER STONE WALL, WAITING FOR
THEM; WAITING FOR THE GREAT MUSIC
TO BEGIN AGAIN AFTER THE SILENCE.

Not everyone agreed with this new national park. Much pushback occurred and not only within the circle of residents. Many of those who owned property and visited also opposed Elkmont being purchased – some said even demolished – for the new national park.

Colonel Townsend had tried for years to oppose the park, or at least, compromise and make it a national forest versus a national park.

An attorney was hired to lead the charge. James Wright, on behalf of The Little River Lumber Company 'railed a hodge-podge group of attorneys, businessmen, and mountaineers at Elkmont to propose the establishment of a national forest rather than a national park'.

Wright, himself an owner of a cottage in Elkmont, was a problem solver and proposed many potential solutions, one being a massive road-building campaign across the crest of the Smokies in hopes of increasing the land's value. This would drive prices higher, and the government may not be able to pay said "fair market value" as eminent domain required.

Along with most others who owned cottages in Elkmont, if there had to be one or the other, Wright and fellow owners advocated for a national forest and not a national park because he was a conservationist and wished the land to return to its heavily forested origins. Many residents agreed. But Wright also pushed for a forest versus a park because he 'believed the area would be contaminated by hordes of crowds'.

Largely because of Wright's efforts, the initial bill allowing for the purchase of land in the Smokies exempted Elkmont from eminent domain. Levi applauded the lawyer and the efforts of the residents, though his reasoning was of a different perspective: "them people who come here to summer are rich. Influential and wealthy. And when they put up a fuss, well, it works. It don't work for folk like us," he bitterly stated, "but I reckon by them and their cottages bein' safe for now, it means we're all safe from that goddamn eminent domain. So I guess those *furriners* turned out to be good for somethin'."

It didn't last. The commissions and committees and groups of the government pushed back.

Still, Elkmont fought on: "cottage owners propose a provision allowing them to sell their cottages at their stated price", even through eminent domain. After all eminent domain requires the government to pay fair market value, and even if their "stated" prices were a bit higher, in their view, it was the least the government could do when pushing – *forcing* – people from their homes!

Though seriously considered by the Commission, that idea did not last either.

Finally, a proposal was proffered to pay the owners half-price for their cottages in exchange for lifetime leases. In the end, the Commission would not agree to any provisions or uphold their initial agreement to exclude the area of Elkmont from the national park. It was finally admitted that the Commission did not, in fact, have the funds to pay the owners their "stated" higher prices, or even half-price, yet it was ruled the owners still had to sell via eminent domain and leave to make way for the park.

The only thing left now for Elkmont was to fight for lifetime leases and to take whatever monies they could from the sale of their vacation homes – even at less than half price - and still be able to use the homes until their deaths.

The Commission said they would consider it.

LEM OWNBY'S FATHER, Tom, died on July 25, 1930, and his beloved mother nine months later on April 5, 1931. Both were laid to rest in the little Elkmont Cemetery a short distance from the family home. This gave the near-blind bear hunter and beekeeper yet another tie to Elkmont, not that he needed it. For he had no plans to leave, government check or not. Threats or not. Oh, those darn government men had tried! But he told them, gently but firmly, that they'd have to drag him out of his old home - and imagine how that would look! He'd yell and scream to every newspaper from here to New York City that a blind man and his wife were taken from their humble wooden home, and the government wouldn't look so good then, would it?

Besides, he figured the government moved so slowly that if a national park ever did happen, it would take so long to acquire all the land and such, he would be long dead and gone before it ever came to fruition. He was only in his forties, but still. Governments move at a pace meant for snails trying to climb the wall of the biggest barn in the Smokies. It'd take years. Or else, like a snail, they'd drop down to the ground and then they'd have to start all over again.

And so, Lem planted crops and a large orchard and acquired additional livestock; kept eating Mimmie's cookies, tending his bees, and managing to keep on making a living while trapping more than thirty bears a year. At seven dollars each, his and Mimmie's lives were quite comfortable.

AMID THE TURMOIL of the start of the 1930s, both Levi and Lem went about their business hunting, raising crops, fishing, guiding, and breathing in their beloved mountain air, while the guests at The Appalachian Club danced, drank tea, hiked, fished, and enjoyed themselves.

No one could completely ignore the frayed cloud stretched as taut as a clothesline that had settled over the land, but Mayna Avent kept on painting and Mrs. Galyon kept on with her Red Cross work and Mrs. Ivah Murphy kept on making her social rounds and relaying all the news she could from all around the world.

The fight raged on, but one side was clearly winning. Residents stood firm: *what about a national forest – can you re-think that idea? Can't we just stay? Can't you just reroute the park and leave us out of it? Can't you just draw a circle around Elkmont and make your park all around us?*

To which, the conservationists and ones fighting for the national park stood their own ground, on higher and stronger slopes: *stop clearing and building and the balance will slowly return. Don't you want trees again? Why, whenever it rains and snows, the runoff floods the river. There's no roots or trees or boulders to stop the flow! Restore it and stability shall return. We cannot just divide the land. It must be an entire area for it to work as a national park. Can't have visitors going in and out of park boundaries and through private lands to get to public trails and parking lots. No. The park must have the land. All of it.*

THE GREAT SMOKY MOUNTAINS NATIONAL PARK had been officially authorized, as a concept, in June of 1926, but that was contingent upon acquisition of land. Anger, hope, bitterness, optimism – all knelt on uncertain breezes until 1930, when it was all but inevitable. North Carolina and Tennessee deeded public lands to the federal government, while private farm owners had largely taken the government money and left. They had no choice.

Lawyers were hired, fights were had, yelling, crying at night in front of all the hearth fires of the Smokies. In the end, the Fifth Amendment of the Constitution of the United States allowed it. It was part of the Bill of Rights. No choice now but to watch the mountains bid goodbye, asking them to find another place within their burly arms in which to settle. Another farm. Another plot of land. Another house outside the boundaries of the park but still within the waves and waves of blue and misty peaks. *There's plenty of land within us*, the mountains soothed. *Come find another place.* But that wasn't the point. They had already found their place. And lost it.

All the while, Elkmont and The Appalachian Club acted as if its place in this new world was solid as a boulder settled into the neck of the river. The club added electric stoves, refrigerators, and heaters to the cabins. It repaired and updated the boardwalk, hired more musicians with banjos and fiddles, hired more guides, spent more money on brochures and advertising, and served up finer dinners and suppers than ever before.

But on any given afternoon, if you perched up a bit higher like the owl, one would see many of the older, established Elkmont residents had moved, died off, and their cabins and barns were beginning to fall into disrepair. Talk of restoring what were now deemed historic structures floated lightly on those same conflicted breezes, but most of the talk turned towards progress. Out with the old, in with the new. And the new was all about the national park.

THE 1930S SAW CADES COVE, Cataloochee, and Walker Valley mostly vacated. A few homeowners in the Smokies managed to negotiate lifetime leases, allowed to remain for the rest of their lives – most famously the Walker Sisters over in Little Greenbrier Cove. But their way of life was greatly impacted; no longer could they rely on neighbors and community – very few remained – and they were largely on their own. No longer could they hunt, fish, fell trees - they were regulated in everything they did because, after all, their land was part of the national park now where nothing could be touched. Nothing hunted, nothing cut down.

The greater good had prevailed.

And that's when, after a year, the mountains answered Levi's question: *And then what?*

Boldly, reluctantly, he listened.

And that's when Levi Trentham, one of the oldest and most loyal sons of the mountains, left the only home he'd ever known.

23

THE PROPHET MOVES - 1930

THE WEEPING PROPHET LIVES WITH
A YAWNING SADNESS THAT DAILY
THREATENS TO SPLIT HIM WIDE OPEN.

∽

Levi Trentham, the mountain man, the Mayor of Elkmont, the Prophet of the Smokies, walked out of his beloved home one morning when the sky was stretched into the bluest banner of heaven he'd ever seen. Didn't bother to look back though. For how could he have ever stepped another stride away from it all if he indulged the urge to turn back?

Ever the mysterious, enigmatic man, Levi bore his grief quietly. It was between him and his mountains. His wife, Emaline, had died two years ago in 1928 after a lifetime shared with ten children and countless grandchildren and great-grandchildren. A legacy long made – quietly. For he rarely spoke of his wife, and she rarely accompanied him to the two clubs or to guide, fish, or hike. Still, by all accounts they had a lovingly practical and patient relationship, and he mourned her greatly when she died. Levi buried her on his own property instead of in the old Elkmont Cemetery on the banks of Jake's Creek. The owl would see history making this the Levi Trentham Cemetery in due time; sooner rather than later if Levi Trentham kept up his mournful mood of late.

For Levi had become a weeping prophet; he had lost his loyal wife, his land was threatened, his way of life near gone. It took a while, but in his usual fashion, he had recovered enough and had resumed living his life as he always had. He was a practical man, mourning in his own way, yet keeping close to his lifelong comforts – spending time with family, living a farming lifestyle, doing chores, and guiding guests of Elkmont and doing whatever needed to be done.

But now, since the national park had become fact, and many of his neighbors - and way of life - were gone, it looked as if he were packing things up.

Selling things.

Burning a huge pile of...stuff.

A man unmoored. Uprooted.

The government had sniffed around his own home and land, closer and closer, with that pungent odor of inevitability. Yet he listened to his mountains, always, even if they gave him blistering and shattering news. And they reminded him that he was practical and resilient enough to realize that such a man as himself – especially at this stage of life and losing his home and land - was much better when he had a woman around to cook, clean, help around the home, and be a grandmotherly figure for his youngest grandchildren.

And so, while The Wonderland Club installed a sewer line, and guests at both clubs and resorts enjoyed themselves at the swimming hole, and the road from Townsend to Elkmont now boasted a gas station, store, post office, and movie theater along its path, the Prophet of the Smokies quietly looked around for another wife.

As was custom, he gently put feelers out to friends and family who jumped at the chance to help: *would so and so's widow be amenable to taking another spouse?*

Why not ask your aunt who lost her husband last year if she'd be open to talking with Levi Trentham? It's been awhile, but he's lookin' again.

Can you arrange for that widow up yonder, the sweet, quiet one, to meet me at the post office to take a walk with me?

I wonder if Levi and Bessie would get along? I think they'd make a good match. And he's got a comfortable house.

Not anymore. He's sold to the government. For the national park. What?!

Yes, indeed. He's gone.

THE PROPHET of the Smokies had seen it. Of course he had. And it was oh so bitter when it happened, but at least he could control some of his departure. He managed to sell his land at a good price, with the promise that his land would be preserved and allowed to grow once again.

Thus far, even today, that promise has been kept.

By 1930, the census showed Levi Trentham living in Monroe County, Tennessee, and owning a farm with his second wife, Bessie Hagler, who was born in 1889. They would have six years together. Two children from Bessie's prior marriage, joined with his ten children and their numerous offspring, and kept the newly married couple busy and occupied, which was the best remedy for a broken heart.

A lifetime lease wasn't in the cards for Levi. Oh, it was offered. Many times. But he didn't accept any of the proposals. Instead, he took the money and left, because how was he to live without chopping wood? Or hunting bears and selling their skins? Keeping bees and making honey? And doing whatever the heck he wanted and saying whatever the heck he wanted on his own goddamn land?

No, that kind of restricted life wasn't the life for a man like

Levi Trentham. He took the full monies and bought another farm, on new land that he hoped the government wouldn't take away. One where he could do all those things he'd been doing his entire life, and no other man could tell him what to say or what to do.

Was he happy?

Well, goddamn it, would you be?

LIKE LEVI TRENTHAM, most of the original Elkmont residents had moved away, but the resort itself, where so many wealthy folk maintained their summer cottages and cabins remained staffed and full, having finally negotiated half of the appraised value of their properties in return for lifetime leases.

But it wasn't the same, and the owl's powers of prophecy pushes us a bit forward in time now, towards when President Roosevelt's Civilian Conservation Corps (CCC) arrived and set up camp in the early 1930s, building roads, trails, restrooms, fire towers, campgrounds, and visitor centers, and restoring the land.

In due time, the Smoky Mountain communities of Elkmont, Cades Cove, Little Greenbrier, Walker Valley, Tremont, Cataloochee, and so many others were transformed into a true national park. Visitors could now park their cars, hike a paved trail to Laurel Falls, drive a paved loop road around Cades Cove, walk inside its churches and the John Oliver cabin and imagine a true mountain lifestyle. Later, they could relax at Chimneys Picnic area with picnic tables and grills and restrooms and parking spots.

All the while, the original residents – the few that were left - could only watch, adapt, remember; heartened memories turned haunted, like nightfall smothering the deepest holler.

Levi Trentham spent his entire life on the land he loved,

happily confined to it for those few years during the Great War when he freely spouted his own special mindset of *goddamn this* and *goddamn that.*

It was the same land that spawned his children, grand-children.

All that was gone now.

The dry, pungent smoke of history chased out the scent of bearskins and rifles and wood stacked high outside a mountain home. Handfuls of anger and bitterness were the only things left, and Levi threw all of it – all of it - into the wind until the sound of life being spawned once again hit him squarely in the chest.

That's when he left.

Because it was gone now, this life he knew. A new and very different one had begun. And it didn't have room for him.

Oh, he'd survive to be sure. New land, new wife, it was all... comfortable. Even familiar. But the wind turned on him whenever he'd dared try to soften or blunt the hurt. When that happened, he re-avowed never, ever to return to Elkmont lest his heart burst with memories that could never let him out of there again.

So, it was quite the surprise when he was called back, not quite to Elkmont, but close enough to his known territory, the one stitched into his very heart and soul, for a unique opportunity. For just when everything was still pushing in on him – his land taken away, a park established, a new life - something else was about to open. Something that answered at least some of the questions which weighed on him heavier than the biggest boulder clogging up the river: *who would be left to honor this place? To preserve it?*

Would all the barns and churches and homes and moonshine stills and orchards with now-bitter fruit and owl nests just...sink into forgotten memories? Unread and uncared for on those moldy shelves of history that not enough people care about? Or would somebody, someday, preserve our legacy? Would anyone cherish our remembrances and ways of living enough to write it all down? Within a book perhaps? Full of our memories and stories and traditions of what the mountains gave us? Or would it all just...go away. Be reclaimed by nature?

And where would that dang owl go?

24

THE BRIDGE – NOVEMBER 27, 1932

BUILD A BRIDGE OF GOLD FOR THY ENEMY;
BUILD A BRIDGE FOR THE TONGUE AS
A NECESSARY PIECE OF FURNITURE.

~

"**M**r. Trentham? Would you come to the newly constructed Henley Street Bridge? It was completed this summer, but we're planning on opening it this autumn. We'd love it if you could make it. We actually want you to be the first one to cross it. You can bring your own ox-drawn cart."

"Why do you want me?"

"Levi. You're well-known all around these parts. Why, you're the Prophet of the Smokies! Your image is even on postcards... you gotta know this by now."

"Yeah, and who said you could use my image?"

"Well..."

"Goddamn right, *well*...."

"Edna Simms's Mountaineer Museum uses you as a logo."

"Yeah, but I told her she could. She's one of us."

"How old are you now?"

"Eighty."

"And still goin' strong, I see!"

Levi narrowed his eyes but was secretly proud. Dedicating a fifty-four-foot-wide big city bridge? In Knoxville? He thought more and more these days about how he'd be remembered, how his land would be honored, and this seemed a good way to add to the already deep legend of his prophecies, his bear-hunting, his general store, his guiding of fishing and hunting trips, and the Ol' Glory and Red Cross incidents. Postcards and guides to the Great Smoky Mountains National Park indeed mentioned him. And he was proud of each and every one of these. Maybe all this will help keep alive the mountain way of life.

"Alright then, Governor. I'll see ya'll in November. Right before the new year."

AN OX-DRAWN cart drew to a stop before Governor Henry Horton, who was announcing to the crowd the history behind the bridge and what it would mean to the future of Knoxville, Tennessee, and the Great Smoky Mountains National Park: "Colonel David Henley was a Revolutionary War officer and federal agent working in our Knoxville area. During these trying times, during this Great Depression and all that we are enduring, this Henley Street Bridge serves as a beacon of hope. A gateway to the Smoky Mountains! To honor America's newest national park."

An estimated crowd of fifty thousand people were on hand on the beautiful fall Sunday of November 27, 1932.

Governor Horton continued with his upbeat and inspirational tone while he dedicated the bridge, emphasizing its connectivity to and from the city and the promise of economic growth in the region. "I wish to thank our state and local authorities for their collaborative efforts in bringing this project to fruition. As we know, America is in the depths of what we are calling The Great Depression, and this beautiful bridge will serve as a gateway, not only to the park and other areas of our great country, but as a gateway towards the future, one with abundance for all."

The governor stepped aside while an old mountain man with eyebrows thick like hedges peered out to the crowd. *Dang. This is the biggest goddamn crowd I ever seen.* Suddenly a bit nervous, Levi didn't have much time to calm the flutters in his stomach, for Governor Horton was introducing him.

"And now, representing the Spirit of the Smokies! Mr. Levi Trentham!"

Levi stepped up to the podium, suspenders holding up a well-worn, but clean pair of overalls. White beard halfway down his chest, eyes flashing with wit and wisdom. Taking a deep breath of the city's blended flavor, he exhaled slowly, imagining his body's return to the country air of his farm in the Smokies where he could look out at his brilliantly peaceful carpet of golden crops and emerald fields. Not like here in Knoxville where there were thousands of people and automobiles and train whistles and people's shoes tap, tap, tapping on the concrete sidewalks, the whole world paved over.

"Good mornin' Ladies and Gentlemen. Sure is a beautiful day here in Knoxville, Tennessee." He drew in his breath once again. The autumn air of the town began padding jagged bits and parts of his heart; yet his mouth felt dry, thoughts near-empty. Who could sum up what this bridge really means to folk like himself? Sure, it was progress. And of course, he knew by now such evolution couldn't be fought. And some of it – only *some* of it, mind - *was* for the better.

But did the world have to have so *much* progress? So much quick advancement that governments could just run a road right through his own backyard? A home and farm one day; concrete buildings and wide paved roads the next? *Abandon all that old goddamn baggage that will hinder progress* was essentially what those goddamn lawyers and conservationists stated in their committees and newspaper articles and in the court-rooms. Oh, they'd said it better, more professionally to be sure, but the message was the same. It was easy for them because their own baggage was in their closets and attics, easily stored or left behind if need be. But the true baggage they spoke of was his very own home and ancestral land. Impossible to pack up and take to the next stop.

Levi thought of all this at the podium, mind racing like a speeding train. He'd had his speech all planned out, but now, that plan was gone. For he was not the same person who stepped up to the podium seconds ago, the one still hanging on to possibilities. No. Fully realizing for perhaps the first time as he gazed out at thousands upon thousands of people, he was a man whose land was...everyone's.

It ain't mine anymore this land. Well, it will always be mine. No matter what goddamn name is on the deed. But now I gotta accept it. I gotta give a speech. I practiced sayin' a good one! I swear to it! But now, standing here on this near-eighteen hundred foot high bridge, I'm gonna speak straight from my heart. I lost my land, but now I need to get folk to honor it. If they can only do that...

Levi cleared his throat and began.

"As Governor Horton here said, you can certainly get to the Great Smoky Mountains National Park using this newly built bridge. It's indeed a gateway. And it's a da...it's a beautiful bridge to be sure. When you come here with your families, I am personally asking you to make sure you honor those who were here before you. Ones like me who had to give up their land."

He could see the crowd listening; his power of prophecy saw that they were even humbled. Ready to do as he asked.

"Governor Horton just introduced me as the 'Spirit of the Smokies'. Said I represent the people of the Smoky Mountains. Well, folks. I'm proud of that. Our souls and spirits *are* here; part of these mountains, part of the very soil itself. And always will be. Honor all who had to give up their farms. Their homes. Their entire lives and lifestyles. Their special culture they began over a hundred years ago. Honor folk like my Pa and Ma. Folk like *me*. Like *us. Honor.* Always."

He nodded at the crowd; people were silenced for a split second longer while they absorbed the impact of the new bridge leading to the new national park.

Then, applause.

All of them, every last soul, stood up from their chairs, and those who were already standing brought their hands up high, clapping endlessly at this old mountain man in suspenders with a white beard. A rousing ovation for the one whose quiet and simple words wove their way into brave and tender hearts, stirring their conscience to do all the right things.

"Thank you, Mr. Levi Trentham! The Spirit of the Smokies indeed! It's folk like you who keep the spirit of these mountains alive. And now, we invite you to be the first to cross the Henley Street Bridge!" Governor Horton motioned for Levi to walk across the newly paved structure.

The old mountain man forced himself to begin his march towards his own ox-drawn cart. Climbing inside like a man twenty years younger, he didn't hear the crowd still clapping, loudly chanting about spirits and prophecies and fortunes and seers. He put aside the newspaper reports he'd heard about over the last few years about the bickering over the bridge – how big should it be? How wide? What construction materials should be used? Accusations of bribery. And who could blame those accusers? After all, there was $1.15 million up for grabs, split between the City of Knoxville and Knox County, both entities and all of America in the middle of the biggest economic depression the one hundred-and fifty-six-year-old freedom-loving country had yet seen.

The bridge was very high, nearly eighteen hundred feet and impressive; yet had none of the majesty of mountain peaks.

He'd been higher – three, four thousand feet on the highest slopes - picking berries, shooing sheep and cattle, hunting. He breathed in again, pulling eighty years of memories and thoughts into his hunched and old body. But his mind was ever-prophesizing. He could've led the cart; could have even walked over the bridge, stopped, and made another speech. These city folk woulda gone hog-wild if he told them a prophecy right in the middle of the new bridge! If he warned them to "tread lightly" and "respect the old ways of the mountains" because "the mountains remember you". And not in that loud, thunderous way, but in the quiet hush of a vanished barn, a dismantled springhouse, the sudden uplift of mist at a crumbling chimney site, of an owl's eyes watching from the lone tree left on what was once a canopied paradise...

But would it matter? Would they listen? Would their newly stirred conscience remain alert from his simple words uttered not ten minutes ago? Some of them might take heed. Enough of them wouldn't. Because they'd do what they wanted anyway, no matter if the mountains held spirits older than anyone knew.

No matter if they disturbed the peaceful places.

No matter if doing so would bring misfortune.

For those types didn't believe in any of that. It was this divide between two kinds of people that made all the difference. One group thought misfortune was all explainable: weather, accidents, unexplained delays, even spirits – these things could all be easily investigated and defended.

The other group, however - consisting of one eighty-year-old mountain man, a few other original residents, ancestors, and those who truly honored them - knew it to be different. Because it was the mountains themselves that resist unwanted changes with all their craggy might. And there was nothing for those logical and scientific men to investigate, for the peaks made sure to cover their deepest struggles with boulders and fires and occasional floods to wash it all away.

Levi wanted to scream at fortune: *That first group is winning!*

But only for the time it took those detached first-group people to forget those who sacrificed so much for the greater good. It would happen quickly. As soon as they forgot, the tug of war would swing again to the side that would always be strongest.

The crowd cheered Levi Trentham, the Spirit of the Smokies, while he slowly, stoically led his ox-drawn cart across the Henley Street Bridge, holding tightly to his legacy, his part in all of this, holding closest to his heart what the mountains gave him. Even managing a slight grin, heaven's smile feeling especially near on this one autumn day in 1932.

25

"I WARNED 'EM" –NOVEMBER 30, 1932

WHAT IS BUILT IN THE DAY SHALL FALL IN THE NIGHT, TILL THE HIGHEST STONE IN THE CHURCH BE THE LOWEST STONE OF THE BRIDGE. – MOTHER SHIPTON

~

"Fire!"

It had been just a few days after Levi walked across the bridge. Dark, nighttime in late autumn 1932, a hushed silence had fallen over the land. No one was around, but Lem Ownby sat up in bed, suddenly wide awake. He may not be able to see more than two inches in front of him, but his sense of smell was as keen as a hungry she-bear with four new cubs.

He and Mimmie were as content as they could be during this otherwise tumultuous time. Lem was in the midst of negotiating a lifetime lease to stay on his land, in his home. He was optimistic, but no deal had been solidified just yet. The middle aged couple were accepting their unpredictable future as much as possible, trying not to think about their own deaths, which, even if they managed to obtain a lifetime lease, would still mean the loss of the home and land when they passed.

They were taking it better than others - James Wright, the very same lawyer hired by Colonel Townsend's Little River

Lumber Company to oppose the national park "was so adamant in his opposition to the creation of the national park that he no longer even wanted a summer cabin in Elkmont and sold his place".

But lawyers and government and wants and needs were no match for Mother Nature or the strong prophecies of men who knew tonight's fiery event to be the action of mountains wrestling with preserving a lifestyle versus regrowing its bald slopes. Even the mountains, stubbornly, still asked: *why can't we have both?*

But even the softly scalloped peaks knew the futility of such question as smoke filled the air, tendrils snaking their way up the slopes.

Mimmie sat up in bed just then. "Lem. What's the matter?"

"Fire!" He repeated. "There's a fire! And from the smell of it – the direction of the wind - it's comin' from the street at Elkmont."

Lem fired off a few rounds from his rifle, summoning neighbors and other residents. Thank goodness there were a few neighbors and friends who stayed, were still around, trying to negotiate lifetime leases. And thank goodness the Elkmont resort was pretty much empty!

All those October leaf peepers had gone; mid-November bringing the first snowfall. But that snow had melted now that it was the very end of November. It had been an exceptionally dry autumn thus far. And the rare lightning storm had occurred just a few hours ago. Could that have been what started the fire? Or could it have been a camper or some careless visitor who had been hiking earlier that day? Leaving embers to be picked up by the wind, birthing a new fire after the wind had had its fun with it?

As Lem ran towards the Elkmont street, he felt the searing heat first, then the blob in front of him turned high orange. Lem ran here and there, shouting instructions: *Get the buckets!*

Ring the bell so the staff can hear! They're sleepin' away in their quarters right near the club! Fire your guns! Once more! We still don't have all the staff outside...any youngins around? Mimmie! Run over and knock on that cabin...make sure no one's there...

The Maryville Times reported it two days later:

> *December 2, 1932 - The fire at The Appalachian Club in Elkmont began quickly, though no one knows exactly how it began. Rumors are swirling that two teenage boys playing with matches while hiking Chimney Tops began the fire, but that is unverified and no arrests have been made. Firefighters arrived and created firebreaks by clearing vegetation to stop the flames. Volunteers, staff, and residents eventually extinguished the fire, but the club was burned to the ground. Nothing is left. Rainfall the next morning extinguished the remaining embers. No guests were at the resort when the fire occurred. No other details are known.*

THE FIRE SHOOK LEVI TRENTHAM, even on his farm in Monroe County, which was just to the southwest of Sevier County where Elkmont and the new national park lay. The Prophet hadn't moved too far away, and as his old stomping grounds lay burning, his powers urged him out of bed, onto the front porch, to stare northeast. No flames could be seen at this distance of course, but he heard the aching creak coming from the familiar peaks of his old companions. The mountains were tender, smarting from too much change too fast.

Levi's mind went back to the bridge, his warning to the tens of thousands of people who would become visitors to America's newest national park – the only one thus far created with public *and* private lands. In just a few more years, in 1935, Shenandoah National Park would join that distinction, but for now the mountains were worried. Would all these new people marvel at its spring and summer finery? Or would they leave trash from their picnics? Would they respect the old ways of the mountains when they walked inside cabins and barns and churches? Or would they carve their names into the wooden planks hand-hewn over a hundred years ago just so they could advertise their awful callousness?

I warned 'em: tread lightly. Respect the old ways of the mountains. The mountains will remember you and ask to please respect their ancient earth. Or else they will throw boulders down their own spines, flood the creeks, stick out their limbs here and there, spark dry leaves - all in a valiant and righteous effort to teach you what your Mama should've taught you. And if she didn't, or you didn't listen, Fate will laugh and stick out its feet to trip some of the more thoughtless folk. Maybe that will make 'em listen.

Such prophecies flew around Levi's mind faster than an owl's eyes can spot its prey. Even Lem Ownby felt the voice - the warning - of the mountains.

Both men sat on their front porches – one still in Elkmont, one further away – yet each could smell the change as The Appalachian Club lay in ruins, wondering, wondering if its charred bones would be completely forgotten in the fumes of history.

THE OWL SAW the first changes after the fire. There was nothing left of The Appalachian Club except for a pile of scorched wood. Summer visitors lamented the ruined hub of the community but vowed to rebuild. In fact, efforts were made that very next summer; monies were raised, plans made, lumber ordered.

In the meantime, the summer residents cooked for themselves, a huge departure from their seasonal routine. Meals had been, for the most part, taken at the clubhouse. Who wanted to cook on vacation? But after the fire, meals were prepared in the kitchens of cottages and cabins. More servants accompanied families that summer and for a few thereafter, to cook, arrange food. Clean up.

All the while, even before the Great Smoky Mountains National Park was officially established in June 1934, the area was drawing crowds - three hundred thousand visitors a year, eager to roam the mountains. By then, the owl's favorite tree would be gone. Like Levi Trentham, the creature fled to another area where there were still a few more trees left.

26

LEM'S LIFE LEASE – AUGUST 1933

IT IS TIME TO YOKE WHEN THE
CART COMES TO THE HORSE.

~

"Some folks are comin' over our way," Mimmie said looking out the window at the worn pathway to their house. "Why, it's...is it Ivah Murphy?"

She put down her sewing and hurried outside. "Mrs. Murphy! I ain't seen you in a coon's age!" They hugged and greeted one another.

"What brings you here? We don't go down to Elkmont's street much anymore. Lem's blind as ever and my old bones can't take the walk too much."

"Ah, Mimmie! I missed your honey cookies!" She laughed, gladly accepting a tin of water and the invitation to sit on the front porch. Sitting in the rickety chair, Ivah swept her hand over their dog laying in the sunshine, gently sniffing her, content with his bowl of water under the tree.

Lem came outside and greeted his old friend, told her all about how even more of their neighbors had just signed life-time leases.

"Well, Mr. Ownby. Lem. That's why I'm here. Because we all heard you signed, and we wanted to see if that was true."

"Well now, Mrs. Murphy. You heard it right. All our neighbors, they done told us they signed their land deeds with an "X" since they can't read or write. They hope it was correct what they signed, but how would they know? They surely had to trust the government people to tell them the truth about what they were signing."

"They got their money, didn't they?" Ivah asked, somewhat alarmed. "Or there'd be a lot more pages of the newspaper talking about how government men were shot in the Smoky Mountains!" She laughed at that but wanted confirmation from Lem.

"To tell you the truth..." Lem sighed and sat down on the step as the ladies rocked on the rickety cane-backed chairs on the front porch. The afternoon had turned cool – unusual for August – as Lem Ownby relayed the deal he had reached.

"...I done hired me a lawyer who's also a judge – Judge Ambrose Paine."

"We know him!" Ivah exclaimed. "A fine man. My husband has worked with him many a time."

"Thank ye. Well, I think so too...so I tol' him I heard of some folk makin' a deal where they received some money for their land, but they could also remain on their land for the rest of their lives. So, I done did that. Signed my own name with an "X"."

"Ah. I see." Ivah felt sad. "And what of your brother?"

"Bert and I – he's still unmarried you know..."

Ivah nodded.

"...well, we done decided to keep our parents' farm and divide it up between us. So, after the judge and the park people – those government men – talked and wrote up their papers and such, we all agreed on a lifetime lease. Bert and I, and

Mimmie, - we can stay on this here land. Until we die. Then...I guess it'll be everyone's land after that."

> *The Register of Deeds recorded it all : 30 acres good and fair cultivated land and 14 acres fair timber consisting of poplar, bass, maple; 180 bearing apple trees in good condition', dirt rick road, wire fence, farm well-watered, 3 room box house; 3 other buildings in fair condition. Improvements $940. Jury of view: $3,500. The deed lists A.M. Paine as attorney, is registered and reflects the final price of $4500. The document states: "see Bert Ownby card 22.5 and 44 acres embraced this price. Transferred to Federal Government 7/14/1933."*

"So, we signed last month. And once it was all divided, I am left with 22 acres, which includes this here house, along with all the outbuildings, our orchard, and ample space for the small crops and livestock we're allowed. It's fine. I am as happy as I can be."

"Mimmie? How do you see things?" Ivah asked.

"Well, the way I see it is, we're left knowing we'll live out our lives on our land. I'm happy that some other neighbors did the same thing – so we're not so lonely out here. We're well into our forties now...both of us. Lem's blinder than ever, but he still tends his bees and still hunts bear with the best of 'em. At least, until they tell us he can't hunt at all anymore on account that it's a park now. And he still talks to all the youngins and brings 'em over for my honey cookies. I can't make 'em fast enough!" She laughed that warm laugh of hers. "Lem loves children. Too bad we weren't blessed with any of our own. But we feel surrounded by youngins...nieces, nephews, neighbor children.

To be honest, it's perfect for us. And I'm mighty glad we can live out our lives right here. Peacefully and quietly."

MEANWHILE, the summer residents and owners of Elkmont were still fiercely fighting to overturn, to undo, to change, to fight for anything the federal government would offer.

Jim Wright, the lawyer, the one who was "so adamant in his opposition to the creation of the national park that he sold his Elkmont cottage" had dropped the fight as futile and moved on. But most owners were very eager to work out a deal so they could continue to summer here, bring their children, grand-children, and families, and breathe the air of their own slice of paradise.

Most had already accepted life-lease agreements in exchange for reduced monies. But they remained in a fighting mood – they were still powerful and well-connected busi-nessmen after all. Together with their active wives, Elkmont cottage owners continued pounding the table over the next couple of decades asking for their properties to be converted to twenty-year terms. That way, if an original owner passed away, their lease would not be terminated – it would pass to their heirs, and the family could remain on the land. For twenty years that is. After that, well, they hoped they could just keep negotiating in the future.

The owl wasn't fooled. His powerful prophecies were even greater than Levi Trentham's. He knew these cottage owners had some fight left in them – a lot in fact. And knew they'd be successful in some requests. But the ultimate outcome...that was already decided.

The only saving grace was that the two rivals – The Wonderland and The Appalachian Club – would need one another and, for the first time, unite.

27

"IT'S OFFICIAL" - 1934

BEAUTY MAY HAVE FAIR
LEAVES BUT WITH BITTER FRUIT.

~

Levi Trentham and Lem Ownby sat together on the front porch of Levi's cabin. The aging blind man and his wife had taken their wagon to visit Monroe County to do some trading of bear skins and to see their old friend. Levi and Bessie were living on their new and prospering farm. They were almost happy except for his deep ache over losing his ancestral land.

Did they really have to leave? That question echoed endlessly, weighing itself right there on the heart. It showed up within midnights, by the hearth fire, always present. But of course, they had to go – it was just like that pioneer woman who kept putting off harvesting the last hen in her coop. *We need the food,* she'd say, *but I will miss the company.*

Levi thought a lot about that story. He needed to leave Elkmont, to be free again, to nourish at least his body. But nothing would ever feel like the quiet company of his *real* land - the one he was born on, the land he grew up on. That land lived in his soul. How cruel is it to face a decision that must be made; one that agonizes you to the very hour of your death, even if it's right.

But Lem and Mimmie Ownby had decided to remain in Elkmont, to watch the world expand around them. They were content to live how they had to live – diminished, contained, emptier. Yet remaining rooted in their soil.

The owl was out during the day, flying between two worlds: the good old days and progress. He hooted periodically at each end, but without its usual vigor.

"Galyon even sold out." Levi offered his friend a tin cup of cold creek water and thanked them for coming all this way. Asked about the prices he was getting for bear pelts and honey this season. The women were inside fussing over this and that: a new grandchild, a new quilt pattern, a new way to cook mutton, lamenting how they swept floors a million times a day and still never got their floors clean.

"He had no choice, Levi. You know that. Nobody had a choice, really. Lifetime leases? They ain't for everyone. Besides, the park done changed everything. Rules and restrictions swirl around thicker than my bees!"

"But you and Mimmie stayed."

"I reckon so." Sighing, Lem told his old friend how even though they had managed to stay, he could never be truly accepting of this new life, this new routine, and all its controls and guidelines. But what choice did he have? He was a blind older man with an older wife who were both slowing down. No children. No heirs.

"It sure ain't the same, Levi. And I'm not so sure it's all gonna work out either."

Levi looked at his friend. They were both older, lines gently curving over wise faces. "Well, I hear the Galyons agreed to convey the property to the park. But they got a pretty good deal outta it, I hear. They made the government compensate their two youngest youngins $242.56 each, plus a lifetime lease for all three of their children."

"To be sure, Levi. It's true. It was on July 14, 1933 - just last year - when Galyon made the deal. Many of the Elkmont families are doin' the same thing. Hangin' on to their cottages and cabins and takin' the government money in exchange for still bein' able to come here in the summers. And maybe a little more money and lifetime leases even for their youngins."

"Reckon them city folk think it's the best of both worlds."

"Ain't it? When you think on it? Gettin' money and still bein' able to do their summers here in the Smokies?"

Levi immediately spoke up, his tone firm. "No, it ain't the same! I coulda done that too! Taken the money and stayed on my land! But no, it ain't the same thing. It does somethin' to a man's soul knowin' their home ain't really theirs anymore. Those city folk can do it 'cause it's only the summers that they're here. And it's all fun and games to them to be in Elkmont. But folk like me...well...I couldn't live there year round, like I been doin' my whole life, and change my routine for the national park folk. No sir. I took the money and went and got my own land again. One that no one – I hope - can ever take away."

"Levi. You sure do make sense. To be sure, our world is shrinkin' – me and Mimmie's. More and more folk are leavin'. And we can't keep much livestock or grow as much as we want – they say take just what we need and no more. We can't even fell many trees for wood for the hearth! National Park rules they say. Well, at least I can still say one thing: I was born here. And I'm gonna die here."

"Goddamn right, Lem Ownby! You stick to that. You stick to that now, ya hear me? Do it for both of us. Take what the mountains give you!"

And with that, Levi Trentham and Lem Ownby went inside Levi's new home on his new land in Monroe County and had themselves a fine dinner of ham, biscuits, green beans, and creamed corn.

SUMMER of 1934 saw Elkmont's owl watching Mayna Avent still painting in her cabin on Jake's Creek. Mr. and Mrs. Galyon sometimes came back to visit friends in Elkmont who still had cottages, and their little girl Hattie kept visiting when she got older, such was her love of the summer paradise. But her family cabin lay vacant, memories sitting by the hearth, overlooking the sparse forest. Even Ivah Murphy and her husband had sold, making rarer and rarer appearances.

Ivah Murphy saddened with each visit when she walked past her old home, walked past the charred remains of The Appalachian Club where so many wonderful memories lay. Despite the beauty of the place – and it was getting even more beautiful since the trees were allowed to grow once again without fear of logging - her heart just wasn't in it anymore. She even missed that feisty mountain man - the Prophet of the Smokies. Even when he had called her dear friend, Mrs. Galyon - and other good hardworking women - *Red Cross whores*, she hadn't taken offense. Well not much anyway. She knew his real anger came from the war. From the early talk of the national park. And they'd gotten along so well most other times; he'd even teasingly said to her before he sold his land and left: *I kinda wish some of you whores would come around again! But like me, you're all gone now.*

Ivah Murphy had given him her sternest what-for look and reminded him that while it wasn't her, but Mrs. Galyon that logged so many hours for the Red Cross, he should be very, very grateful for such women, and should admire her friend's work. He grudgingly agreed and muttered *goddamn it you just may be right* so many times that she finally begged him to stop because he was making her giggle with his cheeky grin.

Then, the two strange bedfellows representing city and country began laughing, laughing so hard they cried over their odd friendship, their different ways of talking, their completely different lives that somehow appreciated each other. And their mutual sadness over losing the one place in the world that felt just...well, it had felt like everything was right with the world when they were held within the blue and misty walls of Elkmont, Tennessee.

OWNERS, residents, mountain and city folk weren't the only ones caught in the upheaval of history. The owl's natural curiosity took a deep dive; he was so bored! Five thousand six hundred sixty people were now gone; only about twenty residents and one hundred mostly wealthy club members and cottage owners were allowed to stay. There was nothing to look at, no one to listen to yelling about *goddamn this* and *goddamn that*. He had heard so many folk over the years talk about Levi's mouth – many thought he was all about cussing just for the sake of cussing and an affront to God.

But the owl knew better - it was simply a way for men like Levi to emphasize a point. Blasphemy and Profanity – two genres full of biblically banned words. But the Bible itself has *piss* and *ass*. And Ezekiel 23:20 has saucy language about the size of Egyptian men's private parts. Levi himself would refer the most religious of the bunch to these facts and further argue his point: *it's all about how you use the words. Ass means donkey. Unless you're not talking about a donkey and then it means, well, you know. As for every other of those cuss words, well, God put them in the Bible didn't He? Damn and damnation and damnable are all over the Bible! They're there to emphasize a judgment. And I use it the same way. To make judgments. So, it's fair to use any word that God puts in the Good Book - and in your heart. Makes sense don't it?*

Even the wise owl couldn't argue with such logic.

As for the preening feathered creature, he watched as the years marched on; as men from the Civilian Conservation Corps – the CCC – continued building roads, trails, picnic areas and visitor centers. Restoring the land. Men were very happy to have jobs during this Great Depression. Thirty dollars a month they earned! Even if twenty-five dollars of that was automatically sent home to their families as part of the program, five dollars a month was still a decent wage for a young man who was also provided clothing, room, and board.

They could sign up for six months and renew every six months for up to two years. It was a win-win for both government and men – the government could provide jobs and stimulate the terrible economy while also conserving land, while the men had their needs taken care of, their families' plights were eased, and they felt good about performing meaningful work.

Colonel Townsend watched all of this from various vantage points: his mill in Townsend, his Little River Lumber Company operating just to the west in Walker Valley, now known as Tremont, his cottage in Elkmont that he still owned. Slowly, as the days, seasons rolled by, the trees rooted once again, turned crimson and back to green, grew up, up towards a blue sky, spearing the sun nailed to its heavenly roof.

28

———

REBUILDING - 1934

THE BRICKS HAVE FALLEN, BUT WE WILL
BUILD WITH DRESSED STONES; THE
SYCAMORES HAVE BEEN CUT DOWN, BUT
WE WILL PUT CEDARS IN THEIR PLACE.

~

"Can't quite recall how it all looked." Lem Ownby smiled ironically.

"Ah, Lem. You never been able to see since you was a youngin'!" Levi scolded his friend lightly.

"Yeah, but I can recall the smell. Which made me see it in my mind. Reckon I recall the feel of the road and the big iron horse comin' into the station to drop off folk...they all sounded like cattle runnin' on a tin roof when they got off the train and they got to runnin' down the platform towards their cottages! It was like they were allowed to breathe and live again for just two weeks, and they knew it!"

The two old mountain men laughed but it was all tinged with sadness. For at its peak, Elkmont, consisting of Daisytown, Society Hill, and Millionaire's Row, boasted around seventy dwellings. Commercial buildings such as barns and storage shacks rounded out the community. Gleaming in the sunlight, the golden days of the mountain resort had been fun. Entertaining. Useful. Inviting. All that was old now.

But today, finally, something was new.

The fire which had destroyed the original Appalachian Club on November 30, 1932, was very fresh in most memories, but during this year, 1934, the club had been fully restored, something the two old men rejoiced in.

The club was sporting freshly hewn wooden walls and finely smoothed floorboards. Larger windows beckoned people over to its sills and panes to admire the views. People still stepped off that grand and steaming iron horse named the *Elkmont Special* and walked down from the station towards their home for the next few weeks, the home that may not have been where they were from, but where they felt they belonged. Where their soul felt wanted.

Down the street towards the north, The Wonderland stood, grand as always, hosting parties and teas and dances and was fully booked every summer and even during the bookend seasons of spring and fall.

"Especially fall when all those goddamn leaf-peepers come off the train." Levi spat out. "I can almost hear 'em oohing and aahing over red and yellow leaves all the way to my farm! You'd a-thought they'd never seen a leaf before!"

Two wise mountain men looked out, pondering how much has changed. Lem was only forty-five years old, and though his face was only softly lined, his small stature and hunched figure, from afar, made him look sixty. Levi was eighty-two, still living in Monroe County.

He was here in Elkmont right now, visiting for just a few days, remembering, looking out at his childhood and over eighty years of memories. Oh, how he missed this place! His new farm was nice, peaceful, but he never felt rooted like he did at Elkmont. And for all his grouching about never coming back, he managed to return once or twice a year.

The old Prophet of the Smokies murmured to his blind friend, almost in a whisper: "It'll be five more years. That's about it. Probably less. It's 1934 and the park has been established. Ain't no goin' back now. Reckon in five more years, Colonel's lumber company will be no more. But even if the park hadn't come in, he'd still have to move his operations further away 'cause there would be no more trees left to fell!"

Lem nodded in agreement. "And when it does close, it'll be yet another change. I admit I've gotten used to the noise! Used to bother me more but...listen...you can still hear the owl hootin' and hollerin'. Hear him? He knows you're back here, Levi!"

Sure enough, the owl who loved the daytime was whistling out his song.

"Sounds like he's sayin' 'who cooks for you?'."

"He he. Sure does! And right here on my front porch where we're sittin' right now – you can listen to the fields and the bees hummin' so bad you just know it's time to gather the honey in June and then again in August. Maybe September if the bees need a bit more time to cap the cells. But durin' the summertime – June, July, and even into August – well, you can hear the hum of humans higher than the buzzin' bees. And I done got used to the train whistle long ago, the buzz of the porch parties, and all them fireworks on the Fourth of July."

"Reckon you recall those folks who visited during the Christmas holidays about a year or so before I moved to the farm?"

"Yessir, Levi. I sure do recall that. It was rare to have visitors durin' that time of the year. So cold and nothin' to do but hike for an hour before warming by the fire. But I reckon they were here for about a week, and we told 'em all about the Christmas Serenades. You recall, Levi, how fun that was seein' their faces when we told 'em what we do 'round these parts for the Christmas holiday?" Lem slapped his knee and chuckled at the memories.

"Lem! I recall fifty years of serenadin' before I just stayed home and then folk started serenaded *me*! What fun that was."

Wistful eyes met unseeing ones as the friends reminisced about that unique Appalachian tradition of running up on a house on Christmas Eve, yelling, singing carols, clanging cowbells, shooting rifles, and then, once the homeowners couldn't take it anymore, they'd invite the raucous revelers inside to give them treats. Apples, candy sticks, nuts, sorghum cookies and hot biscuits, blackberry tea, and coffee, greeted frozen serenaders. Many used this mountain ritual for courting, taking the chance to walk with a pretty girl or handsome boy in the dark. Taking the chance to hang back a bit and plan a future in the muscled arms of the most beautiful mountains on earth.

"Ah, the good ol' days. Thank the good Lord we was able to live that way for a long time. Wouldn't have had it any other way."

"Me neither. But it went by way too fast. Think on it: you gotta go way back to remember when Colonel's railroad and his Little River Lumber Company weren't all over these here parts. Then they done moved on to where they could fell more trees. They employed just about everyone in the town. And now...the park is here. Elkmont has met its end. At least, the Elkmont we know."

Levi and Lem combined well over a hundred years of living history. They'd seen Elkmont morph from the Little River Community to a logging town, to a resort town, and now, part of a national park. The future was uncertain – would Elkmont remain a resort? Would those few life leases for cottage owners be extended? If not, would the park service raze the buildings to the ground? Wiping out any evidence of family, fun, energy, and strong bonds that somehow occur while people stray from the usual routine of life?

Things were indeed ending. The human harp played

mournfully, like it was wailing: *why oh why does the great song of progress have to come at the expense of us mountain folk who lived here for years? Decades?*

Other things were just beginning: the automobile was quickly replacing the iron horse. People liked control over how fast they went, when they arrived, and when they could leave. No more train schedules to confine their plans. That owl of ours looked on from thicker branches, thicker than he'd seen in years. He wondered if the mountains breathed in peace, if restoration of its limbs was what it wanted after all.

Some things stayed the same: city folk still flocked to Elkmont to spend family time and breathe the mountain air. And two tired men, one old and one blind, pondered this and that and what was good and what was bad and what would change and what would never be altered and how loudly one should yell *goddamn it all* because they were sure the mountains would, eventually, make sure that everything remained balanced and as it should be.

"Apparently, the mountains are likin' this." It was late the next morning, and Levi was bidding Lem goodbye. He had to make it back to Monroe County, back to his farm. Bessie was waiting for him, as were his grown children and grandchildren and great-grandchildren.

"How do you know?"

"Trees are growin' again. The balds are fillin' in. And look. There's the owl. Now, I reckon that owl's comin' around a lot more than it used to?"

Lem nodded. "Now that I think on it, yes, it's true. I hear him a lot more lately."

"Well, that's because there's more food here for him. Rats and rodents are all over the two clubs. Especially by the back kitchen doors. He's also got more leaves and trees to roost in. I think he's happy."

"He is. For the most part. Makin' the best of things, I reckon." Lem said looking out wistfully at blobs of green and brown and a hanging tapestry of blue.

Levi closed his eyes for a moment, filling his lungs with Elkmont air. Nodding, he stood up and shook Lem's hand without another word. Bid goodbye to Mimmie with his thanks for a double batch of her famous honey cookies. And then he started down the road in his ox-cart, leaving his old home of Elkmont to return to his new home on the farm, flashes of vivid memories accompanying him on his journey.

Remember, experiences are the most meaningful. Because they turn into memories. It's what the mountains give us.

29

GOODBYE - 1936

...AND THE MOUNTAINS ASSURED THE
COLONEL AND THE PROPHET: YOUR LEGACY
IS NOT IN LEAVING SOMETHING FOR
OTHERS. IT'S LEAVING SOMETHING IN THEM.

~

The year 1936 began with the death of a king.

On January 20th, King George V died at Sandringham; his son, Edward, succeeded him. Little did the world suspect that by the end of this year, an American divorcee would waltz in to rock the eight-hundred-seventy-year-old monarchy. Such a strong love caused King Edward VIII to abdicate, leaving a shaken nation, and his brother Albert, now King George VI, in his wake.

All the while, Agatha Christie's detective novel, *The A.B.C. Murders,* was first published, and on February 6th, the Olympics began in, of all places, Germany, at Garmisch-Partenkirchen in the Bavarian Alps.

At home in America, on February 8th, the first-ever NFL draft was held. Jay Berwanger from the University of Chicago was the first-ever pick and went to the Philadelphia Eagles.

By the time February 1936 was finished, in the remote American mountains of Tennessee where the Smoky Mountains lay sleeping under a heavy winter mist, the world lost a prophet and a colonel.

IT WAS A SATURDAY, February 15, 1936, and snow was plentiful. An old neighbor of Levi's had succumbed to "cold sleepiness" where the body temperature gets low and the "old mind tells a person to go to sleep. Then, they never wake up, having frozen to death". Upon hearing the sad news, Levi's wife piled extra blankets over her husband so the cold sleepiness wouldn't grab hold.

He hadn't been up from their bed in a week. Nor had he urinated. Worried, she tried to bring him soup, hot tea, coffee. But he wasn't interested in any of it. He just slept under a pile of blanketed memories, awakening occasionally to murmur about respecting nature and his own spirit and that both should be respected. Remembered. This and that came out of his mouth and some final "goddamn illness and weather" that were somehow interconnected and to "pay attention to the signs around you so you can live in harmony".

As the dawn peeked out as if making sure it was indeed time to make its appearance on such a gray cold morning, Levi whispered what would be his final prophetic words: "hold onto your stories, your knowledge. Connect to the land whether you're in the goddamn city or out in your fields of corn. Change is comin' but hold onto your heritage. Pass down your wisdom 'cause God knows the *furriners* will need it. In fact, the outside world will hunger for it."

"Levi? Are you in pain?" Bessie asked, urging a bit of stew, a sip of coffee. Levi waved it all away.

"No." Weakly, he took her hand. "Just remember me. I'll go with God by nightfall. When I do, just remember that the greatest knowledge..." he took a breath and seemed to fall into a sleep. It was silent for a few minutes before he summoned the strength for his final thoughts.

"...comes from simple livin' and quiet observation. Them mountains...they will tell you everything. Give you everything. Listen to 'em. Tread lightly. Just listen."

At 3:00 p.m., one week before his eighty-fourth birthday, Levi Trentham, son, husband, father, grandfather, bear hunter, Prophet of the Smokies, Mayor of Elkmont, Spirit of the Smokies, Legend, passed into his Lord's hands.

Bessie watched her husband's spirited soul slip away, a slight smile on his face. His eyes had suddenly opened, and he looked at something. Searched the wooden ceiling with his eyes. Found a point and fixated on it.

And then, he was gone.

Two days later, on Monday, February 17, 1936, Levi Trentham was buried according to his wishes, in his beloved Elkmont. Family, friends, relatives, "almost filled the little Elkmont Baptist Church", what with seven still-living children, sixty-four grandchildren, and one hundred and ten great-grandchildren.

The undertaker, C.H. Biereley, arrived and filled out the Death Certificate.

> *Levi Trentham. February 15, 1936 at 3:00 p.m.,*
>   *Madisonville, Tennessee*
> *Cause of Death: retention of urine due to prostate*
>   *hypertrophy and congestion*
> *Register No.: 798*
> *Male, White, Married.*
> *Trade: None*
> *Informant: Jonas Trentham*
> *Date of Burial: Feb 17th at Elkmont*

Undertaker: C.H. Biereley, Madisonville, Tennessee

WORDS ON AN OBITUARY PAGE. Neat margins containing all the comings and goings and doings of one simple life. But mere verses and phrases could never sum up such a man, would not ever capture the dusty relics of so many seasons, crops – both good years and bad – bear pelts, children, love, grief, railing against scalding reminders of the dishonesty of life's promises, yet with the earnestness of a lifelong believer of hope and freedom.

Levi Trentham loved, laughed, lived his entire life inside the Great Smoky Mountains. He yelled, made friends and enemies, became famous, crossed bridges, and saw into the future more than he wanted to see. Nothing stopped him. He stared, glared even, eyes wide open. For it was there, gazing into the honest eyes of fate, that he realized his final prophecy.

THE FUNERAL WAS SOMBER, yet joyous moments made for a celebration of life atmosphere, for Baptists believe eternal life is reached through faith in Jesus Christ. A few whispered that Levi's mouth got him into trouble and made God doubt his faith, but don't tell that to anyone who knew him well because they would say no, absolutely that is not true. Levi's faith was strong in his own straightforward way; he just expressed himself differently - with urgent and colorful language that merely got his point across in a better way than *gosh darn it* or *what in tarnation* could possibly do.

Christian hymns and reading of Scripture punctuated the service, people rose to share personal stories of Levi's impact and their assurance that his soul was now reunited with God in the afterlife.

When the coffin was lowered into the ground, people lingered. Threw dirt on top, covering the Prophet with the rich and fertile dirt of Elkmont, Tennessee. Where Levi had felt most at home, at one with his land. The gravesite took on an air of a song, mystic chords of memory stretching themselves across hushed voices and a few tears. Bessie joined the large crowd, hugging family, reminiscing, and answering one question that everyone wanted to know, but only a young great-grandson dared ask: what was his final prophecy?

THROUGHOUT HIS LIFE, Levi was a storyteller. Sharing, receiving - stories are the very daughters of prophecy. Experiencing many lives through storytelling is a way for the brain to process many possibilities, many perspectives. Somehow, they coalesce into something that Levi Trentham understood and could see - and most importantly, add to.

It is therefore fitting that his final prophecy was a plea: *keep our cherished Smoky Mountain lifestyle alive. No matter what.*

No matter a national park and millions of visitors.

No matter if trees are struck by lightning, or floods cave in creek banks.

No matter if preserved cabins fell or rotted away; if the national park displaced or even destroyed family farms. If all that is gone, there is still a way: through stories. Stories will remain; they've outlasted the best and the worst of us, after all. If only someone — just one person - is willing to tell them, preserve them. Honor them. Write them down in a book perhaps. Do not let our stories become erased on the grand green chalkboard of history. Pass down your wisdom and practices.

Because who would know how to tell if a newly discovered

herb or plant is safe to eat? *Why, give it to the cow, of course! If it was good enough for the milk cow and the animal was just fine two days later, it was good enough for us.*

Who would be around to tell where the name Trentham came from in the first place? *It is derived from the English, by the way, if you didn't know. From Trentham in Staffordshire, England, which takes its name from the river Trent. Trent means "the trespasser" because the river was prone to flooding, thus trespassing on the land. Ham, of course, is Old English meaning village or homestead. Sometimes, it's spelled Hamm with an extra "m" which meant enclosure or meadow. How would you know that nowadays unless you looked it up? Which is easy enough, but someone, somewhere must care enough to look it up now don't they?*

Who would tell everyone about Levi's famous Armstrong rifle – the one who dared him to get *probably about a hundred bear maybe more* in his lifetime. Courage indeed, of the kind that is not exactly fearless, owing nothing to bravado or daredevil abandon, but was the pure product of experience, skill, and will.

And would anyone remember that large family who were on their way to visit relatives in Elkmont and were stopped by Levi Trentham as they passed near his cabin? There were twelve of them on the road and he saw it all as if looking through a cloud. He called out to them, "Hi folks! Wherever you're goin', please do not cross the river this evening."

"Why not? The water level is the lowest I ever seen it!"

"I know. And the weather is calm right now and it don't seem like anythin' will happen. But don't do it."

"You're our relatives' neighbor right? Levi? They call you some sort of prophet?" The husband and father asked.

"Somethin' like that. But please do not cross the river tonight."

"Thank you for the advice." And they went on their way. All twelve of them. They found they couldn't ignore this strange glaring man in the middle of the mountains. They'd certainly heard of him. Heard from their relatives that the strange prophesizing man was always right and no matter what, he should be listened to. They arrived at their relatives' home the next day wet, soaked to the bones, but alive, for last night, a sudden storm had indeed hit the area with such ferocity that the river flooded to dangerous levels.

Upon arriving at their kinfolk, they exclaimed, "We're here only by the Grace of God. And your neighbor, Levi Trentham, the one who everyone calls the prophet!"

Confused, the family quickly told of their encounter meeting the old mountain man and his determined warning.

"My word! If you'da crossed the river, you woulda been swept away, all twelve of you!"

Even though they were Baptists, that entire family said their Hail Mary's three times that night.

It's up to all of us now to honor Levi Trentham's final prophecy, his final wish.

The best way to do that?

Be in nature.

Breathe in the memories of the mountains. Listen to your inner voice, tune into the forest, the animals, the people before you. There is more to life than what meets the eye. If you choose to reconnect with that part of yourself, you will hear the mountains smile, smell their sweet, craggy faces turned towards the sun. See what the mountains gave them. Feel what they give to you.

Bessie, Levi's second wife, confirmed this. *He don't want you to mourn too much now. His final wishes were truly this: for folk to tell his stories of growin' up, even of him yellin' at Ol' Glory, yellin' at Red Cross women, and yellin' at himself for not saying more. But then, he also wants you to tell all those stories of the bear hunter he was, how he helped chop wood for the logging families who were too busy working on the railroad and felling trees to chop wood for their own families. Of sharing trout with those same families who appreciated good food, breaded with all the Southern style one could muster on a Wednesday afternoon in the middle of summer. Of being a living embodiment of those stubborn blue mountains, the ones livin' just how they wanted, yet adapting as needed. Please,* Bessie asked her family and friends, *Tell the stories. Tell the stories - all of them. That's what he said. Tell the ones you like and the ones you don't like. Especially the ones you don't like 'cause those are the ones that teach the most. Keep this place alive. Keep Levi alive. Keep all of us alive.*

A FEW DAYS LATER, Mrs. Ivah Murphy tearfully made her way to visit Levi's widow who had remained in the Elkmont area with relatives for a few more days. "Oh, we can surely do that – what you said about Levi wanting to keep it all alive! In fact, it's already happening! Let me tell you about the newspaper. Did you see it yet, Mrs. Trentham?"

"Nah, I never saw no newspaper. Did the page mention Levi?"

"Oh yes ma'am. It said in big bold letters: *Levi Trentham, Famed Bear Hunter, is Dead.*"

"Famed bear hunter? Ha! He woulda loved that!" Bessie smiled widely.

Mrs. Murphy dug a copy from her purse, smoothed it out and read it to the widow.

Gatlinburg, Tenn., Feb. 18 – (AP) – Uncle Levi Trentham, 84, famed as a guide and bear hunter in the Great Smoky Mountains, is dead.

. . .

"Read more of it to me, will you? I can't read too well."

"Of course, Mrs. Trentham. The article goes on to say how the little church was all filled up and how many descendants he has."

Bessie marveled at the article. Her reading skills weren't strong, but she could make out the small columns with the big headline honoring her husband and the many words of praise.

"Levi *was* a good one. Always knew where you stood with him. Surely a one of a kind man…" Bessie said, tapping the newspaper before looking up. "Ah, here's Mr. Ownby!"

The near-blind man stepped onto the front porch of the relative's home where Bessie was staying for a few more days. She sighed that she just didn't want to go back to her farm in Monroe County just yet. It would be so empty without Levi…

"Bessie. Good to see ya again. The funeral was…well, it was what Levi woulda wanted. Levi was like a brother to me. Both of us stayed 'round these parts like a pair of stubborn ol' mules. But he moved away. Maybe I shoulda. But I'm still on my land."

"I'm mighty glad you are, Lem. How's Mimmie?"

"Fine, fine. She's right over there talkin' to the ladies." He pointed out the tall middle-aged woman. She still helped her near-blind husband navigate the world outside of his farm and homestead, but within it, he was as comfortable as ever, still tending bees, farming, sitting in his favorite chair by the door so he could feel the breezes come through.

"And how is it in Elkmont these days? Are you lonely? I hear more people have moved out."

"No. Not really. Never lonely. But it's true that there's less folk around these days. Even my Uncle Nathan took the government money and got some land over in Wears Valley, on the north side of Cove Mountain. But the resort and the club are still very popular. Won't be the same without Levi though.

He's been gone from Elkmont for awhile now, but his spirit – I can't explain it – it still lingers around. And the people talk about him all the time! And they tell his stories!"

"Indeed." Bessie hung her head, smiling, talking to her deceased husband. *Your final wishes came true even before you died. Did you know it?*

"You know how we talk about our grandmas and granddaddys. Well, that's the way of keepin' them alive. Tell their stories so youngins know of 'em. Know their wisdom and ways of doin' things."

"Indeed, that *was* his dyin' wish..."

"I know." Lem said with a twinkle in his short-sighted eyes. "We will never forget it."

Bessie marveled as she felt something unknotting inside, like a skein of yarn loosening, soft in her hands. Grief was there but lessened. Sweeter. "Levi's voice still stirs the wind I reckon." She looked out at the beautiful day, slopes reaching towards the sky, an owl perched right over there. All the people whose lives were touched by her famous husband.

"Levi - he's in the creek beds and in his rifle that lays over the mantle. He's by the hearth fire at night. And he's in the memories of those who knew him." Lem held the widow's hand, gripping it tightly as she whispered those words to her husband's dearest friend.

The small crowd nodded heads in solemn agreement; finally, Lem said he'd better get back to Mimmie so they could get on home. Hugging, shaking hands, gratefully taking a few biscuits for the way home, and bidding goodbyes, Lem Ownby looked around as if he actually saw - even with his weak eyes - the soft waves of the Smoky Mountains, as if seeing them for the first time.

Turning one last time to Bessie and a knot of Trentham great-grandchildren. "Youngins. This is important and I don't know if you've been listenin', but if you haven't, now's the time.

One thing your great-grampa - Levi Trentham - did was tell his stories. He did it so well that I reckon I myself can't recall whether the man himself told the stories or if he just listened and repeated as the mountains told theirs. Either way, he shaped how we think about ourselves. And that's the best gift these mountains could ever give. If you choose not to listen, well, what the mountains can give you, they can also take away. It's easy for them to do such a thing you know."

"Well said, Lem." Ivah Murphy whispered softly looking at the peaks, caps of snow atop each one. Youngins nodded, solemn, most of them, enough of them, listening to this older man with the milky eyes.

"The Prophet of the Smokies...goodbye my friend."

"Farewell, the Mayor of Elkmont."

"I love you, Uncle Levi."

"Goodbye, Grampa. We will miss you a lot!"

"The Spirit of the Smokies...he's within all of us."

"And now, in the hands of God." Lem Ownby said, holding his wife's arm. "Before we go, I'd like to add one more name for Levi Trentham: The Keeper of Mountain Wisdom. He holds that honor forever. We're just here to make sure that message continues."

MANY COULDN'T ATTEND the funeral or the days afterwards but sent messages of condolence to Bessie and Levi's large family. Mayna Avent, the artist, wrote that she knew Levi Trentham not as a fellow artist but as a fellow mountaineer, *a colorful witness to the divine simplicity of a life in the hills and hollers and highest peaks. I may see light and shadow and color and transfer them to canvas,* she wrote, *but Mr. Levi Trentham heard stories in the wind, saw truth and wisdom rustling in the trees. Most importantly, he listened and shared.*

Colonel Townsend also sent word:

> Dear Mrs. Trentham, I am too ill to attend, but I hope to feel better soon to pay a visit to you. I will remember Levi as a spirited spirit that could have only happened within the blue walls of these beautiful Smoky Mountains. As much a part of this world as the mountains themselves, he lived and breathed the air of freedom. I am forever grateful to have known him. Rest in peace Levi, and may God be with you. Bessie, please accept my deepest sympathies on your loss. Tell the family the same and I will visit soon.

30

FAREWELL - 1936

AN OAK TREE FALLS; A TITAN DECORATED WITH HARD WORK AND KINDNESS.

≈

"Today, we say goodbye to a titan of industry. A good man whose word was gold. Who took care of his workers and his family; took care of everyone."

Six days after burying Levi Trentham, the Smoky Mountain community reeled with another profound loss.

February 23, 1936, saw family members, employees, friends, and CCC folks crisscrossing the mountain valleys on horseback, in wagons, on foot, even in automobiles, to spread the news.

The Colonel has passed. Eighty-one years old. A legacy. Now, he will join his two wives who have already passed. His third wife, Alice, is grief-stricken but determined to continue her husband's wishes. Continue his beloved logging company's remaining logging rights. Railroads. Sawmills. The Tennessee town of Townsend.

Quite a legacy.

The funeral was the largest many had ever seen. The slightly warmer weather that arrived for Levi's funeral just last week gave way to the bite of a bitter and icy winter, the kind when Earth tried in vain to tilt her frozen face towards the sun, to no avail. No heat could work itself inside.

A leader. Independent and could do just about anything he set his mind to. Had three wives, a large and loving family. Was successful, yet a risk-taker. Cheerful. Confident.

And the Colonel did so much for others that many don't even know about!

The gathering of mourners traded stories and anecdotes. Workers, ones who'd logged the land for decades, lamented on the death of the oak tree that was Colonel Townsend: *One wonders how these good deeds aren't well-known while one lives. But then one always thinks there's time for such things, to talk about this and that and to share what someone else had done for them even when said person didn't have to. Only when you can't say thank you anymore does the urge remind you, overwhelm you, with a need to tell others.*

Subdued loggers and railroad workers - many tearful - shared their own memories. *The Colonel gave college scholarships to some of the logger's children, including mine. That's the only way my two boys coulda gone to college. And now one's an engineer and one's a teacher.*

His first wife, Margaret, brought presents every year for Christmas, but did you know she put up a Christmas tree too? Right in the middle of Stringtown. And it was beautiful! Full of candy and popcorn and even colorful strings of yarn and paper that the children made under her supervision. Glue, yarn, paper, scissors...everything was provided for those kids to have a little color in their lives. Oh, how they loved it! Christmastime was the best time in Stringtown. That was a long time ago, but I recall it like it was yesterday. She even arranged a special movie to be shown on Christmas evening, and for every evening thereafter until New Year's Day.

Townsend also built a baseball field; did you know that? Right next to the school; employees and all their youngins could enjoy America's pastime, as they call the game. He even hired semi-pro players to work just a little bit during the week, mostly office jobs. And then on weekends, he and his workers would watch them play some really great baseball. He figured the town needed morale boosting and baseball was definitely a way to do that.

I remember. But my memory goes to somethin' else: when a local flu outbreak happened…just last year…in 1935…

Heads bowed and *amens* were proffered in remembrance of that horrible time just a year ago when the flu swept through Stringtown and killed thirteen children from Elkmont and nearby Tremont.

The Colonel was always around during that terrible time. He would comfort, let us have all the time we needed to mourn. And he paid for all the small coffins. And all the funerals…

The Colonel also helped Dorie Cope's family when that sheepdog of hers kept rounding up the cows and sheep in the middle of the day and herded them right through the logging operations! He pushed the cows with his own hands and turned his own sheepdogs loose to push them all back to pasture. 'That dog is too good at what he does', he'd say. 'He can round up any herd at any time… too bad that dog can't tell time – can't wait 'til the evening when we're done working!' Oh, but Dorie doted on the Colonel. Gave her a chance to raise a family in the mountains, she said, and that was the best thing in the world 'cause "raising a family in the mountains is far easier than in Knoxville where economic inequality, materialism, and temptations for my children present unforeseen challenges."

He was a man who could fit in anywhere, they all agreed. In the depths of the mountains, in Townsend at the mill, in the boardroom and at the stock exchange, on the steps of car shacks in Stringtown, at The Wonderland Club Hotel, or on the front porch of The Appalachian Club.

I'll surely miss him at the supper – not dinner! - table. His footsteps would make the wood floors creak, and he'd exclaim how every cobbler whether it was peach or apple or cherry was the best cobbler ever made! And then he'd keep a few crumbs to feed the raccoons on the porch after dinner.

They reminisced for days. Former and current workers, staff, friends, family.

He'd come back from visiting The Wonderland and describe it to his workers as he was inspecting the logs, urging all of them to take a break under the shade of poplars: 'It's nice, to be sure. Ladies in their finery just sitting on the wide front porch, looking at the scenery, fanning flies away. They are all perfumed and painted and they ask no questions about us here in the 'logging town' as they call it. They simply want to know about my trains and where they go and if I have a tapestry in my house and then they ask to see my pocket watch and inquire if I'd read Little House on the Prairie or National Velvet which are two of the most popular novels right now and how many trees were left and if my wife and I would like to join them for the dance on Saturday night and perhaps again for tea on Wednesday? Well, with all those questions, my head spun! So I made my excuses, gave my thanks for the invitations, and got right back here. I want to be where my company is. Where my workers are.'

"He was that kind of boss," one employee almost whispered.

And then another one: "Yessir. He was that kind of person."

And finally, "He was that kind of man".

And all nodded and whispered together: *The best kind.*

THE CCC CAMP closed later that same year of 1936.

Earlier in the 1930s, The Wonderland Club had reverted to a more traditional hotel rather than a club. It continued to host lively parties, but also kept a retro, rustic vibe. The two clubs stayed open, even during the next Great War, which everyone now called World War II. After that, the number of vacationers dwindled. Membership and attendance at The Appalachian

Club slowly died off, and by 1950, no events were being held in the clubhouse. Even when The Wonderland closed in 1992, it didn't have TVs or telephones in the rooms.

Logging ceased in 1939. Workers of The Little River Lumber Company - the large and successful company started by Colonel Townsend - cut through the last thread of a massive white oak. This would be the last tree felled by The Little River Lumber Company and the last tree felled in what was now the Great Smoky Mountains National Park.

Workers murmured as the last hums of the last crash of trees split the land: *all this work for nearly forty years. We did a good job here. And now...* Sighs. *And now the land goes back to the mountains. Back to God.*

It was silent. Not even the owl was around. There weren't many trees left where the last of the loggers stood, and the owl had to climb higher into the remaining canopies and higher on the slopes to find adequate shelter. It did not like being out in the open.

When President Roosevelt dedicated the park to America on that crisp day of September 2nd, 1940, tens of thousands of visitors listened, while long-time mountain folk like Lem Ownby and the descendants of Levi Trentham reflected on why visitors wanted to see how they once lived – and were still living. What was the big deal? They'd lived like this their entire lives! Had seen their parents and grandparents live the same way! If these city folk liked it so much, why didn't they move here to see how they felt when a government of free people took their land? How'd they like to feel the bitterness of giving up their ancestral land for the greater good?

They whispered amongst themselves, recalling one of Levi Trentham's prophecies: *'cause if you don't remember the good ol' days, the mountains will only remind you of the bad.* Oh, he was almost as famous for that prophecy as he was about his *goddamn Ol' Glory* arrest and his *Red Cross whores* arrest and his tendency to dismiss many of the goddamn *furriners* rustling around his neck of the woods.

Besides, what did *the greater good* really mean?

To President Roosevelt, it meant: *The old frontier, that put the hard fibre in the American spirit and the long muscles on the American back, lives and will live in these untamed mountains to give to the future generations a sense of the land from which their forefathers hewed their homes.*

But Levi saw it as something else. Which he repeated only to a rare few.

A young wolf, one of Cherokee lore. Eager to prove himself, the young wolf ventures out into the forest at night and meets a wise old owl perched on a thick branch. "Hello, wise owl. Please share your secrets about the best hunting ground!"

To which the owl, holding the stare of the bold young wolf, replies, "There is a hidden valley teaming with prey and pretty things. But watch for the silent shadows at your heels. For where there is shadow, there is no light."

The wolf paused, pondered the meaning, but impatient, impulsive, eager to prove his prowess, he rushed down into the hidden valley, no longer considering any of the owl's warnings.

To his surprise, there was nothing! No obstacles, no threats, but no prey either. When he returned to the owl, he howled in complaint! "Why did you send me into a hidden, but empty valley?"

"Oh, you don't know?"

"No, I don't know! Why?! I demand you answer me!"

"You just answered your very question yourself."

The wolf reared back, ready to pounce upon this brash and annoying bird if he ever even thought to fly away!

"I have no such answer!"

"Ah, but you do. It's the fight of the two wolves within you. Whichever wolf you feed — the greedy, violent, prideful one, or the respectful, kind, humble one — that's the one you will follow. You followed the first one — and you got an empty valley."

After a few minutes of sulking, whining, moaning and grumbling, the wolf opened his eyes to see...nothing. No owl. Not a creature to lash out at. Another hour passed and the wolf decided to take matters into his own hands. He walked back to the valley and found it teaming with prey! How did that happen? Was it the time of day? Luck? No. For he soon he realized it was the second wolf making its appearance.

When he was alive, Levi used to moralize that famous and old Cherokee story: "it's important to possess physical strength alongside cautious courage." But when the time came, he immediately recognized that he had encountered a different kind of wolf named "The Government", who preached "The Greater Good", and goddamn if he didn't grab that wolf by the ears! And held on tight!

In time, however, Levi understood that he could neither hold nor safely let that wolf go. And so, he fled to preserve what was left of himself, exclaiming, "I just hope the damn government and the greater good knows what the hell they're doin'... 'cause," - and he used to pause right here in the retelling of this well-known, altered-for-the-situation story - "it ain't the greater good for *me*."

31

DISMANTLED - 1940S- 1950S

LOOK CLOSELY: YOU CAN SEE HOW
GORGEOUS SHE WAS WHEN SHE
WAS YOUNG; HER BONES, STILL
THERE, LIKE ARCHEOLOGICAL RUINS
BENEATH THE EYES OF A MOUNTAIN.

By 1942, most of Elkmont's buildings were gone, many dismantled for their lumber. One by one, the boards - both crude and well-hewn, bare and white-washed or even painted blue and green – were taken down and burned, charred chips like discarded bones in a graveyard. Levi Trentham would have asked to burn the wood himself, for cooking, for heat – at least he could make some use of it. Waste nothing, he'd say. But he was gone, couldn't use the wood, and thank goodness for that, for it would've broken what was left of his heart to see his hometown scorched by the thick flames of progress.

LIFE CONTINUED. Lifetime leases were renegotiated as the owl looked on, from further away now. 1952 saw the park and members of both Wonderland and Appalachian Clubs giving up their lifetime leases in exchange for fixed twenty-year leases.

They figured they were getting older, and a twenty-year lease would likely last longer than a "lifetime" one.

In the face of all this, residents boldly requested to add to the progress of things: electric service to the entire resort. To which the park readily agreed, which was surprising and strange given they were trying to get the land back to its original state. But it wasn't a big deal. After all, most buildings were gone so it would not be a lot of work to bring electric to less than twenty cabins and buildings and two clubs.

Lem marveled at the leap in progress: "Sevier County Electric Company is installin' lines right now. Reckon we'll see the light all night long by the end of the year."

As for The Appalachian Club, its new frame, rebuilt from the fire of 1932, held up very well under the elements…and all the people! Though attendance dipped for a while, now, there were more tourists than ever, especially since the diesel-powered generators were installed at the northern end of the Elkmont community where the dam on the Little River was built.

One lady wrote home:

> Electric lights and generators make life more
> comfortable here in Elkmont though it's
> lights-out at 10:00 p.m. But on Saturday
> nights, we can leave the lights on until 1:00
> a.m. and not have to dance in the dark. Oh,
> and there are the most peculiar and curious
> people who are talked about quite often.
> Even people who are long gone. For exam-
> ple, I keep hearing about a man named Levi
> Trentham, who many call Uncle Levi or the
> Prophet of the Smokies, and who passed in
> 1936. People around here tell me exactly what
> he would say about things such as electric

> lights. They say, 'well, ma'am, Levi used
> some colorful language all the time and he
> would ask you to turn the lights off even if
> they could be on! Especially during a dance
> when there may be some courting going on.'
> When I asked why, they'd say, 'cause Levi
> always said, 'by candlelight, even a goat is
> ladylike'.

The owl chuckled as the refined woman heard the story and immediately went to the club's lobby, grabbed some paper and a pen, and furiously wrote to another friend all about the shockingly folksy man from the Smokies - long dead now, but still talked about.

Stories preserved.

ELECTRIC LIGHTS MAY NOT HAVE BEEN LIGHTING many cabins, but they were illuminating three hundred and forty camp sites at the Elkmont Campground, as well as its amphitheater where people loved to gather.

The owl turned its head towards the mountain. Too much! Too much light, too many tourists, too many automobiles and visitors. All of them loved the views, the creeks, the river. The food at The Appalachian Club. The Wonderland's views. Fishing, with limits according to national park licenses. Hiking. Watching for bears.

But these tourists couldn't meet Levi Trentham or listen to his stories told with his own folksy flavor. They could hike to Mayna Avent's cabin, but she wasn't there anymore to show how to weave a basket or show off her paintings of landscapes. To explain how to fix the injured eyes of people, at least in portraits, and she wasn't there to guide visitors towards one particularly serene canvas of a cabin with a path leading through the trees.

MAYNA AVENT SPENT her last three years with her son in Sewanee, Tennessee, passing away on January 2, 1959. Named after her grandmother who was also an artist, Mayna had, by now, cemented herself as a southern artist, a talented creative from Tennessee, and the moniker that most made her proud: *Smoky Mountain Artist.*

Remembrances and recognitions were numerous, coming from the very land she loved.

The Tennessee State Museum called her "a pathfinder for future generations of women...an important transitional figure in art in Tennessee and in the South."

Many of her works remain: a portrait of Maria Garland, a cook who worked for a prominent Nashville attorney.

"The Log", a woodcut print showing a bare and craggy tree clawing the sky on the right side of the print. The cabin in the middle, a rust-red path leading the way to the front door, green tree on the left.

"Jake's Creek 1914" – a painting of a sitting Martha Ownby before a window dressed in a dark blue skirt, blouse, with a book on her lap, colorful curtains to the left.

"Indian Pinks in the Mountains" - painted on a large rectangle of tin, a testament to the creativity of Mayna Avent. When canvas wasn't available, she used anything she could to paint. Murky peaks sit there in this particular painting; some in darkness, some illuminated with reds and yellows and smooth brown rockiness. Balls of clouds hover above.

So many others: "Magnolias Just Won't Wait", "The Hermitage", and numerous pastoral and colorful paintings simply entitled: "Tennessee Landscape".

Equally adept at still-life, portraits, landscapes, her love for art and her Tennessee home is inescapable to even the most untrained eye. Rare also is the artist who can create in many mediums, yet she could smoothly switch between pen-and-ink sketching, gouache, charcoal, woodcut, watercolors, and graphite pencil. Anything would do when inspiration struck - canvas, a piece of tin, a door, a piece of driftwood.

Indeed, the legacy of Mayna Avent is a solid one, a satisfying one. She loved what the mountains gave her; took from them all the colors of the world.

But what was to happen to her cabin?

Like so many others, the Avent family was awarded some money and a lifetime lease after the government took it over in 1932. That was all fine and wonderful, the family said, relieved for this short reprieve, but what about now that she is gone? What will happen to the famous legacy of one who saw the shades and hues of the wind and painted the very essence of her mountain home in Elkmont? The palette the mountains gave to her.

32

A LARGE GATHERING
OF FOLK - 1960S - 1970S

EVERY ONCE IN A WHILE, SOMETHING
HAPPENS THAT CAUSES TWO
BRANCHES TO STICK TOGETHER
IN A SEMI-PERMANENT EMBRACE.

≈

960s in the United States was a time of change. While people marched for civil rights, America was also working on putting men on the moon, entering a war in Vietnam, and navigating its place amidst the upheaval of yet another transformative decade.

The Smoky Mountains were no different, steering into its own allotted slot in history. Levi Trentham was gone; his prophecies holding even more significance as the years marched forward.

For instance, he foresaw a "large gathering of folk" for which "the mountains would have mixed feelings". Indeed, the Elkmont Campground was hugely popular by now, bringing "a large gathering of folk" interested in camping, fishing, and the history of the area. Vacationers certainly appreciated the beauty, and the mountains relished showing off their cloaks of rusty reds and oranges, preening with their white dogwoods, pink azaleas, and yellow daffodils, and all shades of greenery.

But then the rocky beasts would shrug their shoulders

releasing an angry boulder or two when some would leave trash, get too close to a bear, or rush through the Elkmont Campground and Cades Cove and Little Greenbrier and Cataloochee and Deep Creek, all because city folk needed to get somewhere when they never even realized they'd already arrived.

Many of these campers had tents, but more and more arrived in their recreational vehicles.

The owl marveled at how these so-called 'RVs' had changed from the first ones in 1904! Those early versions were crude – hand-built straight onto automobiles. But they slept four adults in bunks and had an icebox and simple radios. Darkness was tamed by incandescent lights.

Then came REO's Speed Wagon Bungalow and Hudson-Essex's Pullman Coach. The economy was booming by the 1920s when these models came out, quickly followed by "Brintnall's Convertible Camping Trailer", and the "Covered Wagon", which had six thousand on the road by 1936.

Humans love to be comfortable, and the next decades were ones when massive improvements to RVs were made - televisions, king-size beds, kitchens, showers, storage, and easier drivability. Many of these RVers pulled into the Elkmont Campground in the Great Smoky Mountains National Park to marvel at the waves and waves of blue beauty.

THE AMPHITHEATER HELD all sorts of events, advertised in brochures and on bulletin boards: concerts, dances, welcome home pinning ceremonies for veterans, and a place to gather and eat ice cream in the summer. Visitors still encountered the people who lived in the few remaining cabins lining a narrow street, thanks to yet another compromise. One of the last.

In the early 1970s, the owl perched on a quiet day when it

was dry and the creeks were low, to see the descendants of the original summer cottage owners ask for another twenty-year extension.

"Can't believe The Wonderland and The Appalachian Club are united. But they done got together I hear! For the first time in history. Reckon I can't recall another time when they even talked to one another, much less said 'let's form a sort of club where both of us are members'!" Lem Ownby marveled at how life does surprise us now and again. The front porch of Lem's home became a meeting place for the few remaining residents. His neighbors stuck close to their homes these days, but they also liked to check up on Lem, share the news.

"Indeed, Lem. They done formed what they're callin' the Elkmont Preservation Society."

"That's 'cause both clubs and all their members are hopin' to hold off eviction. Their long-term leases done ran out. And they figured they're stronger together. I hope they're right." Lem sighed, looking out at the swaying trees. "Nowadays, things change overnight it seems."

"I hope so too, Lem. Said in *The Maryville Times* that seventy-five percent of the cottage owners that are left signed off on a document between themselves and the Department of the Interior. They done got a Senator to argue for 'em!"

"Them folk were always rich. And well-connected. It helps!" Lem smiled; the neighbors couldn't tell whether it was in admiration or disdain.

But one of the elderly neighbor men went on while the rest rocked in silence, listening. "Senator Estes Kefauver helped negotiate the arrangement. He argued logically: lease-back rights were given to the cottage owners largely because they accepted lower prices for their property when the government acquired them for the park. As a result, the Senator argued, these property owners showed "patriotic generosity" towards the government, without which the park itself may never have been created. Or at least, it would've been greatly delayed."

"Hmm...makes sense. Was the government swayed? Seems those Warshinton men don't much care for anythin' we say around here. They done want it all under their control."

"Surprisingly, Lem, they *were* swayed! They agreed that the cottage owners made such sacrifice and they done agreed to an extension for another twenty years!"

"Seems too easy. Why, maybe I can go back to the government men and tell 'em I want my life lease extended after I die!"

"Heh. It's worth a shot, Lem. But I wouldn't mess with what you already agreed to. Besides, there's a tangle. Like there always is with most so-called compromises. It's not guaranteed, even though it's signed."

Lem raised his eyebrows in question as the neighbor continued.

"Eight to ten families chose to fight to keep their clear-cut titles. As the newspaper explained it, this means they could own their properties until their children pass...but these children of the original owners could live another fifty years! And it's those children, though fewer in number, who could be the ones to stay ownin' the cottages until...who knows when? Imagine that! The government don't like that at all. But they done granted it. And upheld it too. For now."

"Imagine that!" Lem drank from a tin cup, a long drink of spring water. "Didn't think no government men could be fair ever again. Life does surprise...sometimes."

But twenty years or fifty goes by in the blink of an owl's eye. And the government wasn't well-known for upholding such agreements. In fact, they were getting antsier lately, to take control of everything inside the park. Institutions do not like piece-meal contracts; do not like extending twenty years for some, while upholding clear-cut titles for others. It was a messy arrangement.

However, if – *if* - all these agreements could be upheld that would hold things off even further, Elkmont's dimming days could exhale for just a little bit. If not, the community, the way of life, the summers of fun would be completely gone, left only in the embers of old and feeble memories. The forest and mountains would once again lay exclusive claim to its own fortress.

Uncertain days these were, and Lem Ownby stayed mostly on his own land. He would occasionally appear though, every now and then, to visit some of the few remaining Elkmont cottages. To sit on the front porch of The Appalachian Club. To talk to youngins new to the area, marveling at being barefoot all day and skipping rocks in the river. Those youngins always made him laugh. Made him think of his own childhood. Days gone by. The best days.

Lem could see nothing but shadows now, but he certainly heard the quieter nights, the softer voices, the smaller crowds hanging onto memories of summers spent in the peace of one's own land.

But generally, he stuck to his own domain where he was comfortable and content, at least with his lifestyle. Tending his bees, farming, he remained distrusting of government, bitter over the loss of his land. Oh, he was still living on it, this ancestral soil, but he knew it wasn't his anymore and that clawed at him. Knew it was impossible for the land to stay in his family to pass on to nieces, nephews, youngins who could use the land, whomever he wished.

It was in this mood that he took out all his anger on two Supreme Court Justices on a beautiful spring day in the 1970s.

33

THE JUSTICES – 1976

JUSTICE IS ALWAYS READILY ACCESSIBLE.

~

Lem Ownby was eighty-seven years old in 1976. In his younger years, he'd "trapped thirty bear a year, selling the skins for $7 and selling the bear meat to the hotel kitchens of The Appalachian Club and The Wonderland Hotel - and later - its club."

Bear meat was an interesting addition to the menus, but visitors much preferred country ham, trout, and wild rabbit stew with fresh vegetables pulled straight from the oftentimes muddy dirt. Some were grown right on site, but some were "pulled by an oxen-cart from Gatlinburg. Put on ice and packed in sawdust, much produce was hauled by train from Maryville".

Food hauled into town by trains. In packed crates full of ice and sawdust. Everything was so different from all those decades laying behind him.

And he was tired.

A legend by now like Levi Trentham, the blind old man must've absorbed some of his late friend's foretelling powers, for Levi wasn't the only prophet these mountains gave us.

Lem Ownby's lack of eyesight made him see the world for what it really was, and such harsh reality led to some tough decisions. Mimmie had passed away on December 2, 1967, at seventy-eight years old. At some point he realized he couldn't see well enough to take care of her deteriorating physical condition. As much as it pained him, he finally listened to her doctor's advice to place her in a nursing home for around-the-clock care. The Knoxville Convalescent Home cared for her beginning in 1966. Relatives and friends graciously drove Lem to visit Mimmie about twice a week, until she died.

Lem honored her final wishes: to be buried at Valley View Cemetery in Wears Valley. This used to be her family's center of social and religious gatherings for a long time, and it meant a lot to Mimmie. But that wasn't the only reason. She often told Lem: "I have no desire to be buried inside the park where the bears can eat my bones".

As for Lem, he remained on his land and enjoyed relatively good health. "I lay it to the honey", he'd say when asked about his smooth skin and quick healing abilities. "My favorite is the linn honey, made from the basswood or linden tree blooms. It's light and has a slightly minty taste. Too bad it can't make my eyes see, but it's done good for just about everythin' else."

Honey, his familiar home, his land; all kept Lem company, yet he was essentially alone now in the arms of his beloved mountains, save for just a few neighbors left. The 1970s dawned with a still-angry America over the Vietnam War, uncertainty with inflation and political upheaval, along with seismic social changes. But for Lem Ownby, his anger was squarely directed at the government and its people and its national park that included what would forever be *his* land. No matter what name was on the deed. And anyone associated with such government was not welcome.

❧

"Mr. Lemuel S. Ownby, who everyone calls Lem or Uncle Lem, still lives here in the park. I daresay, he himself says he will be the last person to live in the National Park."

The owl turned its head 270 degrees – the most allowable by nature – and saw nothing to counter such a claim. Indeed, the wise creature was able to see the proud old, grizzled mountain man fulfill that very prophecy in the coming years. Except for Kermit Caughron of Cades Cove who died in 1999, Uncle Lem was the last person to live in the National Park, even outliving each of the famous Walker Sisters. He was also the last official lifetime leaseholder to live in the park; Caughron was on an agricultural permit.

"Anyhow, Lem, who we're going to try to visit today, negotiated a land lease. He got less money for his property but is allowed to stay for the rest of his life."

Two other men nodded their heads, wondering aloud how it truly felt to have eminent domain creep right onto their own doorsteps. But the two men knew it to be something they had to follow because it's right there in the Constitution, the Fifth Amendment.

And they followed the Constitution.

After all, it was their job.

"So, this Uncle Lem as everyone calls him, he's blind? But he is a beekeeper, a great trapper and bear hunter, and continues working his land? That's remarkable!"

"Yes, indeed. I, myself, don't know how he does it other than he says he knows every inch of his land better than he knows himself. People come to his home to buy honey and to talk to him. Lots of folk want to talk to him. And he's usually very obliging. Tells us all about his life, how he used to work at The Little River Lumber Company for a few years until one day he refused to work on a piece of equipment because it was defective and broken and wasn't working right. A rail loader I believe it was. Anyway, he quit right then and there, saying, 'If they can't do any better than this, I'm goin' home.' And he did. He's that kind of man, you'll see."

"Do you think he'll be home? I can't wait to meet him!"

"Absolutely! Keep walking…it's not too far now."

The small knot of men walked uphill while discussing how Lem Ownby got by in life despite his blindness, and later, with the help of his wife, Mimmie, until she passed away. Since then, his brother-in-law, Lee Higdon, who loved to fish for trout and worked as a caretaker for The Appalachian Club, kept him company and checked on him, but Lem was largely alone. But he was still feisty and did not like most strangers or the outside world. He especially disliked the government.

"You recall when those Governors had the conference in Gatlinburg about a year or so ago? Well, they were shuttled around town in big purple cars. And Lem said, 'hope they stay away from here, they're puttin' on the dog in them big purdy purple cars!' Now, understand, Lem never drove a car in his life! Much less owned one. Even if he wasn't blind, I don't think he would've embraced anything to do with the modern world."

"I can't wait to meet this man!" One of the men said.

"What about their children?" The other asked, a bit breathless from the uphill hike to Lem's home. It was rural to be sure, and the path was rocky and rough.

"They had no children. Which is unusual for folk like him. Though he wanted 'em. He and Mimmie made up for it though; nieces and nephews and all the neighbor children were always at their house. He loves youngins. Says there's something special about childhood and if someone is in a child's life, that means all the dreams he couldn't have still have a chance."

The two men nodded solemnly. No children? That meant no heirs. Ah well, there's nobody to leave the land to anyway. Because it's the nation's land now.

"Lem was born in 1889 and grew up growing food, tending bees, hunting bear, and telling stories. He's right up here near Jake's Creek." The man pointed uphill and west. "We're almost there."

The sun was high in the sky, hanging in anticipation of what was to come: government men greeting an old blind mountain man whose very same government had taken his land -the very soil that was as much a part of him as his beard and cloudy shaded eyes that were able to, somehow, see it all.

"There was a time when Mr. Ownby welcomed the logging operations. Met Colonel Townsend and thought it would be wonderful, what with jobs and opportunity." The man stopped and waved his hand. "Look around and imagine it! Before large-scale logging occurred, why, there were trees upon trees! Kind of like it is now. But back then, imagine looking out and seeing a tree here and a tree there, but essentially very bare. Lem used to say, 'who would've thought they'd all be gone?'"

Indeed, it took a long time for what is now the Great Smoky Mountains National Park to fill back in with trees. For the first decade or so, because it had been almost fully logged, one could see bare peaks and animals roaming, trying to find some cover.

The owl was forced ever upward, towards slopes that were too steep even for its preferred prey of rat or mouse. Higher still, the creature found it difficult to find a sturdy tree where he could find a nest. And finding a nest was crucial because owls do not make their own; instead, they commandeer previously constructed nests, or roost in barn rafters, cliff cavities, or hollows in trees. *Kind of like the government with their damned national park.*

Lem Ownby's thoughts echoed Levi Trentham's gritty voice as he tipped his chair back. He sat just inside his home, front door ajar, enjoying the breezes of the mountains. Weaker now, both breeze and man. He could no longer climb ladders to pick apples but did manage to still tend his small orchard and kitchen garden and make his way around his homestead. But he relied more and more on help, which he didn't like, but had to accept.

"Lem eventually changed his mind about logging. He eventually saw, as he still says today, 'the devastation logging brings to the land, streams, and wildlife.' He regretted it greatly. But it wasn't like that at first. Who could've known how vast logging would become?"

The men nodded their heads in understanding, taking in the small homestead. It was amazing how people still lived like this! They couldn't imagine.

"Now Uncle Lem visits with folk from all over who come to the park. Mostly hikers and writers and even the governor came to see him. And he sells his honey. Gives his advice to some – the ones he deems worthy."

"Who does he think is worthy? How does he determine that?" The taller of the men probed for more details on such decisions.

"Ah, there's the rub as they say. It's up to him. He says he can tell whether someone is truly interested in the land and how he lives, or if one is merely curious and can't hold the mountains in his soul for two seconds, hungry as a tick on a hound."

"That's a quaint way of saying it!"

"That's how folk talk around here."

They reached the old wooden home. To the two visiting men, accustomed to that high building in Washington D.C., the rickety run-down home and homestead must've looked like a tiny shanty town. Rustic cabin, barns. A corn crib and a storage shack. Springhouse and smokehouse. And speaking of smoke, the smell lingered in the air, melted into hair and clothes, resulting in a stale and wet rusty-lair odor. Not wholly unpleasant, it was...well, the only word the two men could come up with was *earthy*.

"What are you going to tell him about us when we greet him?"

"The truth. That you two are Supreme Court Justices. I'll tell him the U.S. Circuit Court of Appeals is having their annual conference in Gatlinburg, and I'll introduce you: here's Justice Potter Stewart and Justice Harry Blackmun – they're honored guests of the conference. Today, no activities or meetings were planned, and we thought to visit you."

Mr. Foster Arnett, a prominent Knoxville attorney, owned a cottage near The Appalachian Club in Elkmont and knew Lem well. He often visited and brought friends to Lem's home; dropping in to see if the kind and wise old man needed anything or just to keep him company for an hour or so. Justice Stewart's wife and another Knoxville lawyer, McAfee Lee and his wife were back at Arnett's cottage, enjoying the relaxing views, while the two Supreme Court Justices and Mr. Arnett made their way to Lem Ownby's cabin.

Powerful men all, the court was on a much-needed summer recess. Justices Blackmun and Stewart had just passed judgment on *Gregg vs. Georgia*, upholding the constitutionality of the death penalty and were eager to escape the reporters and newspapers scrutinizing their every thought and word.

"Lem Ownby is a character indeed," Mr. Arnett continued, leading the way around a bend in the gravel path, "but he represents a certain spirit of the Smokies that you just cannot find anymore, even in Gatlinburg. You used to be able to find these types all over. But since the park took over, well, you must venture further and further to find a true mountain man living the mountain lifestyle. They're a dying breed."

"Indeed. We can't wait to meet this man. And see his land, which, from the looks of it, is most peaceful. It's always interesting to see how others live." The two justices were enthusiastic, and Mr. Arnett was proud to introduce two of the most powerful men in the world to his friend as they reached his door, closed now.

"Let me knock. He may be taking a nap. He is quite old – eighty-seven now. But still quick in the mind and can navigate his land better than anyone who could see. Or who is fifty years younger."

The group walked around the house admiring this and that, the way the logs chinked together, the old, dry clay plugging the cracks, the way the whole home seemed to sag a bit to the left, the porch tugging the other way to the right.

"Look. Right over there. There's his honeybee hives."

"There's a lot of them!"

"There used to be a lot more. And there are his flowers. He can't see them, but he can smell them. He's always loved the fruity and sweet smell of flowers. There's the garden over there. And that is Jake's Creek."

The ribbon of darkness snaked its way past the cabin. Mountain laurel and late trilliums were dancing in the sunshine; blues and yellows and pinks all waltzing, bearing witness to two worlds coming together. Two worlds that could only clash against one another.

"Who's thar?" Lem Ownby called through the door, his thick country accent becoming twangier as he aged and talked to less and less people.

"It's me Uncle Lem! Foster Arnett! I have some guests I want you to meet!"

"Well who are they and what do they want?"

"I want you to meet The Honorable Justice Potter Stewart and The Honorable Justice Harry Blackmun, Uncle Lem. They are judges – justices - on the United States Supreme Court!"

The air hung like an unmoving bone-colored cloud. Everything was still. A lone owl stood in a treetop up the slope as bees buzzed lazily and uncaringly around their treasured hives.

"Them men – are they from Warshinton?"

"Yes, Uncle Lem and they are very important people who want to meet you!"

Silence. And then, an old mountain man's voice, gravelly, but clear. And strong. "Don't care. Don't wanna meet anybody from Warshinton. Tell 'em to go away!"

"Uncle Lem...!"

"Them fellows from Warshinton? Don't like them. Don't care for them. They ought to go back home. I don't have no use for those fellows."

Humiliated. Mortified. How could Uncle Lem just refuse to see two Supreme Court Justices? *I know he lost his land to the government, but still...these men had nothing to do with that....*

"Please, Uncle Lem. They came a long way and are good men...good folk as you say..."

Silence.

And after at least ten minutes of a lot of dignified pleading and a little outright begging - to no avail, the two justices began laughing! Soon, they were doubled over in shock, uproarious amusement, their sides tightening from this outrageous encounter.

Mr. Arnett hung his head before two of America's Supreme Court Justices in sheepish dejection. "I am *so* sorry..."

"Oh no matter at all...!"

"No. I am *very* sorry for this. I had no idea...Please forgive me and Uncle Lem for not meeting you..."

"Do not think anything of it, Foster. Why, this is the best thing that has ever happened to us!"

Foster Arnett frowned in confusion. *The best thing?*

"People don't tell us 'no'. This is wonderful!" Both justices agreed, reassuring the friendly lawyer for days afterwards that they'd gotten a kick out of it and that they'd never laughed so hard! Mr. Arnett was finally appeased, though he remained embarrassed for the rest of his days.

As for the justices, their families made sure to send cards to the Arnetts every year at Christmastime, and they would always write, "Give our best to Uncle Lem!"

As for Uncle Lem, whenever Mr. Foster Arnett and his family would visit him in the future - they visited quite often while at their cabin in Elkmont - the old blind mountain man would ask, "You got them fellers from Warshinton with you?"

34

VISITORS

HONEY IS SWEET, BUT THE BEE STINGS.

❦

Later that same summer of refusing to meet two powerful men from 'Warshinton', two women and two men walked up to the home of Lem Ownby. Bees were everywhere and Uncle Lem was sitting on his porch. He smelled the women's perfume before they even saw him.

"Hello sir!" The chippier of the two women cautiously approached. "We're visitin' from Knoxville and wonder if you're the famous Lem Ownby?"

"Yes, ma'am. I am. Don't know 'bout famous though. Glad you're here. Haven't had anyone visit today. Least not anyone as purdy as you smell." He chuckled, which made the woman smile. If she looked up, she would've seen an owl laughing as much as an owl could. Oh, this old man was in a jolly mood today! Just like the staff at The Appalachian Club hoped for when they told the little group of two men and two women to go see Uncle Lem. The guests had asked for suggestions on what to do today and the manager had a ready answer: *you want to see what life is like here? To know what it was like back in the good ol' days? Go see Uncle Lem. Tell 'im the staff at the club sent ya'll. And be sure to get some of his honey. It's the best there ever was.*

"Do you have any honey?"

"Well, *you're* here, aren't you?

Delighted, "Oh, sir! You are a character!" She smiled widely. He could almost feel the joy coming from this stranger, the yearning to know about his lifestyle.

He took her hand and led her and the others around his farm. After a quick tour of the homestead and a short walk into the barn where he kept jars of honey on rough-hewn shelves, the good-natured woman became curious again.

"Mr. Ownby..."

"Call me Lem."

"Okay, Lem. If you don't mind me asking, how old are you?"

"Eighty-seven."

"And blind?"

"As a bat. Yes, ma'am."

"How do you live so well?"

"Ah, that's an easy one. I don't let no one on my land I don't want to. And look around, my dear. Aren't these the most beautiful mountains on God's green earth?"

She did look. Peaks upon peaks, stacked right on top of one another marching like soldiers in fog – hands on each other's shoulders for comfort, and to keep together.

As if reading her mind, Lem said softly, "none of them mountains are alone. Can't get lost that way, can't ever get separated if you just keep your hand on the other's shoulder."

A pause as the others caught up with them. Her husband and friends were roaming around the homestead, looking at this and that, smelling the flowers, marveling at the meat hanging in the smokehouse. The corn in the corncrib.

"It's the mountains. That's how I live out here. That and the honey." He winked at her with unseeing eyes that managed to picture everything. "Yes, ma'am. When I think on it, the way I stay young – *heh heh* - and healthy, well, I lay it up to the honey. And to get that, I got to tell the bees."

"Tell the bees?" She frowned. "Tell them what?"

"Ah. See here. Tellin' the bees is ancient, tracing their roots back to the so-called mystical Celtics – those were sort of our kinfolk, the Scots-Irish. Not exactly the same, but kinda the same heritage. Anyways, some say it's all a myth this tellin' the bees, but to folk like me, it's not only charmin' and ancient as they say, but true.

At the old man's gesture to sit, the woman settled herself into the rocker on the front porch while the others continued roaming the property. Lem waved his hand at them: "Go, go! Explore my land all you want. Before the government kicks me offa it when I die!"

It was rare, but sometimes Lem felt a special affinity with someone. Like Levi Trentham, he could instinctively tell whether a stranger truly cared for the land. For the mountains. For the bees and honey and barns and lifestyle. For how he chose to live his life within God's scalloped waves of heaven.

"So it's like this: tellin' the bees is when beekeepers like me tell their bees about life. Deaths, births, marriages, funerals, and other such things. I told my bees when the government bought my land. I told 'em them government men gave me less money so I can stay 'til I die, but I'm still here ain't I?"

He sighed, tilting his head towards the east where the sun makes its entrance every day. It was late afternoon by now, the sun's heat on the right side of his face. It was a hot one today and he offered the woman some cold spring water which she happily accepted.

"Celtic folk had a lot of myths. Kind of like us in these here mountains. Superstitions they call 'em. But I like to call 'em decorations. They decorate life so it ain't so same, same, same every day. Makes life not so boring."

"Are you ever bored?"

"Never."

"Because you can always talk to your bees?"

"Yes! Ma'am, you're right on that one! Beekeepers since way long ago have been tellin' their bees all about major things in life. Why do they do that? 'Cause bees are messengers between the human world and the spirit world."

"Kind of like that owl up there?" She pointed.

"How'd you notice?"

"I seen him on the walk up here. And if I didn't know any better, I would think he was following me. Seems he's watching *you* all the time too. He hasn't moved!"

"Ah so." Lem smiled. "That creature's been here my whole life it seems! Oh, I know well and good that owls only live five, ten, maybe twelve years, but they do have the ability to inherit memories. And recall what their ancestors saw and knew. At least that's what the Cherokee say."

The woman nodded her head, looking at Lem Ownby, this wise, extraordinary, old, blind man sitting on a shaky front porch as the sun was inching its way down, down, to grab the very highest peak of the Smoky Mountains.

"The government done took my land. But look here." He swept his old hands down his spare body. "Here I am! And there's my bees! I can hear 'em buzzin'. When I go to the Lord, I am sure the newspapers will report on me: 'Lem Ownby dies. He was the last person livin' in the park besides one ol' feller over in Cades Cove.' But what they won't report is the bees. They'll be around. One will land right on my cheek. It won't sting. And no one else will see it. It will mean that my soul has left my body."

She thought for a moment. Felt the cool jar in her hand, the one holding a golden hunk of combed honey which various ancient peoples have called *hunig* and *camb* and *mele*. When she returned home to Knoxville, she would go to the library to look up this tradition of talking to the bees, and she would find that it was very popular and well known in the 18th and 19th centuries in Western Europe and in the United States, especially in Appalachia.

She would also find that the head of household or owner of the home or even midwives and granny women would approach a hive and then gently knock it to get the bees' attention. Once they were swarming, news could be softly murmured to the bees in a solemn tone, whether it be good news or bad or anything in between. This, they would say, keeps the bees informed and 'prevents them from leaving the hive for good or dying'.

"See," Lem continued, rising from the chair indicating she should collect the rest of her party and head back before darkness crept below the mountains, "the bees ain't just bees. They are the deep connection all us creatures feel when livin' right here, embraced in the blue walls of God's Smoky Mountains. I'd rather be nowhere else."

35

THE LEGEND OF UNCLE LEM - LATE 1970S

IN THE CITY, LIFE IS HALF SPENT BEFORE WE KNOW WHAT IT IS.

~

T he story became legendary.

Mr. Carson Brewer, a reporter for the *Knoxville News Sentinel* was somewhat of an expert about the people and places of the Smoky Mountains and wrote about the old blind mountain man a few years after the encounter with the two Supreme Court Justices:

> *I never knew Lem existed until one bright morning in the late 1970s. I was hiking from the Sinks, on Little River, to Elkmont, where my wife, Miss Alberta, was to pick me up. I was within a few yards of Jake's Creek Trail when I saw a cabin in a clearing downhill to my left.*

> *Chickens scattered from my path as I detoured towards the sawmill dwelling in the clearing. Two friendly dogs met me. Bees buzzed around more than 100 hives.*

*And there was Lem Ownby, a short, slow-moving
man wearing bib overalls. I learned later that he
moved slowly and carefully because he was
nearly blind.*

*Lem was not sophisticated. Only once had he been
out of Tennessee. He walked over the mountain
"to buy a dog from a feller" who lived on Tow
String Creek in North Carolina but it was still in
the Smokies. Knoxville was the farthest place
from the Smokies he ever went and usually went
there only when his wife, Mimmie, had to go to
the hospital and then, a nursing home.*

*"I never took a dose of doctor medicine in my life till I
was fifty-five years old." He said he had eaten
honey "might nigh every day" for more than fifty
years. He spent five weeks and one day in St.
Mary's Medical Center in Knoxville when he had
pneumonia in 1970. He didn't like it; couldn't
stand the water and wouldn't drink it. Somebody
finally had to bring him water from the mountain spring that's piped constantly to his back
porch.*

*Lem also didn't like the rainbow trout stocked in the
Great Smokies stream in later years. He preferred
speckled. His favorite honey was linn.*

AS THE YEARS MARCHED ON, Lem's grandnephew, along with his
caring and patient wife, pled with the park service to let them
keep a trailer on Lem's property to keep an eye on him, to cook

meals, to take care of the upkeep of the home. Lem didn't like the idea – he didn't like feeling like a burden – but had to admit, life did get better with some help. His relatives even arranged with the park service to install electricity and a telephone, and other upgrades to the home. But he resisted these changes, and they never happened: *I don't need no lights or telephone. Who would I call? And this here runnin' water I got still works fine for me. This here spring water has six different minerals and folk come a long way to get some.*

His fame rose when a Knoxville artist, Terry Chandler, came to town with the purpose of paying tribute to the people who lived in the Smokies before the national park. Chandler painted Lem standing in front of his house leaning on his walking staff, beehives in the background. The limited edition of five hundred prints quickly sold out. The painting was titled: *Uncle Lem.*

Writers, painters – all made Uncle Lem a legend. Soon, reporters from Sevierville and Maryville and even Atlanta and Nashville showed up. Lem greatly enjoyed telling his stories: how his mother prayed before the mantle clock that his family purchased before the War Between the States and how it held special powers. For instance, family lore revealed that when she prayed especially fervently one day, every one of her brothers returned home from war on that very day. Within the hour even. Some said her brothers wouldn't have been old enough to fight in the war. But over 100,000 boys who were 15 years old or younger had served. Perhaps she was really praying for her father who served in the Ninth Regiment, Tennessee Cavalry? Or her uncles who served in the Union Army? Or perhaps it wasn't that way at all and she was just praying? Or watching the time?

No matter. Stories become embellished and expanded as needed. To teach and to remember. Lem often pled this idea: "stories of my ancestors - where and who we come from - why, they're even more famous, more important than me denyin' to greet two Supreme Court Justices from Warshinton!"

He would chuckle, and then add: "Now, there was one governor who I *did* let into my house here in Elkmont. His name was Governor Lamar Alexander, and he came with some other men. I thought about denyin' 'em, but I guess I was in a better mood that day. Anyhows, I let 'em in and they started askin' me why I never left when the government came in. And I told 'em, 'cause I was born here. And then the Governor, who was sittin' on my bed mind, tol' me he was from East Tennessee and how we hadn't had many governors from East Tennessee before. And I said, yeah, but we hadn't had many that didn't steal either. And that's when he laughed and said something or other about how he's different and not like that and can be trusted and a whole bunch of other stuff. So, I looked him in the eye – now, I can't see hardly at all, but I think I knew where his eyes were – and I said, I ain't heard nothin' on you. Yit."

36

THE FALL - DECEMBER
1983 - JANUARY 1984

TELL THE BEES; THEY WILL
NOT STING MY CHEEK.

~

"Uncle Lem fell."

"Oh no! What is he? Ninety-four now?"

"Yes. Ninety-four years living in these here mountains."

"What happened?"

"Well, as I hear it, during that ice storm last night, he fell on some ice. Reckon I hear he was on the front porch and then began walkin' towards Jake's Creek and just fell."

"He's always so careful when he walked. Ninety-four... This ain't good."

"His nephew, Roy, found 'im. Lyin' right where he fell. Cold. Helpless."

The owl saw what happened. It was as reported: *Uncle Lem Ownby fell today, December 28, 1983. He suffered some broken ribs. Bruises.*

And then came an update: *pneumonia, treated for three weeks. He improved and doctors were going to send him home. But then, on January 12, 1984, he suffered a stroke, and on January 16th, Lemuel*

Stuart Ownby, farmer, keeper of bees, blind mountain man, husband, uncle, legend, died at Knoxville Presbyterian Hospital.

IT WAS REALLY the loss of his home that led him to God. Not the loss at the hands of the government – he had learned to live with that – but the loss of being able to see it for the last time. For he overheard a conversation that a doctor told one of his nephews the day of his stroke, "your uncle will never be able to return to his mountain home".

Once Lem overheard those hushed words, it was a matter of mere days. He decided to go to "the better place" he often spoke about.

Newspapers reported his death and word spread about the death of a "legend" and "the end of an era." You can almost hear Uncle Lem scoffing at some of those headlines! But he would've appreciated others:

The waters of Jake's Creek still sing their music. But for the first time in nearly 95 years, Lem Ownby is not listening.

Uncle Lem was sort of a monument. He was the epitome of a true mountain man, the last of a breed. Uncle Lem was our last tie to a way of life in our mountains before the coming of the park.

GOVERNOR LAMAR ALEXANDER even released a statement:

> It's hard to talk about Mr. Lem Ownby in a
>   couple of sentences. Everyone who loves the
>   Great Smoky Mountains should have had a
>   chance to meet him. I almost missed my
>   chance, but I saw him over Thanksgiving
>   when my wife, Honey, and I started a forty-

mile walk with Peter and Barbara Jenkins that began from Lem's house and went through the park. He told me that he would be 95 if he lived until February 24th. In a way it is both ironic and appropriate that he died the year of the park's 50th anniversary. He was older than I am now when it was created. And he simply never left. He was an independent mountain man. His seven uncles were Union soldiers, and he was a link with what makes East Tennessee special. While we were visiting he told me that his uncles came home to Jake's Creek from the war on the same Sunday morning, while his mother was praying before the mantle clock in the kitchen corner praying for their safe return. I guess I will never forget what he had to say about Governors. He said that most of them had stolen something, but he hadn't heard anything on me yet. I am glad to have had the chance to talk with him and to learn a little bit from him.

LIBRARY OF CONGRESS STATEMENT:

>The Library of Congress is seeing renewed interest in its February 1980 entry about Lemuel Ownby, the "last life-right resident remaining in the Great Smoky Mountains National Park".

>In 1980, Kathleen Mascill, a Collector for the

Library of Congress entered a recorded conversation with Lem. Her entry is entitled: "Recorded Ownby, "Uncle Lem" (Speaker)", and his soft lilting voice talks about several topics. He tells of his lifelong eye problems, but says he was able to get around just fine. He also speaks of churchgoings, big snows of sometimes thirty-two inches high, bees buzzing in the house, and that he didn't go to school much. He can recall no hard times during the Depression as they always had food. He even had his own grist mill and turned corn into chewing tobacco. One time he sold a hundred bushels for 40 cents a bushel. He was asked at a later time if the park enforces the restrictions on the residents. And he said, 'you betcha! A neighbor cut down a tree and was evicted. Another one shot a bear who got into his smokehouse and was evicted'.

About five and a half minutes into the recording, you can hear his family's mantle clock chiming in the background.

Last Smoky Mountains Hermit Dies

ELKMONT, Tenn. -- Lem Ownby, who once turned two justices of the Supreme Court away from his door, is dead at 94 -- the last of the Smoky Mountain men.
'Uncle Lem' was the lone survivor of a handful of

independent mountaineers allowed to stay when the government formed the Great Smoky Mountains National Park 50 years ago.

'Everyone who loves the Great Smoky Mountains should have had the chance to meet him,' Gov. Lamar Alexander said in a statement Tuesday.

Few got the chance. Ownby was such a recluse that he refused to see Justices Potter Stewart and Harry Blackmun when they knocked on his door one spring day in the mid-1970s.

Ownby was completely blind the last few years of his life but that didn't keep him from walking the familiar paths around his home. Friends said he once shot a bear from the sound of the animal chomping his apples.

His only income was money from the sale of honey from his bee hives, and he sold that only to friends.

Ownby sold his 44-acre farm to the government at less than its fair market value so he could stay in the mountains. His wife Mimmie died more than 15 years ago.

'He was an independent mountain man,' Alexander said. 'His seven uncles were Union soldiers and he was a link with what makes East Tennessee special.

EAST TENNESSEE. Legend. Mountain man. Link to the past. Independent. Special. Those were words describing Uncle Lem, but how can this man be put into those few powerful words? How can we truly understand the joy of his mountains, the pain of selling his beloved land to the government because he had no choice? Losing his eyesight, his wife, yet staying steadfast in his own wants and needs and desires in life?

It was eight o'clock on Tuesday evening, January 17, 1984. The day after. Family, friends, neighbors, national park service employees, and an old and curious owl, all gathered at Archley's Funeral Home in Sevierville to bid goodbye to Uncle Lem Ownby. Reverend Roy Gose, pastor of Valley View Baptist Church officiated the funeral.

The owl perched, stooped just a bit to hear the accolades. Hours went by. The same large crowd would return the next day at 1:00 p.m. for the graveside service at Valley View Cemetery where he would be laid to rest beside Mimmie. The church was the same one that was dismantled and moved from Elkmont so long ago; reassembled in Wears Valley.

Lem Ownby now lay for eternity in the shadow of his former life, his soul risen towards the future.

Whatever it may hold.

THEY LINGERED. So many people at a gravesite, outside all day long in the cold sting of a Smoky Mountain winter. So many sharing stories of what Lem Ownby meant to them. To the world.

He taught us to adapt. To fight for what's right.

Uncle Lem was a very independent person, and the thought of losing that independence caused him to be ready for life's next great adventure.

He sold me some honey every summer when we visited the park. I didn't even know anyone lived here before the park opened. It makes me sad to know they lost their homes and land. But he told me he was born here and he'd die here. And then he'd brighten and ask me in that twangy accent of his, 'kin I innerest ye in some good ole pure mountain honey?' Now, I admit it took me a minute to under-

stand him, but I bought ten jars every summer for $3.50 each. Don't know what he did with the money, but he smiled every time.

A good man.

Smart. Clever. Funny. I recall when he and Levi Trentham would get together. Mind, we're right outside the church and I can't well say what Levi Trentham used to say, but let's say he took the Lord's name in vain a few times in just about every sentence. But Lem would just listen and wouldn't use the same language, 'cause he was more God-fearin' than Levi, but I could see a smirk forming at the corners of his mouth. And I could definitely see the spark in those unseeing eyes that seemed to see everything.

Can't imagine how he managed bein' blind. But he did. Better than any seein' man!

Uncle Lem was my real uncle. I know everyone called him that, but I was one of his true nieces and boy did I love visiting he and Aunt Mimmie! Those cookies...they were the best. And Uncle Lem taught me to talk to the bees too. He taught me most everything I needed to figure out this life. It's simple really: he just said take what the mountains give you. And then, give back just a little bit more.

He sure loved youngins. Always takin' the time to talk to 'em more than the adults. Seems he was makin' up for not bein' able to have youngins of his own...

Oh, speakin' of youngins...did you hear? All that honey he sold? We all wondered what he did with all that money? Well, turns out, he left a Will!

I, Lemuel Stuart Ownby, after debts, funeral expenses, and necessary taxes have been paid, Will, Devise and Bequeath all the rest and residue of my estate of whatever kind and character and whatever situated to the Tennessee Baptist Foundation to be held in trust forever. Because of my love for the Lord and my interest in children, I direct that the income from this trust is to be for the care of children in the Tennessee Baptist Church's home. This trust is to be entered on record of the Tennessee Baptist Foundation as the Lemuel Ownby Memorial Trust and it's to remain for all to come.

To MANY IN the outside world, the old blind mountain man who lived in a shack was pitiful, reclusive, even odd. Oh, the owl had heard it all! Isolated. Backwards. Hillbilly. Living in the sticks. Why doesn't he move to town where he would be more comfortable? Have electricity. Running water. People around to help?

Ah, but if you have the bees to talk to, one is never lonely. Talk to the bees. Tell them how you saved up $54,000 for a trust to benefit children; the children you were never able to have. The ones locked up in your heart as the most fervent of dreams gets locked into memories.

Talk to the owl. How you sold honey at $3.50 a jar, for how many years and years to save $54,000 to help others. The smallest ones. The innocent ones who need it most.

Talk to the mountaintops whether capped in snow or an aura of fresh green blossoms. They never fail to listen, these stone giants. They will always listen. And they will always guide a good hurting soul.

Uncle Lem knew all of this. But more importantly, he lived it. And when family and friends and many who merely knew of him or had met him once or twice gathered to say goodbye, one and all repeated their pain, not only for the man himself, but for the way of life he represented. A way of life that Levi Trentham and Lem Ownby and so many others created from anything and everything the mountains provided.

Levi – the Prophet, the spice sprinkled onto life in the Smokies. The Mayor of Elkmont. The Spirit of the Smokies.

The Keeper of Mountain Wisdom. Bear hunter. Husband, father, grandfather. Master of his chosen vocabulary.

Lem – the quiet, smart, blind man who saw it all. Beekeeper. Bear hunter. Husband. The last lifetime leaseholder in the Great Smoky Mountains National Park.

Uncles, both; no matter if they were truly, officially, kin or not.

Gone.

And now, who is left to keep our Appalachian traditions alive? Where to place the hand-hewn wooden vessel that holds the secrets of farming and bees and bear traps? What about planting according to the Three Sisters Method? Where you place those three "sisters" of beans, squash, and peas next to the almighty corn crops to suppress weeds and keep pests away?

And what about onions to ease a mountain cough? Eat it whole or put slices in a glass of milk and drink it. Roast it if you wish; drink the juice. Mix onion and sugar and spread it on a biscuit. Rub camphor oil and turpentine together and rub it on the chest. Cherry bark tea. A bit of sawdust mixed with moonshine. And if all that fails, stick a table fork into the head of the bed of the sufferer, eat the hind leg of a fat dog, or find a cat without a white hair on its body and take a tablespoon of blood from its tail.

Works every time.

And when everyone is feeling good - a good that comes from breathing in the mountain air and touching the dirt - we can talk about how it was, back in the day, walking to school: "going in the front door of the school and out the back" as Lem described his own schooling, but being smart enough, clever enough to let the scenic and gentle mountains teach you everything you need to know.

And what about The Appalachian Club, that thriving club where porch parties and dances and now-famous people dined on trout and ham and biscuits that could make you scream at the treetops that the buttery top of a biscuit is a pillowy arrow pointing straight up to heaven itself.

And then there's The Wonderland, where the showy peacocks said it had only one fault: it was perfect. Otherwise, they'd say, it was perfect. *See? Here, we use our imaginations and wit instead of overcast musings and memories like that club down the street!*

As for that club down the street, they'd always have a quick retort: *memories mean we have longevity and longevity's the answer. If you live long enough, everything will turn your way!*

Oh yes, who will be left to let other people roam back into the experienced memories of those who lived and vacationed here? The ones who Levi would chuckle to himself and whisper: *I taught them everything* they *goddamn know about these here mountains. Just not everything* I *know.*

Muddy wit. Humor so icy sometimes, it hurt to breathe. Such personalities made sense in these isolated walls. The independence. The freedom. The decision is all yours: "I don't ever vote," Lem used to say. "I bet you there's not two cents' worth o'difference in Carter or Reagan or any of them crooked fellers up there in Warshinton."

Indeed, decisions are all yours within the waves of mountains, the ones standing like soldiers, ever unmoving, ever watching what you will do next. They will let you do whatever you want! But they will not help your good or bad decisions. Not if it's insufferably humid and hot, not if it's bitterly cold. Daily struggles are many and the mountains will just sit there.

But they will smile at you. Just enough to let you know it's exactly where you want to be.

Finally, they will turn their stony faces and look you dead in the eyes, speaking directly to your soul: *We have a story of our own to tell. But it's up to you to listen and pass it on. Preserve our tale. Our way of life has changed. In fact, it's pretty well gone. But it's important to remember. Even moreso as our years of modernity and technology march onward.*

Are you with us now on our mission to preserve and honor Levi and Lem? And Ivah and Mayna and Mimmie? Bessie and Emaline and the Colonel and everyone who got on their knees to till soil or pick a carrot or pound a steel spike into a railroad line?

Are you with us to preserve the creeks and trees for the bears and the deer and the owl?

One mission.

One club.

37

THE LAST FIGHT

COME OUT OF YOUR BUG-
HUTCHES AND BARNS AND FIGHT!

≈

The Elkmont Campground remained at full capacity since its opening in the 1950s. Families slept under the stars in tents, brought their recreational vehicles, and marveled at the owl as it flew between trees. Green tunnels hung overhead as children hiked to waterfalls and climbed The Wonderland Hotel's steep steps. They couldn't go inside anymore; it closed for good on November 15, 1992. The front porch sagged a bit, paint chipped off its walls; a general neglect showed itself as if patience had finally given up. But campers and visitors still looked up at the once-grand building and wondered how life was back in its golden days, when people danced and laughed and watched a large owl flying to the beat of a banjo.

There were no leftover brochures, no out-of-date guides, no old timers left to tell the stories. If only there was something - a book perhaps. If only there were someone who took the time to find out and write it all down. So we can read about how it really was. Before it's all gone.

Cabins still lined the Elkmont street, mostly empty now, but a few residents fought on and stood their ground. The last of the leases expired in 1992, but the remaining families were ready for another round.

This time however, the park stood its ground. And they had the higher ground. The power. All further extensions were refused.

A shut door didn't stop the residents though; they kept knocking. And that's when what was once considered unthinkable – the two rival clubs uniting – became even stronger.

The Elkmont Preservation Committee had formed some time ago; the Wonderland and Appalachian Clubs coming together to fight for their shared land. They even managed to laugh at times: *remember how we wouldn't even talk to one another on the Elkmont Special as we pulled into the same station?*

Admitting - and proving - that they were stronger together, the preservation committee managed to re-negotiate their expired twenty-year leases and clear-cut title claims. Three angry, but powerful families fought on, obtaining extensions until December 31, 2001.

Elkmont's Preservation Committee also obtained Elkmont's rightful place on the National Register of Historic Places. At least nothing else could ever be taken down, burned, demolished. But all properties were now fully owned by the National Park Service.

Nowadays, people flock to sit on the front porch of The Appalachian Club when they visit the most popular national park in America. They walk through colorfully restored cottages and imagine laughter and visiting and sitting on stone patios overlooking the creek. What would it have been like to live in Elkmont? To see the logging town grow and become a resort? What would it have been like to visit this place in the early 1900s? To stay for two weeks falling asleep to the music of the creeks and winds? To see those mountains for the first time, layers upon layers of blue craggy beasts warming your body during the day, wrapping you in its mighty cloak at night.

What would it have been like to visit that famous artist's home? The one further up on Jake's Creek?

THE AVENT FAMILY used the cabin until 1992 when America faced high unemployment, inflation, and a new president. Clinton was his name. A Democrat. Things were happening in Washington and not just in the White House - the Redskins won the Super Bowl, and the city of government was in celebration mode. The world was also changing - Disney World opened in Paris; McDonald's opened its first restaurant in China. The space shuttle, Endeavor was launched, and Bruce Springsteen began a world tour.

In the mountains of Eastern Tennessee, life moved at a faster pace too, but not fast enough to ever forget the past.

Before she died in 1959, Mayna Avent herself wrote eighteen pages full of praise for her mountain home. It was her contribution for an eventual application to the National Register of Historic Places. Even decades ago, she knew the park would eventually deny extending leases. And then what? So, she fought her biggest fight on paper. A canvas of heartfelt musings.

Taking the cause over was her great-grandson, Bryant, whose own mother, also named Mayna – they liked to keep the name in the family – worked tirelessly to have the Avent Cabin listed on the National Register of Historic Places. This designation would ensure the cabin's preservation. But it was a long, arduous and unsure process.

"Can you hand me that paper?" Bryant's mother would say.

"Which one? There's eighteen pages here!"

"The floor plan. The one with the sketch of the kitchen and

rooms." And he would hand over a long paper with detailed descriptions of the cabin's construction.

"Letter of Support", stated the first paper the family filed. Five more letters - one from the Curator of Art and Architecture for the Tennessee State Museum, emphasizing "Mayna Treanor Avent's role as a Tennessee artist and describing the cabin as culturally significant as her studio and source of inspiration."

Another paper filed: "Included will be a 'notebook of laminated pages that includes a biography of the artist, photos of her work...'"

Papers upon tedious papers. Applications. Amendments and clarifications. A field visit to view this artist's cabin and to see what shape it was in. If it was worthy of being included in the registry.

It worked.

On February 7, 1994, in the fourth decade after her death, the Mayna Treanor Avent Studio was accepted and placed on the National Register of Historic Places. Now this famous and kind artist's inspiration would be preserved along with the entire remaining town of Elkmont.

Visitors can walk up the peaceful path by Jake's Creek and marvel at the view from the spacious windows: magnolias and mountain laurel in spring bloom, quiet and gentle white snowy hills in full winter splendor. All under the watchful eye of a wise old owl.

Thank goodness for these valiant efforts of preservation, because the original plan was to get rid of every cabin, every building, everything. Burn it all. Dismantle it. But enough folk fought for what was important. And just enough people listened.

Now the National Park Service and Elkmont Preservation Committee had to develop a plan to preserve the remaining cabins and club. Their plan was thus:

"preserve 19 buildings, including all 17 cabins and the 'lodge from The Appalachian Club' as the 'Elkmont Historic District'. Our plan will incorporate displays of times gone by, such as stoves, fireplaces, even a scattering of furniture. Many items, including the very buildings themselves, need to be restored as time ate its way through wooden beams and porches and interiors."

Unfortunately, The Wonderland Hotel was not part of the plan. Its main building fell into severe disrepair and collapsed in 2005. Today, an owl perches on a lone sign, the only thing left save for steep stone steps leading once to a mountain paradise.

TODAY, over twelve million people from all over the world visit Elkmont. The Ghost Town, some call it. Many will marvel at the beauty. Will wander into a cottage that was once a summer home. They will step into a little log cabin originally built in 1845 by a father who sired a prophet; now sold to the government. *Sold,* that prophet would snicker across the winds of time. *It wasn't sold! It was goddamn taken!* But many wouldn't know that. They would walk and look at the hearth, the ceiling; wonder at how a man named Levi Trentham lived out here and why people like him chose this place above all others.

38

FIREFLIES

LET YOUR LIGHT SHINE BEFORE ALL MEN.

~

L em Ownby had always loved fireflies. Every year in late May or early June, the winged beetles would show off, causing youngins to yell about *the lightnin' bugs that were lighting up the world!*

When Mimmie was alive, their front porch would become a hive of activity - busier than the bees - when folk gathered to watch the mating of these curious creatures.

"Now, I can't see too good, but I do see little flashes here and there. It's when the males wanna attract the females. They flash their lanterns which are yellow-green and they flash 'em twice every second! Makes the whole mountain light up like the sun."

Levi Trentham used to love the fireflies too, a spectacle occurring only once a year. What made it so special was they did it all together all at once – in perfect synchronicity.

"Them lightnin' bugs give off four, maybe up to eight flashes at a time, but they do it all together! In harmony!" Levi used to marvel as he watched his garden benefit from the two-week display. Lightning bugs feed on snails and slugs, which can destroy vegetables and flowers; during those two or so weeks of late spring, all he'd talk about was their amazing display and how the pests were nowhere to be seen on his peas and carrots and lettuce.

"The mountains give us these here bugs. They're really beetles though and spend most of their lifecycle in what they call the larval stage, which lasts about one to two years. This is the amount of time they spend on the forest floor feedin' on snails and worms and small insects. Now, once they grow and mature, they done turn into adults. Now's the sad part. From there, they only live for another three to four weeks. But it's the most fun part too. At this stage, it's all about matin'. And I mean it's *all* about matin' – they don't even feed! Most never feed at all, ever again!" Levi and Lem would laugh together, watching and discussing nature's strange courtship habits.

"The males, they flash while they're flyin' around trying to find a mate, lightin' up trees and grasses, while females are usually stationary, and then they flash in response. I seen this my whole life and it always amazes me!" Levi Trentham would shake his head, every year, marveling. He knew that these synchronous fireflies are one of the rare species that live in the Great Smoky Mountains. There are other species living here that flash, but to do it in harmony, in synch with one another, is a feat that only around nineteen species of fireflies can perform.

Bioluminescence is what it's called. Jellyfish, shrimp, glow-worm beetles, and some fish can do the same thing; the product of chemical reactions that result in the release of light with little or no emission of heat. It didn't matter that Levi and Lem knew nothing of the chemical luciferin, and the oxygen, along with the enzyme luciferase, in the abdomens of fireflies. It mattered nothing that they had no idea that the light is a "cold" light, with nearly all the energy given off as light, but without heat.

All they knew was that by early June – sometimes late May if the temperature was warmer than usual – it started with a few bugs lighting up, followed by two to three weeks of their Smoky Mountain world pulsating with light. And love. For the males must display their prowess in unison because they must make sure the females are responding to one of her own kind. After all, there are other firefly species lighting up the night - and some are predatory. She must be able to recognize the ones that light up all at once. Those are her type.

She will also know her type if they won't flash in heavy rain or if the temperature drops below fifty degrees. That will shut down the action for the evening and then, she must wait.

Owls can eat fireflies if they are desperate, but they emit a distasteful chemical. The feathered creatures mostly prefer mice, eating three to four mice per day. The bigger species – like the great horned owl - can eat forty mice per day.

The owl didn't eat any of the bugs that lit up the night, but he did watch as thousands of people gathered every year to set up chairs, wrap themselves in blankets against the chilly summer nights to watch nature's light show.

For Levi and Lem, the annual firefly spectacle was simply another way the mountains showed their majesty. It was part of life. But to visitors from cities and towns, their mouths opened in awe at the thousands and thousands of beetles trying to mate in their last weeks of life. Their final act.

This event became so popular that by 2006, a lottery had to be created. For those who hit the jackpot, they would head to Elkmont, hypnotized by tiny dots of yellow-green light, the reflective glow revealing wonder in eyes both young and old.

After mating, females lay their eggs on the ground. Days later, perhaps even a few weeks if they're hearty, the synchronous fireflies die. Visitors go home and tell their tale of how the fireflies of the Great Smoky Mountains National Park lit up the night. And they will talk about how they walked inside a small cabin in the Elkmont area of the park and tell everyone how people – an entire family - used to live in that small cabin that is now on display.

Can you imagine? All those people – they had ten children! – living in such a place. No running water. No bathrooms. Cooking over a fire. Or a stove in later years.

And can you imagine the man who lived in that little cabin? It was that old mountain man who everyone said could see inside the mind of the mountains. They called him a prophet. And can you also imagine, a blind man used to live right up there! His cabin is no more, but somehow...we feel his spirit. It's especially strong when the bees start buzzing. We tell those bees to stop and go somewhere else, but they don't listen to us.

We would've loved to meet those men and their families. They represent a way of life that just doesn't exist anymore. We wish we knew how they really lived their lives. What they thought. I know there's some stories out there, and the rangers told us what they knew about the people who used to live here...Levi and Lem they were called. Maybe someday someone will write it all down so I can read all about it. I'd love our kids to read something like that, to hear the stories. That way, they can experience the good old days when life was simpler. Even for just a little while. Because if we keep these memories alive, this special way of life doesn't die off like the fireflies do after they live, love, and then their lights go out forever.

Seasons cycle through, just like they are supposed to.

Springtime is when the earth throws off its heavy winter cloak to reveal itself decked out in its finest attire. Color, light, and warmth weave themselves into a showcase of vibrant yellow and white flowers, while tan fawns take their first steps. Brown balls of fur practice eating the first berries of the season with their protective mothers. Mountain laurel bloom. Rhododendrons splash themselves up and down the slopes with their audacious pinks and purples and reds.

Summer reveals more berries, plump orbs which attract everything from bear to deer to turkeys, basking in the abundance. Crops grow, and everything needs weeding.

Fall is the showiest of seasons – carrot and crimson leaves staring you right in the eyes, daring you to look beyond the yellows and blazing oranges and reds towards the bluest of skies. Colors fill your soul; there is no way to feel anything but satisfied with nature's grand spectacle.

Finally, a dusting of white covers the land once again; the quiet time begins. A time to sit, whittle, clean, bake, cook, stir, and sweep, read the Bible and Almanac and Sears Catalog and wonder where that owl is and hope it's in his nest because a storm is coming. We know because we read the animals. Especially the bees. Because they not only listen to us talk to them, but they also talk to us too. What with their heading back to the hive when they detect a change in air pressure. They stop all foraging and gather to protect the queen and larvae. They tell us when cold weather is coming by creating clusters in the hive to keep warm, the outside bees fluttering their wings to insulate the bees inside the cluster. Then, they rotate. Each individual creature working to make sure the whole hive survives. Just like a community.

Which is just like the mountains. Where individual freedom runs deeper than roots, yet everyone is invested in their communities. People listen to themselves but listen to others as well.

If *you* listen, you can still hear the tales, the lifestyle, the nuances of farm life, the love, the bitterness, the adaptability and resilience, the prophecies of Levi Trentham and Lem Ownby and all the others. Prophecies which are actually just the mountains answering the important questions, contributing their own thoughts and experiences, urging you to remember, please just remember, what happened all along their craggy spines and ridges.

Oh, to be sure, sometimes they'll sass and cuss and talk back to you, and those times are when you should sit up and take notice for it is usually in their most desperate hours that they backtalk in that tone that a mountain mother uses when you were young and careless in the garden and spilt half the milk in the pail on your way to the house because you were running when you should've been walking.

It's when the government of your own country takes your land and nothing, nothing, nothing at all will ease the hurt even if it's for the greater good. For whom? *Not for us,* their long-time residents would say. The ones with bib overalls, bear pelts and rifles slung over shoulders, some of them blind, but able to get around just fine. The ones in cotton dresses tending gardens and children and animals, cooking and administering mountain medicine which comes with a healthy dose of experience and love and hardiness. *But even if the park and all these changes weren't good for us, we will sacrifice. Because we must. The only thing we ask,* the mountains will plead, giving you the most explicit instructions, *is that you keep alive the good folk who once called this place home.*

39

———

LEGACY

WE GET OLD TOO SOON AND WISE TOO LATE.

~

"An owl is a sight to see. Winged vessels of wisdom, folklore; symbols of fear and the fantastical. Many visitors report seeing owls in the park, especially while visiting Elkmont," the newspaper reported.

Twenty or thirty people the young reporter stopped to ask, "Why do *you* visit the Great Smoky Mountains National Park?"

It was easy to find those willing to talk. After all, fourteen million people and counting visited the national park every year! And they replied with many different answers: *the beauty. The animals. The mountains. To see the Walker Sisters' cabin. To hike and picnic. Play in the creeks. Skip rocks and tube down a river. Wander Cades Cove and walk into the cabins and churches and see how they lived. Respect the history. Walk back in time even if for a moment while we're on this family vacation.*

Some had someone specific in mind when they visited: *We want to see where this Black Bill Walker lived — the one who had three wives at the same time! We want to see what they saw when they lived here. We wonder how they all lived together.*

We want to see where Levi Trentham lived. Walk inside his home that's now part of history. He was a prophet you know...I believe most of what he said.

And we want to see where Lem Ownby lived. His cabin is gone now, but it was right up there. We can see what he saw. Or didn't see. He was pretty much blind...how did such a man live out here in the sticks? He was quite the character, but I admire him. Stayed true to his land and himself. Imagine refusing to see two Supreme Court Justices? That must've sent them into next week's tizzy! But I hear they loved it...because no one ever told them no. What a life...it seems like a life that could've been lived a thousand years ago...

And then the young reporter at the old newspaper would insert some of these quotes and end his piece with a bit of nostalgia and one question for readers to ponder, a very effective rhetorical device:

Levi Trentham lived his life in the sun, saying what he wanted, doing what he wished. Raising a family and living the lifestyle that was in his heart. Lem Ownby spent much of his life in physical darkness, yet he clearly perceived the richness of mountain life with uncommon clarity. Those two hearty hearts, full to overflowing, sought a vent and nothing relieved them so effectively as pouring their thoughts out towards craggy peaks. Will *you* honor their story?

To which everyone who read the piece folded the newspaper in half and placed it on their laps to think.

To answer.

Those who responded right away had already found their soul while surrounded by the softly scalloped peaks that held a deeply rooted mountain culture: *Yes. I want to see an owl in the wild. To remember the legacy of the land and these mountains that sat back for millennia waiting, waiting, until some hearty and good humans decided to settle right along their spines and nestle within their deeply loving arms.*

I want to know about how they lived their lives until other folk came in to change it all. How they adapted. How they viewed the future – an uncertain one. One forced upon them. Because what else was there to do? Oh, there are so many lessons here! Ones we should teach to our children around the dinner table and in schools. Should we fight progress and discard all its baggage? Change with the times? Embrace improvements and advancement even at the expense to ourselves? Perhaps it is all of these, or should we just select the best bits out of each option?

SOME CALL it a ghost town but that's not correct. There are no ghosts, because the past isn't quite gone yet. Oh, to be sure, it's not anything like it was. Not like when families would step off the *Elkmont Special* and be greeted by a man with a beard and overalls, and a rifle and bearskin slung over his shoulder, asking only certain people if they'd like to go fishing or hiking.

No more were the days when mothers wouldn't have to cook and she'd usher her children down the road towards The Appalachian Club for the best peach cobbler they'd ever had.

Visiting, tea on the porch, dances, banjos, stories...all gone now, locked up inside wooden beams and stone steps and chimneys. The only things remaining: 17 cabins and one larger building where you can peek inside and see the splendor of bygone days at The Appalachian Club.

No, indeed. Though it may appear so, the past isn't quite gone yet.

The families of Elkmont are lucky for they are vessels of memories of days gone by. We are lucky too, for we still get to walk down a narrow street in the middle of the Great Smoky Mountains National Park and glimpse a past that was bustling, happy. A collision of two worlds that worked itself out as it always does.

And if you stop and listen, you will hear one final commanding prophecy from the mind of Levi Trentham – spoken not with curses this time, but with the quiet conviction that you too will understand what the mountains gave him.

Come on over to Elkmont, Tennessee.

Stay long enough to see the beauty. The rugged brutality of nature.

Long enough to imagine, if only for a moment, what it was like when an old mountain man, an artist, a blind beekeeper, a business-man, loggers, and tourists all shared this town. Divided into sections, segregated into two clubs, but somehow forming one community. One legacy.

Stay long enough to read the story - whether in the buzz of a bee or the pages of a book. Whether you hear it in the trees or in an old timer's antics that begins: "back in my day..."

And when you smile and feel that nostalgia in your heart –

Stay. It will do you good.

Stay long enough so that when you are far away from everyday life and finally sitting still in our burly, ancient arms, our peaks and boulders and trees begin to speak.

When the wind passes through your soul, and the mountains tell their tales –

Stay long enough to dream.

To dare.

To find hope in the sifted embers of a past, existing now only to guide us to the most beautiful days we have not yet seen.

One history.

So many pages.

So many sections.

But always the same book.

An owl's wisdom nesting on every page.

We move through history together; we cannot escape it. But

we can all stop and linger a while amongst its pages - the ones in the middle of millions and millions of other tales – where our story breathes the freshest air on earth.

Here, the mountains whisper: *Sit a spell. Let us tell you some mighty good tales about truly wonderful summers at The Appalachian Club in Elkmont, Tennessee - when wildflowers peppered the air and the bees danced.*

As it was. As it will always be.

Remember what the mountains gave them.

Remember.

Honor.

Cherish.

And then –

Remember what the mountains gave *you*.

ABOUT THE AUTHOR

Catherine Astl holds a Master's Degree in English - Literature and Curriculum from Southern New Hampshire University, a Bachelor's in English-American Literature from University of South Florida and is a graduate of the International Summer Schools Shakespeare and Literature program at the University of Cambridge, Cambridge, England. She also holds an Associate of Science degree in Legal Assisting and worked as a civil litigation trial paralegal for 27 years before switching to teaching English.

Catherine lives in Wesley Chapel, Florida, where she spends time with family and friends, reads, writes, travels, and scours bookshops to add to her personal library of 2000+ books which is always expanding.

After writing a trade magazine column, two non-fiction books and two novels, all of which received much acclaim in the academic and literary fields, Catherine began focusing on the stories of the people who lived in the Great Smoky Mountains National Park before it was a park.

Catherine is hard at work on her next Smoky Mountain historical novel.

instagram.com/Catherineastl

amazon.com/author/smokymountainauthor

facebook.com/catherine.astl

www.ingramcontent.com/pod-product-compliance
Lightning Source LLC
Chambersburg PA
CBHW060520160726
47991CB00001B/108